Yudit Avi-Dor

## About the Author

EDEET RAVEL was born on an Israeli kibbutz and completed grad-uate studies in English at the Hebrew University of Jerusalem. She now divides her time between Canada and Tel Aviv, where she is involved in peace work. She has been publishing stories and prose poems in English and Hebrew since age sixteen, and is the recipient of several writing awards, including the Norma Epstein Award for her poetry and a Quebec Council for the Arts writing award. She holds a Ph.D. in Jewish Studies from McGill University and has taught creative writing, English literature, Holocaust studies, and biblical exegesis. She has one daughter. This novel is the second of a trilogy dealing with the Palestinian-Israeli conflict and its effect on the people who live in its midst.

# LOOK
### *for* ME

Also by Edeet Ravel

*Ten Thousand Lovers*

# LOOK

## *for* ME

*A Novel*

EDEET RAVEL

Perennial

*An Imprint of* HarperCollins*Publishers*

HarperCollins books may be purchased for educational, business, or sales promotional use. For information please write: Special Markets Department, HarperCollins Publishers Inc., 10 East 53rd Street, New York, NY 10022.

FIRST EDITION

*Designed by Elias Haslanger*

Library of Congress Cataloging-in-Publication Data
Ravel, Edeet.
    Look for me : a novel / Edeet Ravel.—1st ed.
        p. cm.
    ISBN 0-06-058622-2
        1. Accident victims—Family relationships—Fiction. 2. Women political activists—Fiction. 3. Separation (Psychology)—Fiction. 4. Military spouses—Fiction. 5. Missing persons—Fiction. 6. Women novelists—Fiction. 7. Married women—Fiction. I. Title.

PR9199.4.R39L66 2004
823'.92—dc22
                                                                    2003068931

04 05 06 07 08    ❖/RRD    10 9 8 7 6 5 4 3 2 1

And take upon 's the mystery of things
As if we were God's spies
—*King Lear*

# LOOK *for* ME

ELEVEN YEARS AGO my husband caught fire while on reserve duty. He was not a combat soldier; his job was folding laundry. There are women who wonder, when their husbands leave for the army, whether the good-bye kiss at the door is the last one, whether they'll ever see their husbands again. I was luckier: what could possibly happen to someone who served his country by sorting shirts and towels? I didn't have to live in limbo between one check-in phone call and the next. Or so I thought. But on the last day of reserve duty my husband caught fire, and before I had a chance to see him, he vanished.

# Saturday

I WOKE UP AND DIDN'T KNOW WHERE I WAS. This happens to me frequently: I emerge in stages from a deep sleep and I can't remember what time of day it is, or what life I'm living. Am I in my parents' seven-room flat in the desert, waking to a breakfast of rolls and butter and nine percent cheese, or living with neighbors who are tiptoeing around my sofa bed so as not to disturb me, or in my army cot, facing a day of cleaning toilets because I'm in trouble with my sergeant again? Or have I woken in some altogether unknown place, where people wear black capes, say, and hop from place to place instead of walking?

This process of relocating myself never lasts more than a few seconds. I knew where I was: the bedroom of our U-shaped flat near the sea. It was Saturday morning, the beginning of September, and I had a demonstration to photograph in Mejwan. Odelia was coming at eight-thirty to collect me.

I sat up in bed. When my husband lived with me I'd wear one of his T-shirts to sleep, but after he vanished I started sleeping naked. I wanted to feel closer to him, wherever he was; if he came during the night I would be prepared. It was just a fantasy, of course. I knew Daniel would not appear suddenly at the stroke of midnight, the way some of the characters in my novels liked to do.

I slipped on my bathrobe and raised the blackout shutters. Bright sunlight flooded the room and settled on the dusty heart-shaped leaves of my climbing plants. "Leaves deserve to be noticed," Daniel had said, cryptically at first, when he painted one of the bedroom walls black. He hung a mirror in the center, and arranged the plants so they framed the mirror and spread outward until they covered the entire wall, heart-shaped green against night-black, our own reflection peeping at us from the midst of a leafy jungle.

I put on the kettle and while I waited for the water to boil I wrote down a dream I'd had in a notebook I kept for that purpose. I'd decorated the notebook with a color printout of Raphael's *Madonna with the Fish,* which seemed somehow appropriate. I began recording my dreams when I was fourteen and my mother died in a traffic accident. For several weeks she came to life each night as I slept, and in the morning I would try to recapture our nocturnal encounters so I could relive the experience, and also because I wanted to understand the dreams, which were often perplexing. In one she was riding on a seashell and she called out, "Don't forget Lord Kitchener!" In another she told me to wash my hair in a kneeling position, never while standing.

This morning, just before waking, I dreamed that I was at the Munjed checkpoint, a checkpoint I'd photographed a few times. I was climbing the watchtower to get a better angle, and the border guards were telling me to watch out for electric wires. I wondered whether they were afraid they'd be blamed if I was electrocuted, or whether they really were worried about me. I tried to find a good angle for my photograph, but realized it was hopeless because there were seven thousand Palestinians below, lined up and waiting for their IDs, which had been confiscated. I called down to the guards, "How come you've detained so many today?" and they answered, "It's the drugs we've taken, they multiply everything seven thousand times." I tried to figure out how their hallucinations could affect my own vision, and the effort to introduce waking-life logic into the dream woke me.

❖

I left the army to marry my husband. He was the lead singer of the band at my cousin's wedding and I could not take my eyes off him: his dark brown hair and David Bowie eyes, that smile of his as he sang. It was an extravagant wedding at one of the most ritzy halls in the country—my aunt and uncle were wealthy, and their daughter was spoiled. The small, laid-back band was noticeably out of place in this gilded setting: three musicians perched on a little wooden platform, all wearing jeans, short-sleeved white shirts, and black vests. One of the musicians was a multitalented albino with shoulder-length white hair; he played drums, sax, and keyboard. The other was chubby, with raisin eyes and sweet dimples, and the confidence to shake and bounce about as he strummed his guitar.

There was dancing at the wedding, of course, but the band didn't follow the standard wedding repertoire. No zesty religious chants, no inspirational nationalist classics, none of the traditional tunes that were considered a must at any celebration. Instead, Daniel sang contemporary songs about waking up in the middle of the night with a feeling of dread, or going to airports to watch planes taking off. He sang my favorite song at the time, "Seer, Go Flee." When he came to those words I knew I had to have him. *Seer, go flee. For there is no mercy in this city, and no place to hide. Seer, go flee.*

I waited until the band began to fold up and then shyly approached him. I didn't want to say anything in front of the other two musicians, but I knew that if I didn't speak up they'd all be gone in a matter of minutes, leaving me alone in the empty auditorium.

Daniel looked at me. He seemed amused for some reason, maybe because of the contrast between my uniform and the confused, unsoldierly way I was standing next to the platform. "Can I help you with something?" he asked.

"I was wondering . . ."

But now all three performers were looking at me.

"It's private," I said.

"Oh, private." Daniel smiled. He stepped down from the platform and walked away from the others. "Well?" he said.

"Well . . . I'm due back at the base, but . . . if you take me home I'll go AWOL. If you're free, that is," I added. It had just occurred to me, with a mortifying shock, that he probably had a girlfriend waiting for him at home. I pictured their flat: candles, incense, Klimt posters. There, amidst the poetry books and leftover hashish crumbs, on a velvet blanket spread over a mattress on the floor, they would have a long and glorious night together.

He burst into laughter.

"I don't think I've ever received such a compliment in my life," he said. "AWOL . . . no, I can't be responsible. You'll be in deep water."

"You don't have plans?"

"I was planning to go home and sleep. And you should get back to your base, or you'll have hell to pay."

"Oh, who cares, they hate me anyhow. I can't clean any more toilets, I've done them all twenty times this week."

"What's your name?"

"Dana. The bride is my cousin. I guess she's not a bride any-more. I guess she's a wife now."

"Dana. Well, Dana, what are we going to do? Encourage you to be derelict, or urge you to do your duty?"

"You don't have other plans?" I asked again. After my despair-ing vision of the flat and the girlfriend (black hair, sensuous mouth, aloof but generous), his availability seemed too good to be true.

"Not at the moment."

"Don't pay any attention to my uniform. I only wore it because I don't have a dress."

"I guess I'm too weak to resist."

"I'll wait until you finish packing up."

"That's okay, Gabriel and Alex will look after everything. Let's go, my car's just down the block." He waved to his two friends.

❖

I finished recording my dream and drank two cups of *café et lait,* a coffee drink Daniel had invented and named. The kitchen had a name too, the Dining Car, because of its narrow oblong shape and its position at the end of the U, between the living room on one side and the bedroom and bathroom on the other. The flat had originally been three separate units on the ground floor of the building. There wasn't enough space in this middle section for a table and chairs; instead, Daniel had built a counter along the wall, bought two wooden stools, and hired an artist friend from work to paint a mural on the wall above the counter. The mural showed two train windows, through which appeared a comical landscape of cows and barns. I loved the painting, and I loved the kitchen. But in fact we rarely ate at the counter.

Daniel preferred to eat Japanese-style, kneeling at the low table in the living room.

I finished my *café et lait* and had a shower. Showering at our place was a particularly pleasant experience because the bathroom Daniel had built for us was very luxurious. We sacrificed space in the bedroom in order to have a large bathroom, but Daniel said he was tired of the closet model he'd grown up with, and he brought all his creativity to bear on this project. The room was tranquil and luminous, like the crystal floor the Queen of Sheba mistook for a pool in King Solomon's palace, but it was also warm, with a white clawfoot tub, a cushioned window seat, and multicolored ceramic floor tiles. Some of the tiles had come loose and I kept them in a pile by the sink. Whenever my neighbor Benny came to visit he'd glance at the tower of tiles, stacked snugly at the corner of the counter, next to the toothpaste. Among the many things Benny found exasperating about me was my refusal to let him glue the tiles back. "I want Daniel to have something to fix when he gets back," I explained. "So he'll feel at home."

In the novels my father sends me from Belgium, September is an autumn month: the days grow cooler, leaves turn, people become pensive. We like to pretend that here, too, September brings a gentle foreshadowing of winter, and that today and yesterday were exceptions, but we know we're lying to ourselves. The weather forecast promised a sweltering *hamseen* day. I extracted a pair of blue cotton trousers and a short-sleeved black top from amidst the household debris strewn on the floor. The place was a mess, as usual. Then I prepared my camera, covered my face and arms with sunscreen, packed water and a hat, and slid my mobile phone into my front pocket.

It was still early, so I sat down at my computer and worked on my latest novel. I pay the mortgage by writing anonymous novels in which beautiful women with euphonious names swoon into the arms of sardonic but ultimately pliant men, always dark, always handsome.

The guidelines have changed over the years; the list of words they want me to use and the types of sexual acts they want me to describe have expanded. But basically the rules are the same. The plot has to move slowly but inexorably toward a satisfying climax (romantic conquest, marriage) which is also the resolution, and the characters have to speak like imaginary people in a textbook on earthlings, a textbook used on a distant planet by creatures who have never met any earthlings but have done some research and guessed the rest. I wrote without thinking, my mind wandering.

*"Give me a sign, darling," Angeline said. "Give me a sign that you will stand by me. Anything at all, that I can keep next to my heart."*

*"Take this ring," Pierre said, removing the gold and emerald ring from his own finger. "Wear this ring around your neck and each time your heart beats my sword will—"*

I listened to music as I wrote, the songs Daniel and I loved, and also new ones that had come out since he left. *Mercy, mercy on us all.* Or funny songs that Daniel would have enjoyed singing. *Why did you tell your mother I come too fast? Why didn't you tell her about that time in the car, or about the tattoo I got just for you?* More cynical songs had also come out in recent years. *Back in high school they shared you in the shed like a package from home, but they're not the sort who get caught, they're the sort who get medals.*

At eight-thirty Odelia knocked on the door. I saved the few paragraphs I had written and we walked to her car.

❖

I followed Daniel to his small, tinny-looking car, the kind you expect will shatter, cartoon-style, into a thousand pieces, leaving a heap of metal in the middle of the street. But miraculously it worked.

"I don't know," he said as he drove down the dark streets. "You're sort of young. Is this even legal?"

"You can't be much older than me!"

"I'm twenty-nine."

"Really? You don't look it. I guess because you're a singer—performers always look young. Anyhow, I'm nineteen. Nineteen and two months. My birthday is March 15. The Ides of March."

He smiled. "The band's just a hobby—a way to earn some extra cash. I'm an architect. I'm saving up so I can build my own house, one day when I'm eighty. I live with my grandmother, by the way, so be warned. But she won't bother us."

"Oh." I was disappointed. A grandmother wasn't as bad as a girlfriend, of course, but could definitely put a damper on my plans.

"She's nearly blind," he reassured me. "And I'm sure she's asleep by now."

"How come you live with her?"

"She doesn't want to go to a residence, the idea terrifies her. She was in the camps; I guess she's getting a bit mixed up and she thinks we want to take her back there. We drove her to see a residence, it was such a nice place, but she had hysterics the whole time. We can't afford a full-time nurse, of course, so I look after her. I don't mind, it's better than living with flatmates. What about you, Dana? Where do you live?"

"Oh, it's a long story. Nowhere, really."

"Nowhere?"

"It's a long story—I'll tell you another time."

"The mystery soldier from nowhere."

Daniel's grandmother lived in a four-story apartment house on a quiet street lined with palm trees.

"It's a bit cramped," Daniel warned me as we climbed the stairs to the third floor.

I watched him unlock the door, and it seemed to me this was the most erotic and exciting thing I would ever experience, no matter how long I lived and no matter how many wonderful things happened to me. Daniel unlocking the door at that moment, unlocking it for the two of us, his beautiful hand on the key, the key turning: the entire universe was compressed into this small motion, and I was the person who'd been chosen to witness it.

All the lights were on in the flat. A narrow hallway lined with old books opened onto a living room decorated with ugly, flimsy furniture from the fifties. It was the sort of furniture I always found heartbreaking: the square, bright orange sofa cushions, the sofa's thin wooden arms, rickety side tables, matching scarlet and green horse-head lamps, the shortwave radio from the Mandate period, the mandatory maroon carpet on the stone floor. There were two doors along the wall on the right. The farthest one was half open and evidently led to a bedroom: soft, irregular snores drifted out of the room like crooked musical notes. Daniel smiled at me. "No need to whisper," he said. "She sleeps like a log." Even there, where Daniel's grandmother was sleeping, the light had been left on.

The second door, closer to the entrance, was a two-paneled folding door with horizontal slits, painted white; beyond it lay the kitchen. The toilet and bath were adjacent to the hallway, also on our right. The flat smelled of a hundred years of chicken soup; I was sure no amount of paint and plaster and detergent could remove that smell, and who would want to? This way you'd always know where you were.

"Cute place," I said. "Where's your room?"

"Off the kitchen. It was a balcony—I turned it into a bedroom. I thought I would have to chop off my feet in order to sleep there, but in the end it worked out fine, I got to keep my feet."

"Don't say things like that. I visualize everything."

"That must be hard."

"Sometimes. How come all the lights are on?"

"It's the only way my grandmother can see anything. Even with the lights on she can just make out the outlines of objects."

"Do you read to her?"

"I'll make coffee and then I'll answer all your questions."

I followed him into the kitchen and sat down at what appeared to be a bridge table. Daniel struck a match and lit the stove, put on water to boil. "What did you say your name was?" he asked.

"Dana."

"Dana, Dana, Dana. I don't know how I'm going to remember that name. I might get it wrong the first few times, don't get offended. I might call you Lana by mistake, or Tina."

I laughed. "How am I going to know when you're joking about things?" I asked.

"I don't know. Maybe we could have a code. I could pull my earlobe, for example."

He made regular coffee for me and *café et lait* for himself, then sat down facing me at the bridge table. I asked to taste the *café et lait,* and I liked it, so he spilled my coffee into the sink, handed me his mug, and made himself another cup. "You're my first convert," he said.

"What's in it?"

"Cheap instant coffee, cinnamon, cocoa powder, hot milk, honey."

"This is a bridge table."

"Yes, my grandparents were obsessive bridge players, it was their whole life, practically. They got tired of folding up the table all the time, so they decided to sell their kitchen table and use this for everything. Would you like cookies? Pastries? Pretzels?"

"Don't even mention food. I'm absolutely stuffed from the wedding. I may never be able to eat again. I like all this fifties furniture. It's touching, you know? Those horse-head lamps! They're funny," I said.

"I think in my last nightmare the horses came to life and began reciting passages from Proust."

"I think they're nice."

Suddenly we were both embarrassed. We had no idea what we were doing there, sitting at Daniel's grandmother's bridge table, drinking *café et lait* and discussing furniture.

"I hope you don't think I'm crazy," I said. "I just . . . liked you."

"Have you changed your mind?" he asked, worried.

"No."

"Maybe you should call your base, tell them at least that you're sick."

"No, I can't, they'd never believe me. I'd have to bring a letter from a doctor saying I was in a coma or something before they'd believe me."

"You're going to get into huge trouble."

"It can't get any worse."

"It can always get worse. What's going on there?"

"Oh, I'm not getting on too well. I'll tell you about it another time."

"More mysteries. Another time as in . . . ?"

"As in, after . . ."

"After you know me better?"

"Yes." I rose from the table, opened the door that led to his room. Daniel's bed took up nearly all the available space in the converted balcony. The upper third of the walls consisted of sliding glass panels; the sky was visible through the glass and I was reminded of a medieval triptych, except that here the scene changed all the time. Now, against a black background tinged with the yellow glow of city lights, a single white star or satellite shone like a jeweled belly button. The only decoration in the room was a movie poster for *Stranger Than Paradise*.

"I loved that movie!" I said. "I saw it a million times. You're the only person I know who also saw it."

Daniel made a noncommittal sound, something between "mmm" and "huh."

" 'I am the winner,' " I said, in English with a Hungarian accent.

" 'He is my main man,' " Daniel said, also in English.

" 'Poor guy, can you imagine working in a factory?' "

I pulled off my uniform, then my underwear, and lay down on the bed.

❄

Odelia always looked neat and delicate. She was wearing a beige knee-length skirt and she'd tied her hair back with an elastic band. She was the only one who came to these demonstrations wearing a skirt; it was a disguise. "The soldiers have a different attitude if they think you're religious," she would tell people.

There were no traffic jams on the highway because it was the weekend. "What's happening today, do you know?" I asked her.

"I'm not sure. I heard three towns were put under curfew, Mejwan and the two towns next to it."

"Three towns? Last I heard it was two."

"I heard three. Some people went down there to stay the night, in case they don't let us in. Better than nothing."

"I forgot to bring an onion."

"The organizers are bringing a whole crate. Don't worry!" She smiled at me. She was a calm person, though her permanently wrinkled brow made her look like a high school student trying to work out a complicated math problem she'd been assigned for homework.

"How are you, Dana?" she asked.

"I'm okay. I'm fine."

"How's your father?" When my father comes to visit, he stays with Odelia, in her guest room.

"Happy. He sends his regards, by the way. How are things with you?"

"Another lay-off at work, someone we really liked. We've been depressed about it all week. I think I'm next . . . How's Vronsky?"

"Same as always." Odelia was convinced that my friend Vronsky, a bone specialist with whom I had dinner every Wednesday, was in love with me and that we should get married.

We drove for an hour. As we approached the capital, the landscape widened into mute green hills and incongruous sprinklings of small, distant neighborhoods, sterile and symmetrical, which had sprouted on the hills in recent years. We entered the city and headed for Liberty Bell Park, our usual meeting place. Odelia tried to remember the way and her wrinkled brow became slightly more furrowed than usual. The streets were full of Hassidic families, the men brisk and determined in their long black coats, the women strolling leisurely amidst broods of children. I tried to repress my hostility toward them; I knew it was wrong and irrational. Our problems were not their fault.

After a few uncertain turns and a phone call to a friend who lived nearby, we found the park. We were a little late, but these activities always started later than planned. Odelia parked her car on the street and we walked to the graveled parking lot. Five sturdy-looking tour buses stood side by side at one end of the parking lot and two minimalist army Jeeps were stationed on the other. Between them, a large crowd of demonstrators mulled around, waiting for instructions: they all looked scrubbed and relaxed, as if they'd just stepped out of a shower and discovered that while they were soaping themselves the conflict had nearly resolved itself, and only needed this one last push.

The soldiers had deserted their Jeeps and were talking to the organizers, trying to persuade them to cancel the demonstration: the towns were under curfew, the entire area was sealed off. It was the usual ritual, the army on one side, the demonstrators on the other. No one expected a new and startling outcome:—*Yes, you're right, we'll cancel the demonstration, we'll change our plans and go home, because you've asked us to.*—*Yes, go ahead, we'll lift the curfew and let you through, good for you that you're making these efforts.* We boarded the buses and set off.

The army Jeeps followed the buses as we drove through the city. We didn't take the main road to Mejwan; we knew it would be blocked. The hired bus drivers were instructed to drive instead to a barren field on the outskirts of Ein Mazra'a, the town adjacent to Mejwan. Everyone got off the buses and pulled out signs from the baggage compartment, which slid open at the side of the bus like the belly of a whale. *Arise, go to Nineveh.*

We walked single file along a path that cut through the field; trudging with our signs through this landscape that we loved, pale beige stones, pale beige earth, a thousand shades of pale beige and a thousand patterns of stone and earth, motionless under the pale sky. Up ahead, the houses of Ein Mazra'a, with their tiny black square windows, looked like dice scattered on the earth, and the pink-flowered thorns that grew close to the ground seemed to be breathing softly around our ankles.

On one side of the path a solitary donkey strolled amidst a car graveyard: twenty or thirty cars and trucks and vans, all of them white except for one red station wagon and the remains of a yellow school bus. They were in varying stages of disuse and ruin; some were nothing but rusty metal shells crushed into the ground, while others were perhaps still salvageable, missing only doors or wheels.

I stopped to take a photograph of the donkey wandering among the car carcasses, and another one of the remains of a house, now a heap of broken blocks and cement fragments with wires coming out of them like twisted insect legs. The house must have been demolished some time ago, since nothing remained apart from the broken blocks and shapeless cement fragments with the wires poking out. Golden grass covered the spaces between the house fragments and even the fragments themselves. In the distance we heard the explosion of a stun grenade. Tear gas was sure to follow.

❂

I had never so much as kissed a man before Daniel. The boys I knew in high school didn't appeal to me, or maybe I was too preoccupied with staying afloat to notice them. Shortly after my mother died my father moved to Belgium to marry his childhood sweetheart, taking with him only a single suitcase of clothing and his chess set, leaving me the rest. He asked me to come along, but I refused: what would I do in Belgium? I didn't even speak the language—what did they speak in Belgium, anyhow? French? German? I persuaded him to go without me. He didn't need much persuasion; he trusted me. Scandalized neighbors and relatives and family friends competed with each other to feed me and worry about me, and I drifted from sofa bed to sofa bed. I enjoyed the endless attention and eased myself into the role of orphaned and deserted daughter, at first with a slight sense of disorientation and then with total submission to hedonism.

But my life was disorganized, and I never knew where I'd be from one day to the next. It is possible that boys who might have been interested in me gave up and went after girls who were easier to locate. My friends and I often planned overnight hikes, and on the last summer before our induction almost everyone paired up. I'd hear soft sounds of pleasure coming from the sleeping bags next to me and sometimes I watched the swaying hills and bumps formed by my friends' movements; it all looked very charming, but I wasn't envious. Now and then a boy tentatively slid an arm around my shoulder and I tried not to hurt his feelings as I gently moved away. I told him I was too confused to date; the real reason was that he was too bony or too confident or too talkative. And so I was still a virgin when I entered the army, one of only four in our barracks. I was well informed about sex, though, because the more experienced girls in high school were very forthcoming with details and advice, and in the army a few conscripts gave some memorable demonstrations of various erotic options.

I didn't tell Daniel I was a virgin, but he guessed at once. I still don't know how he guessed, and neither did he. "I just had a feeling," he said later. Maybe the look on my face gave me away: I was self-conscious but also defiant, and I probably looked pleased with myself, as though I'd just won a prize for public speaking or for coming in first in the sixty-meter dash.

"Is this your first time?" Daniel said, standing in the doorway and looking at me lying there on the bed, waiting for him.

"Sort of," I said.

He laughed. "Sort of?"

"I know a lot," I said proudly.

"That's a relief," he teased. He was very amused.

"What about you, do you have a girlfriend?"

"Fine time to ask!"

"Well?"

"I'm between girlfriends at the moment."

"Do you like me?"

"What a question. You're very strange, Dana. It is Dana, isn't it? Here, get under the blankets." He joined me fully clothed on the bed and covered us with the sheet and bedspread. He was careful not to touch me.

"My mother never let me get into bed with my clothes on," I said, stupidly.

"That was a rule in our house too, but we ignored it."

"No one ignored my mother. She wasn't the sort of person you could ignore."

"Where is she?"

"She died in a car accident—she got stuck in a traffic jam and a truck behind her was speeding and couldn't stop fast enough. He smashed into her car. My father's in Belgium. I've been living with neighbors and relatives for the past five years—that's why I don't really have a permanent home. I grew up in the south, in the desert, but we moved when I was twelve, two years before my mother died, for my father's work. And I hate my sergeant, but not as much as she hates me. That's the story of my life, so far. Not very mysterious, as you see."

"What's going on now? Why me?"

"I don't know. I liked the way you sang *Seer, go flee*. Your voice is like a blanket—a pale blue cotton blanket with bright red diamonds. I guess I love you."

"Love at first sight?"

"Not really. I had the whole evening to look at you."

He laughed so hard he began to cough, and he had to sit up. Finally he calmed down. "Are you always this impulsive?"

"I'm not impulsive. But you know, there are only three other virgins in my barracks, one because she's religious and two because they're terrified of their fathers. So, don't you think it's about time?"

"You're just lucky. You're very lucky, because I could be a total jerk. A total jerk who didn't have any feelings for you at all."

"No, I can tell you aren't a jerk. And I can tell you like me, too."

"You can't really tell these things, Dana. Trust me."

"I can. Maybe some people can't but I can."

"You can't assume you know a person just because you like his voice and you have some chance association with it."

"It's not a chance association. Voices have colors and shapes for me, and textures. Not always, but a lot of the time. I used to think everyone was like that, but now I know I'm just weird."

"How about we just talk for now?"

"Well, all right. But can't we at least kiss? I want to try at least one new thing."

"Surely you've kissed before?"

"Not really."

"God help us."

❖

I fell behind because I was taking photographs, and I was one of the last to enter Ein Mazra'a, an orderly town with green trees and small apartment buildings, many of them unfinished, surrounded by scaffolding or simply left as they were, dark compartments gaping at the street from cement shells. The army ordered us to turn back. Military vehicles zoomed past us, their sirens howling through the streets. That's what the army did, it created crises before any existed; it created a military emergency out of the void, the way God created the heavens and the earth.

The organizers dropped onions on the ground, smashed

them open with their shoes, and handed out the pieces, in anticipation of tear gas: onions helped a little if you held them to your nose. We slid the shiny white crescents into our pockets. Then the organizers instructed us to sit on the ground while they negotiated with the army. We placed our hopeful signs against the wall, where they acquired a life of their own, like sentries from toyland.

At first the streets were empty because of the curfew, though we saw Palestinians watching us from their balconies, women and children mostly, women and teenage girls, watching from their balconies and roofs, happy to see us but still unsure, waiting for events to unfold. Then all at once the men began streaming out of the houses and their children followed them. The women stayed indoors for the most part, or stood in doorways, but the men and children came out: boys of all ages and very young girls wearing pretty dresses: purple velvet or bright cotton prints. The men and boys had short trimmed hair and tanned arms, and wore light-colored jeans or white cotton slacks with polo shirts that were open at the collar, eight or nine buttons running down from the collar, the small lapels folded to the sides. The shirts were striped or else solid colors with American cartoon figures and meaningless messages in English. All their clothes were carefully laundered and ironed; I'd never seen a Palestinian in grimy or stained clothing, unless they were working and wearing their work overalls.

Everyone was chatting and laughing, the children and the men. They greeted us happily and took the signs from our hands and waved them in the air. The children posed for me, smiling broadly into the camera. Their smiles made me dizzy, as if I were walking on a narrow, tilting ledge, or in space. So easy, to get along. And instead this endless fighting, hundreds upon hundreds of dead and mutilated bodies, year after year.

Finally the army allowed us to proceed a little further in the direction of Mejwan. Three months ago a peace worker we all knew, Idris, had run out of his house in Mejwan to look for his child. He was shot first in the leg from a distance and then at close range in the back by a lone red-haired soldier. I wanted to take a few photos of Idris and his family, and I hoped we'd be allowed into Mejwan. He was paralyzed now from the waist down.

We walked with the Palestinians. Then another barricade was set up, and this time the army was not going to move. We stood on one side, they stood on the other. A soldier and a Palestinian man got into an argument. I couldn't hear what they were saying, only a few isolated words: *no right, stop, move back, freedom*. The man's rage grew, his frustration grew, and he kicked the soldier with his soft, dusty shoe, a sad black shoe, and the soldier pushed him with the butt of his rifle so that he fell backward. A child, possibly his son, picked up a stone and threw it at the soldier. A soldier who a few days earlier may have been someone I had photographed on the beach, stretched out on a towel, asleep, and whose trembling lips may have filled me with pity.

Panic and disorder tend to break out without warning, and the first moment is always terrifying, because we react instinctively with fear when we see or hear a large crowd running. Everyone was trying to escape the tear gas. Across the street a man carrying a young woman in his arms was looking frantically for a car: the woman was having some sort of seizure. I took a photo of the two of them, even though I couldn't see very well because my eyes were burning. I needed to find shelter as well. I was standing near a half-built warehouse, and I saw that people were running up a wooden ramp that led to the upper story of the building. I ran up the ramp with them, hoping it wasn't a mistake, hoping it wouldn't be worse up there: what if we were trapped inside with the tear gas? Luckily, there were two open sides on the upper story, one facing the sidewalk and the other facing the army barricade. There were also two window openings in back. Every few seconds I took a break from taking photographs to hold an onion crescent to my nose; it seemed to help. A boy in his mother's arms was shrieking with terror. He wore shorts covered with tiny yellow and red and navy blue hearts. His small hand lay on his mother's black hair, which fell in waves against her white blouse. The walls were made of rough cement blocks, and here too there were bits of wire coming out of the cement; a strand of the mother's hair was caught on one of them.

A stun grenade exploded and there was more crying, not only the boy now but also two other children, a girl of about seven and her older sister. I huddled with them in the corner. I knew the stun grenades weren't real grenades, but the sound was frightening all the same and it made you cower. The Palestinians were more afraid than I was, because they weren't entirely certain the army would hold back even if we were there, and they feared for their lives.

From below a soldier began to shout. He pointed his weapon at us and ordered us to come down. I saw the soldier's face. He was young and he was the sort who didn't want to be there, I could tell. Some soldiers were keen, they liked what they were doing and believed in it. Others wanted to be with their girlfriend on the beach, or surfing with a friend.

And then, as if out of nowhere, a demonstrator emerged from the darkness, walked over to the edge of the warehouse, to the side where there was no wall, where down below the soldier was pointing his submachine gun at us. I was sickened by the weapon, a weapon I had once held myself, but which was now pointed at me. The demonstrator looked down at the soldier near the barricade and shouted, *Enough, already, enough!* Five stun grenades had exploded by then, one after the other, and several more tear gas canisters. And now the soldier was threatening us.

The words of the demonstrator, there in the dim crowded shelter, amidst the crying and fear, brushed against me like peacock feathers, the kind I used to play with when I was a child, and I wanted to shut my eyes and enjoy the sensation. Even after he'd spoken I felt the words moving softly around me, and I almost forgot to photograph him. I focused my lens: red baseball cap on a short black afro, white T-shirt, jeans, running shoes. His sign in one hand, his onion in the other. *Enough, already, enough—*

*Well then, come down*, the soldier shouted back. It unnerved the soldier, that there were people up there; he felt exposed, afraid. He might have shot at us to get us to come down to the street, where the air was sharp and heavy with tear gas, but he couldn't risk hitting someone from his own side, and in this way we protected the Palestinians with our bodies.

The demonstrator turned to me and said, "Let's go." We made our way down the ramp and out onto the sidewalk, and the others followed us. The air stung my throat and I pressed the onion to my nose again. The street was deserted; everyone had run for shelter.

"Are you all right?" he asked me.

"Yes, are you?"

"Fucking assholes . . . Your eyes are red."

"They don't bother me."

"I've seen you before," he said. "You always come, I've seen you many times."

"I haven't seen you."

"You're too busy taking photographs."

I smiled, and when I smiled he said, "You're in bad shape."

I didn't answer. I stared past him. People were slowly coming out of their hiding places, tired and upset.

"You wrote me a letter when I was in jail," he said.

"Who are you?" I asked.

"Rafi Atias. And you're Dana Hillman."

"Oh, yes. I remember. But how do you know me?"

"I'm clairvoyant."

It was a stupid question: we all knew one another, we were the same people who showed up at these things, again and again. Apart from that, I was famous. Once a year, on the anniversary of Daniel's disappearance, I placed a full-page advertisement in the newspaper, which read, *I will never ever ever ever ever stop waiting for you,* with the word *ever* multiplied so that it filled the entire page, and I was known for this annual plea. It cost me an entire romance novel, but I didn't care. I had also been interviewed several times on radio and television, and I gave those interviews in the hope that Daniel would hear or see them and believe me and come back. I had recently placed my eleventh ad.

I tried to remember what I'd written Rafi when he was in jail. *Your courage . . . gratitude . . . refusing to fight . . . example to others*—the usual clichés.

"A girl had a seizure, they were rushing her to a transit—do you know what happened to her?" I asked him.

"She's okay, she's in the ambulance. I'll go check on her." He disappeared into the crowd. People were buying fruit at a kiosk; it helped them feel in control again. Then we all sat down on the sidewalk, looked at one another, and said nothing.

❖

Daniel and I stayed indoors for three days. We were afraid to break the spell, afraid that the world outside might somehow rouse us from the sweet dream we'd fallen into, and threaten us with omens or actual misfortune. Granny was happy to have me there and tried to give me some of her jewelry. She was thin and very bent; her back had been broken in the camps. And yet she didn't seem to be in any discomfort. Daniel told me that she had lost the ability to experience pain, which was actually quite dangerous, because she didn't know when she burned herself or when anything was wrong with her. It was a rare but known phenomenon, he said, the inability to feel pain, and it had a medical name, though very little was understood about it.

I couldn't communicate with Daniel's grandmother because in recent years she'd forgotten all her languages apart from Russian. Daniel, who had taken a few courses in Russian so he'd be able to talk to her, did his best to translate. He had also found a young Russian woman, Elena, who was willing to come over every evening and read to his grandmother. Elena was formal and prim, like a governess in a Victorian novel; according to Granny she was well educated and had a wonderful reading voice. They were now halfway through *The Possessed,* which Daniel was reading as well, out of curiosity.

I phoned the base to say I was sick, but I didn't have a doctor's note, I had not followed correct procedure, and I was afraid to go back.

Things were not working out for me in the army. My life after my father left had been easy; I was coddled and indulged. Flash floods of distress came over me only at night, as I lay stretched out on the temporary sofa beds of various surrogate parents, feeling slightly sick from too many homemade french fries dipped in hummus—my favorite food, and therefore always included in either the afternoon or late-evening meal. My mother would have been appalled by this diet, and I was slowly expanding out of all my clothes; they were ripping at the seams and I held them together with safety pins.

The army jolted me out of this epicurean reverie. No more french fries, for one thing, and the mashed potatoes in the mess hall were watery. All the same, I was hopeful at first. This would be a good chance to get back into shape. I was also excited by the prospect of living in close quarters with the other conscripts. When I was little, an only child in a seven-room flat that offered a view of the vast, theophanic desert from every window, I slept with a copy of the children's book *Madeline* under my pillow. I'd imagine the two rows of beds in which the lucky girls at Miss Pavel's convent school were safely tucked, and I'd transport myself to Paris, to Madeline's dormitory. I often fell asleep clinging to this fantasy. I would not be Madeline herself; she was too extroverted for me. But I would be her best friend, and I would tell her my secrets. In school I had many friends, but no one became my true bosom friend, as they were called in the novels I read. No one knew more about me than I was willing to disclose.

Now *Madeline* was coming to life, more or less: girls in rows of bunk beds above me and on both sides, putting away combs and makeup in the little compartments assigned to us, chattering, laughing hysterically at nothing. One girl laughed so hard she began to snort and the snorts made us laugh even harder. Then a male officer came into the barracks to say a few words. We couldn't stop giggling, and he was embarrassed and confused and suddenly self-conscious, though he tried not to show it, and he would probably have succeeded if you weren't looking hard, but I was. He told us to settle down, we weren't in nursery school. When he left we all began to sing spontaneously. One of our sappy nationalist songs; I suppose we did it in order to calm down. *Our homeland, O our homeland.* Everyone in my barracks was nice. Maybe I was lucky, or maybe we had to be nice to each other because otherwise the whole experience would have been unbearable.

But the pleasures of getting proper exercise and living with girls my age were eclipsed by the difficulties that beset me almost immediately. I didn't like getting up early, and I didn't like obeying orders, especially orders that felt like bullying, though I was told that my attitude was the problem, and I agreed: my attitude was indeed the problem. I lacked enthusiasm, I lacked patriotism, I was selfish and failed to see the larger picture, which was that you couldn't have a good army if everyone slept in and the sergeant was a pleasant person—and if we didn't have a good army, where would we be? One time my sergeant told me it was a good thing my mother had died so she wouldn't have to see what a loser her daughter was, and I cried. My friends tried to console me, and one of them, Sheera, gave me a gold locket and told me to keep a photograph of my mother inside and wear it around my neck. I tried to reform, partly because I wanted to and partly to avoid cleaning more toilets, but I didn't succeed. My heart wasn't in it. Somewhere, it seemed, my parents had failed to instill in me the right values. Or so it was suggested. I was very hurt by the accusation, especially since my mother wasn't around to defend herself, but they were right, of course. My parents were skeptics.

So Daniel and I left his grandmother's flat, finally, in order to set a date for our wedding. Armed with proof of an impending marriage, I returned to the base to clean some more toilets and collect my things. "You're lucky," the officer who released me said. "You're lucky you found someone to take you off our hands. And maybe we're lucky too . . . Well, congratulations."

I handed in my uniform and left the base. I was free again.

❁

I sat with my back against a storefront, next to two young Palestinian men. One of them spoke to me. "I can't go anywhere," he said. "I can't move, I can't work." He was still hopeful, he thought things might improve, but his friend had given up entirely. His friend stared into space, his eyes set; he didn't believe anything would ever change. I asked for permission to photograph them. They were an interesting pair: one of them energetic, ready to try new things, the other convinced that they were all doomed forever and amazed at the naïveté of anyone with faith in the future. I knelt on the sidewalk to get a good angle and took several photographs of the two friends. The angry man's face was closed and still, but his friend smiled for the camera. I had rarely met a Palestinian who was uncomfortable in front of a camera. Palestinian men and children liked being photographed no matter where they were; the men stared straight into the lens, and the children lined up in front of me with smiles as soon as they saw my camera. Women preferred to be photographed indoors, though some women were shy even then, and would urge me to take pictures of their children instead.

"What are your names?" I asked.

"I'm Ismail. This is Fayez."

Ella, a journalist who wrote about Palestinian affairs, sat down beside us and handed out nectarines. Ella had won several international awards for her writing, though none here. She was a passionate person, but her articles were controlled and professional; she could have been reporting on fluctuations in stock prices. After all, the facts spoke for themselves. There was no need to do anything other than record them.

"What's happening?" I asked her.

"I guess we'll be going home," she sighed, biting into her nectarine.

"You've cut your hair." She'd had shoulder-length hair for as long as I'd known her, but it was cropped now. Her new haircut made her look a little like Ingrid Bergman.

Ella smiled. "Lice. It was driving me crazy, the shampoos didn't work, so I got up in the middle of the night and chopped it all off."

Ismail heard us and said, "Stay away from me!" and the three of us laughed. His friend, Fayez, wanted to know what we were laughing about, and Ella repeated what she'd said in Arabic. Fayez nodded, and though he didn't smile, his eyes relented a little. He was amused in spite of himself.

The organizers announced that the demonstration was over and we would be going home. Ismail cried out, "Why, why!" He wanted us to stay, try harder. After all, we were citizens, immune from danger; surely there was something we could do: throw ourselves on the soldiers, maybe, or sit on the road and refuse to move, even if it took days and weeks, until something was done.

I looked at him helplessly. He saw my distress and tried to console me. "At least we have no dead this time, thanks to you."

His friend grumbled something in Arabic.

"What's he saying?" I asked.

Ismail was embarrassed. "He's asking me what I expect you to do. Don't listen to him. He's in a bad mood."

"The girl who had the seizure, is she all right?" I asked. Rafi had vanished; I didn't know whether he was still in the ambulance or merely lost in the crowd.

"Yes, she made it."

Ella said something in Arabic, and we all shook hands goodbye. Ella's words seemed to have had an uplifting effect on the two friends. "What did you say?" I asked her as we walked away.

"Just wished them well."

Ella and I walked with the group through Ein Mazra'a to the stone field. We took a longer route this time, and the Palestinians gave us cold water to drink. When we reached the borders of the town they said, Well, that's it, we can't go further, our IDs are orange. Thank you for coming, they said. God will bless you. Thank you for your courage. We want to be your brothers, and to protect you.

We crossed the field to the road, where our large solid buses were waiting for us. They looked like alien spaceships in their incongruous complacency.

Ella and I were on separate buses. "Take care, Dana," she said.

Everyone climbed onto the buses and sank down on the cushioned seats, sweaty and satisfied. This was the way it was: we left the Palestinians behind, we left them in hell, but people were laughing and talking, because you had to survive and you did it by contracting into your own narrow life, your own personal life, distinct from the conflict and the deaths and the suffering. And besides, the event had been a success, within the confines of goals that were also narrowed and thinned down: there had been a demonstration, even if we had not reached Mejwan or seen Idris. We had walked side by side with the Palestinians, we had shown that it was possible. And at least the activists who'd stayed overnight had visited Idris. He was in constant pain, they said, and money had to be raised for a stay at a rehabilitation facility in England. He'd been a sports instructor and youth leader before he was shot. The army had promised an investigation, but nothing ever came of such promises.

Through the streaked bulletproof window of the bus I watched the last demonstrators put away their signs. I was keeping an eye out for Odelia. Rafi sat down next to me.

"I'm saving this seat for my friend," I said.

"Odelia? She's on the bus behind us."

"Oh. okay, then. How's the girl?"

"She's fine. Now let's see what the orders are for today." He took a sheet of paper out of his pocket. It was covered with notes, handwritten in green pen.

"Things I have to do," he said, smiling. "My wife makes lists for me."

I looked out the window again; I tried to ignore him.

But he said, "I've wanted to talk to you for a long time."

I turned toward him. "I have seen you, come to think of it. You had shorter hair. You had no hair at all."

"Yes, my hair grows fast, I'm due for another haircut. Where do you live?"

"Opposite the City Beach Hotel."

"Really? The manager there is a good friend of mine. We were in the same unit. Coby, do you know him? Tall, dark hair, glasses?"

"Yes, I've seen him around. I use their fax machine sometimes."

"Give him my regards."

"Okay," I said.

"Did you take a lot of photos?"

"Four rolls."

"Am I in any of them?"

"Yes, one." I didn't want to look at him, I didn't want to think about him. He gave up and didn't speak to me again.

The buses arrived at the park and by then everyone had to pee. We found bushes and trees. Rafi was using a tree not far from mine. And when I rose and pulled up my underwear I saw that he was looking at me, and not smiling, and not turning away.

❧

My father met Gitte when they were both sixteen; Gitte's parents owned a jewelry company with interests in South Africa and the family moved there for a few months. Gitte and my father took violin lessons at the local music academy on the same afternoon, and my father began waiting until Gitte's lesson was over so he could walk her home. They fell in love, and after she left they exchanged passionate and frequent love letters, until Gitte stopped writing and finally confessed that she had met someone else. In fact, so had my father, and he was relieved. He'd met my mother. The two of them tried to escape apartheid by moving to Israel, which later made them laugh at themselves. "From the frying pan into the falafel," my father used to say.

My father was an engineer, and he loved to sing classical choral music. He dreamed of joining a choir, but had to content himself with singing in the shower or providing vigorous vocal accompaniment to the Munich Bach Choir in our living room. He seemed particularly inspired when he washed the dishes. *Denn alles Fleisch es ist wei Gras, und alle Herrlichkeit des Menschen wie des Grases Blumen.* This was fine when I was very little, but he soon became a social liability and I gave him strict instructions to restrain himself when my friends were over. My father was not a demonstrative person; he was shy when he wasn't singing, and he let my mother run the household and make all the decisions. But we read the newspaper together. From as far back as I can remember he would sit beside me on the carpet, spread the newspaper in front of us, and comment on the stories: "Unabashed corruption," he'd say. "Shortsightedness, insanity." He explained things in simple terms so I could understand them, and by first grade I probably knew more about our parliamentary system (and its many defects) than any other seven-year-old in the country.

His brother was a doctor, and the two of them, my father and his brother, took me to refugee camps when they went to do volunteer work there. My uncle, an energetic man with a good sense of humor, would do the driving. He liked to sing too, though his specialty was drinking songs or folk classics like "Waltzing Matilda." I would sit in the back and watch the view change from city to town to village and finally to refugee camp.

No one I knew visited the camps, and I didn't tell anyone at school that we went, because the one time I mentioned it, there was a big scandal. In third grade we had to write a composition on the topic "How My Family and I Contribute to the State." My father suggested I write about our visits to the camps, and I took his advice, though I knew we were both being deviant: he in his suggestion and I in my compliance. I described the poverty, the living conditions, and what we did. My uncle saw patients and distributed medicine (which he stole from the State, but I didn't mention that), and my father fixed things that were broken. I played with the local children, who competed to have me visit their homes—a dizzying assortment of structures crammed together and piled up like boxes one on top of the other. In these neat little rooms I would stuff myself with sweet baklava and empty my bag of toys on the floor. The Palestinian children spoke Arabic and I spoke Hebrew, but at that age language is malleable. We spent hours exploring the possibilities of the treasures I'd brought: marbles, dolls, trucks, airplanes, cards, Pick Up sticks, dominoes. I gave a detailed account of these visits in my essay, and concluded, *In this way we contribute to people who are under occupation, we show them that we are not all horrible, and we help the State see what it's doing wrong.*

My parents were called in, and my mother, who was not in the habit of keeping her thoughts to herself, had a huge fight with the principal. She called him an impotent, narrow-minded pimp, a poor excuse for an educator, a limp, spineless State puppet. She said she felt sorry for him and sorry that her daughter had to be exposed to his stupidity. Then she swept out of his office like a diva and slammed the door. I was sitting in the hallway outside, and I felt both proud and dismayed. I admired my mother but I took after my father, who was averse to conflict.

I was happy about our move to the city; I had just reached the age at which small towns become irredeemably boring. My mother's death two years later left my father literally speechless: for several weeks he walked around in a daze, confused and unable to concentrate on anything. When he finally began speaking he was mostly incoherent, and he sat and stared into space for hours, a puzzled look on his face. I think he contacted Gitte because the only life he could make sense of was one that had not included my mother. Gitte was divorced, lonely, and excited to hear from him. Letters with foreign stamps began arriving at our place; shortly afterward my father flew to Belgium for a week, and when he returned he announced that he was going to marry Gitte, and that I would be happy in Belgium. I didn't believe him.

He became convinced, later, that his anachronistic flight into the arms of love was irresponsible and that, like Anna Karenina, he had made a drastic choice. For as a result of the disorder in my life after he left, I did not graduate from high school. I failed all my subjects apart from English, which didn't require any exertion on my part. I was bilingual, not only because my parents spoke English at home, but also because I loved to read novels about the mystifying world of adults and the best ones came from my parents' bookshelves: I was particularly fond of Iris Murdoch and George Eliot, but I was also a Miss Reed addict.

He blamed himself, but I felt he'd made the right decision and I was happy for him. His letters suggested an ideal life: a two-hundred-year-old house with sweeping staircases and secret panels; a place in the local men's choir; close friends who came over for dinner and chess. He often spent his evenings reading by the fireplace or, when it was warm, on a patio facing the tulip garden; his French was improving and he'd picked up some Flemish as well. As for Gitte, she had not disappointed him. He said she spoiled him, and his letters were full of *cassoulet* and *soufflé à l'orange*: his tone when he described these dishes was reverent. It was obvious that he and Gitte were generally compatible. They both liked theater and books and conversation and, oddly, knitting; my eccentric father had taken up knitting, which he found "relaxing, touching, and spiritually satisfying." This late romance was the inspiration for one of my novels, though of course I had to change most of the details. My father was transformed from a slightly overweight, myopic engineer to a young, dashing horse breeder (who obviously did not knit). My mother became delicate and innocent, a flower taken in her youth. As for Gitte, I had never met her, and so was free to invent her both in fiction and in life. My father sent me a photo of the two of them next to their large house, but the photo was taken from a distance, and Gitte is wearing a wide-brimmed hat which throws a concealing shadow over most of her face.

❖

Benny was sitting at my kitchen table when I came home from Ein Mazra'a. He lived upstairs from me and had a key to my flat, in case I lost mine; sometimes when I wasn't home he went inside and waited for me. I was on friendly terms with everyone in my building: my legless and maddening neighbor Volvo, who had moved into the small one-room flat adjacent to ours shortly after Daniel left; Jacky, former rock star and prince of the city; Tanya, former prostitute, now a successful fortune-teller; and Tanya's mother. Benny lived on the top floor, next to two large flats that had remained empty for as long as anyone could remember because of some dispute that had been tied up in the courts for decades.

Benny was a restless, impatient person. He drove a taxi, and lately he'd been struggling to make ends meet; the tourist industry had nearly vanished and the collapsing economy affected everyone. On the other hand more people were taking taxis because they were afraid of being blown up on a bus. That helped a little, but not enough.

Benny had other worries, too. He had a very emotional relationship with his ex-wife Miriam. The two of them still fought and still had sex, behind her boyfriend's back. He hated her and loved her and couldn't rid himself of his desire for her. He vowed to quit smoking and he vowed to stop seeing Miriam, but he hadn't had much success with either plan.

He was burly and hairy, though in recent years he'd started balding, much to his dismay. His real age was forty-one, but he liked to tell people he was thirty-five. He did repairs in my flat, bought me small practical gifts like coat hooks, and worried about my safety. Often he gave me long, mournful lectures about my political views, trying to explain, patiently and hopelessly, why I was wrong to help and trust the enemy. He pitied the Palestinians too—but their miserable situation wasn't our fault. It was their fault, because they had terrible leaders and because they hated us and would never accept us and because they would always want all the land, including our State. And for the past seventy years they'd been trying to kill us; even before the State was founded they'd already started with their wild attacks, plunging knives into women and children, slicing off their heads.

At other times he spoke just as mournfully and hopelessly about Miriam. He worried that she was neglecting their children; he didn't trust her new boyfriend. A self-centered pig, he said, who was drawing Miriam away from the children, and she was too blind to grasp what was going on. What she saw in that poor excuse for a human being, that petty crook who was born with his brain in his arse and his nose in other people's arses, he would never know. Benny was a devoted father, and sometimes when I walked along the seashore with my jeans rolled up to my knees I'd see him sitting Buddha-style on a blanket, surrounded by his four small children. One would ride on his broad shoulders while the others poured sand over his crossed legs or tried to impress him with their acrobatics. He'd grin at me from the midst of his clan, but he'd never invite me to join him.

"Benny, I'm too tired for a visit today, I'm worn out from the demo." I took off my shoes and flopped down on my bed.

He sighed. "Why, why, why do you do these things? Where were you, anyhow?" He sat down at the edge of the bed.

I told him about the demonstration. It had not been reported on the news, he didn't know it had taken place.

"The last place on earth I would want to be, the last thing on earth I would want to do," he said, shaking his head.

"I'm sure there are a zillion things you would want to do even less," I said. "Swallowing a live cockroach. Getting into a booth full of scorpions. Shooting a child."

"You have an answer for everything." He sighed again. "So I can't stay? I just had another visit from Miriam, I need someone sane to talk to."

"I'm sure I'm as messed up as Miriam. Come back later, I'm going to sleep."

"Your eyes are red."

"From the tear gas."

"I can't understand why you do these things to yourself. On behalf of people who are trying to kill you, people who cheer every time a bus with someone like you on it explodes."

"Please, Benny. I'm tired."

"Okay, I'm going, do you need anything?"

"Just sleep."

"What does tear gas feel like?' he asked, curious.

"It stings. Your lungs burn. You feel like throwing up, or at least I do. You get scared."

"Poor Dana."

"No, poor Palestinians."

Benny sighed heavily. "You have a good heart, Dana, but you

refuse to see the writing on the wall. I'll drop by later, unless business picks up."

"Great." I shut my eyes, and the sound of Benny shutting the door as he left was already mingling with a dream.

❂

First Daniel and I fixed up our flat, then we married, and then we fought.

When Daniel and I bought the three rooms that became our ground-floor flat, they looked as if they'd drawn inspiration from those black-and-white Time-Life photos of inner-city blight: broken sinks, cakes of dirt in every corner, spotted mirrors nailed to the wall. Prostitutes had lived in the building, and they'd left behind not only mirrors but also their shiny damask bedspreads. Daniel was horrified when I suggested we wash the bedspreads and use them as sofa covers.

The building was also stained and run down. But this was prime seaside property, and even the smallest of the three flats was very expensive. Daniel's parents were heavily in debt, so my father came to the rescue. "It's the least I can do, duckie," he said.

Daniel's younger sister Nina moved in with their grandmother, though she chose to sleep in the living room and to use the converted balcony for meditation. Nina was twenty-two and recently divorced; she was also unemployed and "off men" for the time being. Moving in with Granny suited her; in any case it was better than going back to her parents' house. At Granny's she could play tapes of her guru's teachings and listen to Ravi Shankar to her heart's content. She had even started giving yoga lessons to Elena, the prim Russian woman who came to read to Granny, and who, as it turned out, had back problems.

Daniel and I set up a tent in one of the rooms and lived in it while we worked on the flat. We broke down walls, retiled the floor, plastered and painted. Daniel was good with his hands, and he engraved small angels in the molding along the ceiling. The walls were replaced by arched passages: Daniel didn't like doors.

When the flat was ready we folded up the tent and bought a bed and olive green sofas and a faded olive and pink Turkish carpet for the living room. Then we invited everyone we knew to celebrate our marriage. My father arrived without Gitte, who had lost her parents in an air crash and was afraid of flying. She sent profuse apologies and a charming tapestry of tiny happy people enjoying themselves in a park. The wedding party lasted all night: over three hundred guests crowded into the two empty apartments on the third floor, which we had illegally taken over for the evening. Eventually the party spread to the beach, where we danced to live music and stuffed ourselves with catered food until sunrise.

In the early morning, after all the guests had left, Daniel and I walked slowly back to our flat and flopped down onto the new green sofas. The caterers had tidied up, more or less, but gifts lay scattered everywhere, a sea of boxes and packages. The smell of grass and hashish and ordinary cigarette smoke hung heavily in the air.

"The emperors of hash and grass have fled," I said, "leaving a trail behind them."

"You're more stoned than I thought."

"I'm not. I didn't smoke."

"It's enough to breathe in the air here."

"It's childish to humanize objects. I read that somewhere. But I can't help it. You've married a childish person, Daniel."

This was Daniel's cue to say something affectionate and reassuring, but he didn't answer. It was the first time he used silence against me, and I understood that we were moving toward a fight, though I was still hoping to stop it.

We were not used to discord. Until then we had only wondered, day after day and night after night, at how alike we were: the coincidences were almost alarming, and had we been inclined toward mysticism we might have posited fantastic phenomena: twins in another lifetime, carriers of sibling souls. We had the same hairbrush and toothbrush; we owned the same scarf, which we had both picked up at the same street stall. Our handwriting was nearly identical. In high school we had both given oral presentations on manipulation in the media, and a week before we met we had clipped the same cartoon from the newspaper. We even had male and female versions of the same name.

And now, married, exhausted, trying to hold on to my happiness, I said, "I wonder how a person knows. I wonder how you know when you see someone that this person is right for you, just by watching them sing and tell dumb jokes onstage."

"You must have a sixth sense, Dana. I had no clue at all."

"I know."

"I barely noticed you at the wedding."

"Don't rub it in!"

Again, Daniel said nothing. "You told me you thought I was cute," I reminded him, still hoping to recapture the bliss I'd felt only seconds before. But it was no longer possible to avoid the tension in the air, which was sliding and slipping around us like a filament of barbed wire.

"I just wondered why you'd come in your uniform—I thought you were probably one of those people who wanted to show off that they were in the army."

"I didn't have a dress!"

"Yes, but I didn't know that during the wedding."

"What else? What else did you think?"

"That's it."

"And what about when I came up to you? What did you think then?"

"I figured you were horny."

We'd had this conversation before—lovers always go back to the first innocent moments that spawned their love—but he had said kind and flattering things. "Weren't you at all attracted to me as a person?"

"I didn't know you."

"You thought I was some sort of desperate, pathetic loser?"

"No, I just thought you wanted sex."

"So . . . when were you sure?"

"Well, I'm sure now, of course."

I got up from the sofa and stared at him. I felt the fury rising in me. "Now! You weren't sure until now? Can I ask why you suggested getting married three days after we met?"

"You're the one who suggested it, Dana. And I agreed, partly to help you get out of the army. I figured we could always get divorced if things didn't work out."

I burst into tears. I was heartbroken, and nothing he said could console me.

"I said 'partly,'" he reminded me. "Partly to help you, partly because I thought I could fall in love with you. I'm not as impulsive as you are, Dana. I'm more cautious."

"So it was all a big act," I sobbed. "You were just pretending all along! You acted as if you were in love, otherwise I would never have brought up marriage!"

"I wasn't pretending, I loved having sex with you."

I stormed out of the flat and began walking along the main street: I didn't want to be alone. It was too early for the usual bustle, but here and there I passed people heading out for early-morning jobs or returning from night shifts, and soon the stores and restaurants would be opening. I knew Daniel was following me but I didn't turn. Finally I flopped down in exhaustion on a chair at a sidewalk café.

A few minutes later Daniel caught up with me. He ordered

coffee for both of us and sat down facing me across the round white table. He said, "I'm sorry, that came out wrong. I was afraid of my feelings for you, Dana. I didn't trust you, and it had nothing to do with you, but with me—it's hard for me to trust people right away. I'm not like you. What if I let myself go and then you left me? What if it was only a whim on your part? What if you did this all the time, went up to people and offered yourself? I couldn't know. But you know how much I love you now, I've told you a hundred times. Men get nervous when they love a woman this much. It's nerve-wracking, it makes us mean sometimes. You must be tired, Dana. Let's take a taxi home and get into bed and say a prayer of thanks to the gods." And right there, sitting at the table, he began to sing. He sang me one of his favorite songs. *Praise is due to the Creator for the dark and the light and the things that fly and the things that crawl and Noah and Cain and the fools and the prophets and the kings and your feet and your elbow and your smile and your light and the dark.*

It was impossible to stay angry after that. We took a taxi back to our new flat as he'd suggested, and we got into bed and thanked the gods.

❖

I didn't wake up until evening. I was hot and sweaty; I had not turned on the air conditioner before I fell asleep. I was also confused by my dream: Benny was crouching by the bed, stroking my hair. It was a dream I often had, especially when I fell asleep during the day, and it baffled me a little. The sensation was pleasant and I yielded to it easily, though at the same time I always thought, *Good thing I'm asleep and this isn't real life.*

I turned on the air conditioner and returned to bed for a few minutes because I needed to come. Usually I fantasized about Daniel, though not about actual encounters we'd had: my fantasies involved an imagined reunion in unfamiliar, faraway settings. On rare occasions Daniel was absent and I found myself conjuring surprising images of people I didn't know.

When I was finished, I took off my black top, poured cool water over my shoulders, put on one of Daniel's T-shirts, and went to check in on Volvo, my legless neighbor.

Volvo moved into the flat next to ours shortly after Daniel left. I saw at once that he was going to be difficult. His goal in life was apparently to impose his dark mood upon the entire world, and he reacted with bitter satisfaction to news of suffering and disaster. Since he had broken off all contact with his family and with friends he'd had before he lost his legs, it fell to me to look after him.

I did my best to make his dismal one-room flat habitable, and I arranged for a series of volunteers to come during the week. When no one was available, I helped him bathe and kept him company. On top of all his other problems, he had hemorrhoids, an ailment on which I was now unfortunately an expert. In the beginning he tried to drag me down with him by explaining that all happiness was immoral because what about the person next to you who had lost his legs? But he failed to convince me and he gave up and liked me for resisting. When he was in a particularly gloomy frame of mind he asked me to read him pornography, though he insisted that his interest in such things was purely scientific: he wanted to study the effect of sexual material on a man who had lost his sexuality along with his legs. I refused, and we compromised on *Lady Chatterley's Lover*, a few selected passages from *Ulysses*, and the work of a well-known local poet who was famous for, among other things, his lurid, transgressive writing.

I knocked lightly on Volvo's door, but there was no answer: he was asleep. I returned to my flat and switched on the television to see whether by some miracle there would be something about the demonstration, but the local news stations were occupied with the funerals of yesterday's restaurant victims. One mother had lost three children; she was brought to the funeral in a wheelchair and despite everyone's efforts she passed out. This was followed by a commercial promoting a cure for male impotence, which showed an overweight middle-aged man getting ready for sex and rejoicing in his recovered prowess. I flipped through the channels and landed on a game show in which two teams, women against men, were given sixty seconds to think of songs with specific words like *happiness* or *land*. An attack of masochism prevented me from turning off the television; I wondered whether Daniel was watching this show, wherever he was, and whether he was thinking of me, of the way we liked to laugh at what he called Torture TV.

I finally pulled myself out of the stupor I'd sunk into and wondered about dinner. I wasn't very hungry, so I made myself *café et lait* and checked my e-mail.

There was a letter from my father; he wrote every two or three days. His letters were nearly identical, not because he lacked imagination but because his life was repetitive, and he liked it that way. He wrote,

> *Dearest duckie,*
>
> *I was very pleased to hear from you. Before I forget, it's Gitte's birthday in three weeks, so please send her a little card. She kept the one you sent last year (with the pressed flowers) on the mantelpiece for months. It means a lot to her, so please don't forget, thank you darling. It's raining today, and we are sitting by our third fire of the season. For a while we had some trouble with the fireplace and a man came in to have a look, but the problem appears to have solved itself, or was scared away by the appearance of the man, the way my toothache always vanishes in the dentist's waiting room. Gitte is con-*

*cocting some new dessert in the kitchen and the fabulous smell
is making me hungry. For the hundredth time, darling, I wish
you would come and visit. You would love it here, and a vacation will do you good. There are many young people in the
neighborhood who would be very interested in meeting someone from Over There, and in seeing your photographs, etc. I've
said this before, and will probably keep needling you until you
give in. Alain and Sylvie are coming by later for dinner, to be
followed by a vigorous walk in the woods if we can get off our
lazy arses. We are all getting too fat. I miss you terribly, so
please come. The choir is taking a day off today, some sort of
important soccer match everyone has to watch and we couldn't
find another suitable time. The Messiah will have to wait. There
is nothing new to say about the dismal news so I will not say
it, except keep me up to date with everything you do. Be well,
have fun, go out dancing. Love, Dad. Love from Gitte. Many
many hugs and kisses. P.S. I've put two novels in the mail for
you, haven't read them yet but they look good.*

I replied at once. I gave my father a detailed account of the
demonstration: the walk through the field, the woman who'd
had a seizure, the two Palestinian friends. At the end of the letter I wrote without thinking, *A guy from the demo sat next to me
on the bus. He was in jail a few months ago for refusing to serve and I
sent him a postcard, but I didn't recognize him at first, because he used
to shave his head.* I looked at the two sentences, quickly deleted
them and sent the message.

The phone rang. For a second I thought it might be Rafi, and
I was afraid to answer.

But it was Beatrice, my freckled red-haired friend. I didn't
hear from her very often. She was an activist and also a phi-
losophy teacher, and she had a very hectic life, running from
one international conference to another while she tried at the

same time to raise a family, correct student papers, organize events, and write books. Sometimes in desperation she dumped a pile of essays on my bed and begged me to correct them for her. She visited about once a month, and usually stayed the night.

"Darling, Dana, how are you?" she asked. "I heard about the demo, I couldn't make it. Are you okay?"

"Yes, I'm fine."

"Good. It's been absolutely crazy. I haven't seen you in so long, maybe I'll drop by next weekend? My car broke down, it's just been insane. I need some quiet time with you, dear."

"Come on Friday, but call first to make sure I'm home. We're going to South Lifna, I don't know how long we'll be. Some rabbis are coming with us, so we're supposed to get back before sunset, but who knows."

"Perfect. I can't wait, dear. We'll talk on Friday. *Yalla,* bye, love."

I met Beatrice five years after Daniel left. I was taking photographs of a candlelight vigil at the Women's Reconciliation Tent, and Beatrice came up to me and asked about my work. At the end of the evening she insisted on giving me a ride home. "There's a chicken sandwich in my bag," she said, when we were in the car. She turned the ignition. "See if you can find it, I'm famished." I looked inside her huge, messy bag, which was stuffed with books, papers, makeup, hand lotion, sunscreen, and a lot of other junk. At the very bottom I found the sandwich, wrapped in tinfoil. She offered me half and we ate as we drove. "Delicious," I said.

When we reached my building she asked if she could come in.

"Of course," I said.

She wanted to see my photographs, and she was very excited about some of them. She was an excitable person in general. We sat on the living room floor, and she spread the photos out on the faded Turkish carpet until we were surrounded by a sea of images.

When I first took up photography I tried to capture the patterns and moods of people on the beach. I loved the dots of color sprinkled against the sand—no artist could have deliberately planned more intriguing compositions: streaks and splashes of brick red, bright yellow, pale blue, lollipop orange, black crescents on lime green. And I loved the way people let go at the beach: their bodies expanded with joy or wistful contentment or, at worst, resignation. The photos were of families and couples and solitary men or women; small naked children playing beach tennis or balancing on the edges of chairs; tubby people and thin young couples; a dark young man asleep on his stomach, his leg curled up toward his chest, sunk in the sand, exhausted, unable to bear the exhaustion, demanding comfort from the sand and finding it.

But most of my photographs were of the conflict, the physical ugliness of war, the people lost inside it. War destroys the landscape: for example, the metal lockers and cement blocks at checkpoints, crumbling stone and pieces of bent metal everywhere, human cages, watchtowers, ripped asphalt, barbed wire, floating garbage pinned to the barbed wire; shredded rubbery camouflage, flimsy and amorphous, like the khaki skin of a sea monster; improvised structures at military posts, all of them cheap, makeshift cement squares, slightly askew, because who can be bothered with architecture in wartime? No one worries about beauty when people are killing each other. Inside the mess and chaos floated an endless multitude of faces and bodies, extraordinary because of the extraordinary circumstances. They left their signatures on the landscape in the form of competing graffiti. Palestinian graffiti was trilingual: *Long live the PFF, I am the son of the PFF* (Arabic); *Come and see what you have done* (misspelled Hebrew); *American Occupation of Palestine*

(English). In response, young soldiers sprayed available surfaces with their own defiant strokes: the name of their unit, a Star of David, a fighter plane.

"How did you get into photography?" Beatrice asked.

"It's a long story."

"I'm going to publish these photos," she said. "Good thing I married a man who has not only a heart but also money! Now, what about your personal life?" she asked.

"Nothing much going on."

"That's what I was afraid of. You can't live like a cloistered nun, you know."

"Yes, yes . . ." I said vaguely.

"Don't 'yes yes' me, dear. Are you having any sex at all?"

"No."

"Since when?"

"Four years, seven months. There was someone a year after Daniel left, just a onetime thing, it was a disaster."

"That's scandalous. Someone like you! Don't you miss it?"

"I miss Daniel."

"You feel you have to be loyal to him." It was a mild reprimand: she clearly didn't think much of my approach.

"I can't help the way I feel," I said apologetically.

"Listen, dear. Would you feel it's less of a betrayal if we slept together?"

I considered her question. "Yes," I said at last. "Daniel wouldn't mind. It wouldn't bother him."

She looked at me a little pityingly, as if I were slightly backward. "I'll stay the night, then."

"All right. But I'm not experienced with women."

She laughed. "I'll let you read the manual first." She phoned her husband and told him she wasn't coming home. "Dudu, my love, I'll be back in the morning, I'm staying with Dana, poor sweet thing," she said, smiling at me. "Don't forget Hagari has her project, and there's that pizza in the freezer . . . yes . . . yes . . . fine. Bye for now, honey."

"He sends his regards," she told me, putting her phone away. "So, let's have some fun."

I didn't know how old Beatrice was; she never told anyone, and it was impossible to guess, partly because she was covered with freckles. There were times when I thought she was in her early forties, but then under bright morning light, just waking up, her russet hair spiky and silly on the pillow, she seemed older. She never discussed her past, she only talked about her current projects and her hopes for an end to the endless war, but I knew she had lost a son in the first Palestinian uprising. Sometimes she let me read her poems, which she scribbled on receipts, student papers, or any handy scrap of paper. The poems were ruthless: *the sergeant twists in his muddy bed one last oh fuck / in the evening nothing remains but the television fantasy of one more hero helping his country / over there lie the remains of the Palestinian girl he sported with this morning.* Nothing about Beatrice suggested that she harbored such poems and she seemed rather embarrassed when she showed them to me. I had a sense that I was the only person who saw these poetry scraps before they were stuffed into drawers.

We had an easy friendship, casual and simple. But I knew that Beatrice didn't approve of the way I conducted my life. She believed in looking ahead. It seemed to me that there was a price to pay for detachment, even if it helped Beatrice survive. In any case, detachment was not an option for me: Daniel was alive.

❖

Daniel was not interested in politics, as far as I could tell. When I brought up political subjects, his eyes would glaze over or else he'd start kidding around. "Saint Dana," he'd tease me. But I wasn't a saint; I acted as I did in order to stay afloat. I was living in the midst of a Swiftian farce and the only way for me to stay sane and keep my perspective was to become Gulliver. That was probably the reason I'd never joined any party or group. When I was growing up my father took me to demonstrations, and after he left the country I went on my own. I was a few feet away from the grenade that killed a demonstrator and wounded others, at one of our largest peace rallies. A Jewish extremist had thrown a grenade into the crowd. I heard a deafening explosion, the air filled with smoke, and everyone began running and screaming. For a while I was nervous about taking part in demonstrations, but the fear passed. You never knew how or when you'd die. No one can control fate, not by staying home and not by going out.

Daniel, on the other hand, had never been to a demonstration in his life before he met me. After we were married he came along a few times, but found the small subdued gatherings boring and hopeless. He liked to joke about the conflict. "The solution to the Palestinian problem," he'd say, "is the body-double plan." Each of us would have a Palestinian body double, and we'd switch places on Mondays, Tuesdays, Wednesdays, and alternating Thursdays. On those days the body double would take on the name Moishie Lipshuitz, for example, and move into Moishie's house, and Moishie would move into his double's house and take on the name Raid Ahmed Bashar. People could be matched by profession, taste in the opposite (or same, as the case might be) sex, and hair color.

If that didn't work, Daniel said, we could all leave. We could desert the entire region and spend the rest of our lives on Club Med cruise ships, only they'd be renamed Club Mid. Some of

Daniel's jokes were macabre and in poor taste; they were about things like recycling body parts and obligatory victim suits, with pictures of corpses on them, which all citizens should be forced to wear, in order to garner sympathy from our critics abroad and also to raise money. Instead of relying on posters of a child with missing limbs lying in a hospital bed, the foreign ministry could print an aerial view of the entire population dressed in victim suits.

When I came to know Daniel better I understood that he felt there was something trivial and tedious about endless analyses of the situation, endless conversations in living rooms. A few months after we married there was a problem with an Arab at the firm he worked for. The army approached the company and asked them to design a big military complex. It was a great contract for them, huge. The army said this guy, Isa, who was one of the architects, couldn't be part of the project, or even part of the firm, because he didn't have clearance. The firm didn't want to fire Isa, but they promised to keep him away from the project. They took away his keys to the filing cabinets and moved him to an isolated office. He had an entire floor to himself, but he was all alone there. Daniel quit in protest, and one other woman left, too. Daniel didn't tell me about any of this while it was going on. He just came home one day and announced that he'd quit his job. "Why?" I asked. "Too many racist cowards," he said. I had to ply him with questions to get the full story.

✳

It was time for the sea, my drug and my salvation. The sea kept me from drowning myself, a notion I had never seriously contemplated, but I knew that if I did, the sea would be there to hold me up and send me back. Every evening I walked the one hundred steps from my flat to the beach, to the soft hot sand or the soft cool sand, depending on the season. There were times when I didn't go out until late at night, but my favorite time was dusk, when the waves turned into white satin and pale blue silk with gray transparent strips of light shimmering under the fading sun.

I stepped out of our building and waved to Marik, a young immigrant with smooth skin and slanted eyes who guarded the gleaming new City Beach Hotel across the street. Poor Marik sat on his stool all day, sullen and languid behind an incongruous office desk that was taken out to the street every morning and removed at midnight.

I once had a very embarrassing experience with Marik. One sweltering summer night I had left the house wearing a long cotton dress. I rarely wore anything but jeans, but I had a yeast problem at the time and the doctor had recommended loose clothing until it went away. So I bought an ankle-length Indian dress; I wanted it to be light and colorful because I didn't want to be mistaken for a religious woman. I wasn't wearing panties; they only made matters worse, and the dress was long enough to provide a feeling of security. Unfortunately, on my way back from the beach, just as I reached my building, I stepped on a sidewalk grate, the kind that produced such winsome cinematic results when Marilyn Monroe encountered it in her white skirt. In my case, the dress blew skyward above my shoulders, leaving me completely naked on the street.

I didn't understand at first what had happened, which made the dreadful moment last even longer. I tried to pull down my dress, without success; my second idea was to crouch down. Only then did it occur to me that I had to move away from the grate under my feet. Luckily it was already dark, and the street was deserted, but Marik was still on duty. He had ducked inside the hotel in a panic.

I decided to ignore the event entirely, and made a point of waving to him as usual when I left the building the following morning. But Marik never recovered, and though he continued to nod back in his usual sullen way, after that day he looked mortified every time he saw me.

I waved at him now, then headed west, toward the sea.

Though I had walked down this street ten thousand times on ten thousand evenings, the pangs of my unrequited love for it never diminished. The buildings on my side of the street were weather-stained in competing layers of black, sepia, ash, bone, peach. Geometric patterns emerged from the edges and rims of windows, doors, security bars, the metal rods of air-conditioner supports, the fat, hairy trunks of palm trees next to narrow electric poles. A multitude of details interrupted the patterns: black and gray graffiti, abandoned scraps in the alley, crevices and cracks in the walls, the tips of new sunny-white buildings peeking from other streets. In the midst of this collage a naked neon woman reclined on a white panel like an oblivious angel; she had once reigned over Bar Sexe. The caged cavern under the sign no longer led to a bar but was still an important meeting place for certain citizens who, as I quickly discovered, did not like to be photographed.

Further down, behind a brash pop drink sign, our miniature La Scala maintained its dignity, despite the yellow and maroon sheets nailed to its arches. The real La Scala's arches are on the ground floor, but here the four arches had been reproduced on all three stories, and the building, which stands at an intersection, curves gently around the corner. I often thought about the surge of enthusiasm that lay behind the design of this building, when the city was very young. And though the arches were now smudged and dingy and someone told me that people did drugs behind the yellow and maroon sheets, the faith that had inspired this doomed project still had the power to move me.

I walked past the defunct Bar Sexe, past our miniature La Scala, past the chairs scattered on the sidewalk outside the little convenience store, past the store's mounted television, set permanently to the sports channel, across the street to the paved boardwalk, with its patterns of concentric circles echoing the movement of the waves, and down the stairs to the beach. The change from walking on a hard surface to sinking unpredictably with each step was always a surprise. At this time of night the sea was black, except for strips of pearl white foam along the edge of waves, and navy blue shadows where light from the street or moon happened to fall. There were couples lying on blankets here and there, a few joggers, and one or two determined late-night swimmers. A voice said, "Mia?"

I turned and saw a man with a long oval face standing behind me. He was dark-skinned, tall and very broad, like a weight lifter.

"Pardon me," he said. "I thought you were someone else."

Normally I would not have answered because I had a rule about pickups and the rule was that I didn't do them. A year after Daniel vanished I had yielded to the relentless pressure of friends and acquaintances, and allowed someone to follow me home. I met him at a little video store down the street from my flat. There was barely room to move between the three crowded shelves, and our bodies kept brushing against one another as we looked for movies. Finally he spoke to me. I suppose it was partly his height that misled me about his age, though it's also possible that I was too detached to worry about how old he might be. I didn't discourage him, and when I left the store he trotted next to me like a colt. He came into my flat, and then remembered to ask my name. I didn't want to tell him. "What do I look like?" I asked him. He considered. "You look like a Simone," he said. "That's me, Simone," I said. He let it go; he was too excited to insist. I liked him: his soft green eyes, his anxious shoulders, the way he talked about his collie and his trip to Italy on the way to my place.

But in bed, he barely knew what he was doing—though he wouldn't admit it and tried hard not to show it. I had to explain some things to him; he was embarrassed and pretended he'd known all along. Everyone had told me I needed to see other men, but it didn't work. The experience had no relation to anything that was going on in my life, to who I was or how I felt. After he left I soaked the sheets in soapy water and called Odelia. "I wonder why everyone thinks adultery is such a good thing," I said. I told her about the boy and about the sheets soaking in the tub. "Washing sheets after the guy leaves . . . that's always a bad sign," she agreed. And then she apologized, because she'd been one of the people advising me to date. "Do what you feel is right," she said.

For weeks afterward he called me every day, came knocking at my door. It turned out that he was sixteen and in high school. He was desperate, and it took a lot of energy getting rid of him, and I hurt him. I promised myself that this would be the last time, and it was.

But that night, after the demonstration in Ein Mazra'a and the two intrusive sentences in the letter to my father—that night I wanted distraction. And though I had no intention of letting this man follow me home, I didn't send him away.

"I've seen you here," the man said. "I've seen you walking here at all hours, as solitary as a wolf in the forest."

I continued strolling along the shore, where the tide had created a smooth shelf of wet sand, flat and generous, giving us back the imprints of our shoes as we walked.

"Once I saw you with a camera slung around your neck," the man said. "You were taking photographs at dusk. Is it okay with you that I'm walking next to you? Tell me if it isn't. I don't want to intrude."

And this is where normally I would have said, "It isn't okay, go away, I need to be alone."

But I said, "I don't mind."

His spirits lifted. "You're very kind," he said. "You have a compassionate heart. It really shows on you, it sits on you like a coat. A coat of many colors," he chuckled.

"What are you doing here at this hour?" I asked him.

"I just came back from reserve duty, I came for a jog, to clear my mind," he said. "To breathe in some sea air. You can feel the heat coming from the waves, but it's a pleasant heat."

I took another look at him, and it was true, he was dressed for jogging: running shoes, shorts, T-shirt. He looked reliable; he looked like someone you could trust to pick you up in his large arms and carry you if you fainted or had a seizure from tear gas. He would know not only what to do but also how to do it, because he was clever. You could tell these things from his eyes, his hands, and especially his way of speaking—not just his voice but also the interesting words he used, his perfect grammar. It was pleasing to the ear, his poetic use of language.

"You use nice words," I said.

"Nice words?" He was puzzled.

"Yes."

"No one ever said that to me."

"People don't notice things."

"*I* never noticed," he laughed. "What sort of nice words?"

"The way you speak, the phrases you use."

"Come to think of it, I did very well on the vocabulary part of my psychometric exam. I remember they remarked on that, they were impressed. I just have a good memory. Maybe one day I'll write a novel. About reincarnation. A man who was a warrior in the days of the Bible, reborn today . . . a hero from ancient times, like Samson, let's say. Fighting the Philistines.

The whole story of Samson repeated, because he's a reincarnation. Do you believe in reincarnation? I do."

"I support the Palestinian struggle," I told him.

"Oh well," he said. He didn't care. He only cared about whether he was going to get anywhere with me. "This is romantic," he said, "walking along the shore with you."

"It would be, if I knew you," I said. "If I knew you and we were in love. Then it would be romantic. As it is, I can't think of anything less romantic."

"We were destined to meet, it was preordained," he said. He couldn't think of anything else to say.

"How do I know you're not a psychotic rapist?" I asked him.

He paused, surprised. "I'm safe," he said.

"Do you have children?"

"Yes, a son. I missed him while I was away. I'm glad to be back from reserve duty. He's in kindergarten. A very naughty boy. Naughty, but clever. You know what he asked me the other day?"

"No."

"Where is yesterday's time? Is it gone, or is it in our thoughts? That's what he asked. Isn't that clever?"

"Yes."

"It's nice to be home."

"Where were you?"

"In Dar al-Damar. I'm in a special unit."

"What do you do, in civilian life?"

"I teach programming."

"You could be lying," I said. "I don't know you. I don't know anything about you. Maybe you just escaped from prison. Where you were serving time for killing your wife with a chain saw."

"I'll show you my ID if that helps. My army ID too, if you want, I think it's still in my pocket. I'd show you my business card but I don't have my wallet on me—I just came to jog."

I laughed. He was very happy when I laughed.

"Okay, show me your ID," I said.

He pulled his ID out of his pocket. His name was Aaron and he was forty years old. Then he showed me his army ID. He looked about eighteen in the photo.

"Well, now that I've seen your ID and I even know your serial number, I guess you can come over."

"Thank you. You can trust me."

"I was just kidding."

"Why not? Why not? This is perfect—you, me, a perfect night."

"No," I said.

I didn't say anything more. Aaron went on talking about how much he loved the sea, and then he talked about his son, but I wasn't listening. He gave up and walked silently next to me.

We reached the southern end of the beach. "I have to go now," I told him. "It's getting late."

"Do you have a boyfriend waiting for you?"

"No, I live alone. Good-bye."

"Maybe I'll run into you another time."

"Maybe," I said. I climbed the stairs to the boardwalk and walked back to my flat.

✸

Daniel and I lived together for seven years and two months. Daniel designed buildings and I worked at an insurance office. I enjoyed my job: I typed letters in English, handled overseas phone calls, brought lunch for everyone, and watered the plants. The office was full of interesting exotic plants because our employer, a bald, friendly man who was, however, capable of ruthless decisions when it came to client claims, was an amateur horticulturist; he had taped instructions about each plant to the wall and it was a compliment that he trusted me with their care. "I can count on you, Dana," he used to say.

In the evenings Daniel and I nearly always went out: to concerts, comedy shows, plays, lectures. We wore matching outfits and everywhere we went there were people we knew. We had friends who were artists and musicians, waiters and drifters, students and left-wing lawyers; we got together with them for dinner or at parties that lasted all night. Daniel invented our own private language, called Kamatzit, in which the syllables of words were all vocalized with a short *a* sound, in honor of my name.

We tried to have a child, and I finally succeeded in getting pregnant, but I miscarried in my sixth month. Daniel was convinced that he had saved my life by harassing everyone in the hospital and insisting they take me in and look after me instead of letting nature take its course, as they suggested, and I was angry at him for being rude and alienating the entire hospital staff, but we were both just stressed out and disappointed. The experience brought us even closer, if that was possible. We breathed the same air and a few times we had the same dreams at night. Once we both dreamed we were in a field filled with rabbits and we were feeding them lettuce; another time we dreamed we were on a sailboat with Asian sailors.

Before Daniel I had hardly thought about men, or about how they might be different from women. I now felt that there was such a thing as maleness (men were never cold, for example); this uncharted territory was interesting, and also moving. I watched Daniel, the things he did, the way he looked at the world. I watched how he held a coffee mug or undressed, I noticed his attitude to his body, his work, other people. I had dreams in which I found myself on a planet inhabited only by men and I tried to pass for one as well, and no one guessed I was really a woman because I'd come to know Daniel so well.

When I came home from the beach it was past midnight. I realized that I hadn't eaten all day, so I boiled two eggs and made myself a sandwich. Then I undressed, turned on the air conditioner, and lay in bed. On some nights, as soon as I shut my eyes I saw a tangled dam, the kind a small, industrious animal might construct out of sticks and leaves and mud. The image interfered with sleep and in fact was no more than a visual projection of insomnia. When that happened, I would summon three memories and try to slide with them through the dam and into sleep.

The first memory was of a sandstorm. I was twelve; we were about to move to the city and our flat was full of boxes. The ones my father had packed were neatly marked *dishes* and *books,* while my mother's packing style was reflected in her less disciplined scrawls: *junk from drawers* and *junk from office.*

We'd been warned that day that a sandstorm was coming our way; there were continual reminders on the radio, and our teachers instructed us to roll wet towels and place them under doors. And yet somehow from one moment to the next it slipped my mind, and shortly after I came home from school I decided to walk to the corner store to buy a snack. My parents were still at work and there was nothing tempting in the fridge or pantry. I left the building and began crossing the parking lot. All at once it came. I didn't understand at first what was happening—I only knew that I couldn't open my eyes or breathe or move. I kneeled on the ground, pulled off my shirt, and wrapped it around my head. The sand burned my skin, sank into my hair, entered my mouth and nose through the shirt. And yet I found that if I covered my face with the palms of my hands, inside the shirt, I could breathe, and I was after all, alive, a tiny living cocoon, breathing inside my hands, inside the shirt, inside the sandstorm. I decided that it was precisely because people were so small that they managed to survive on this huge and dangerous planet: how much air did we really need, and what did we need apart from air? Eventually someone noticed me; I felt strong arms lifting me into a car. I was rescued.

The second memory was a remnant from my army days. I'd been sitting on my bed trying to clean my weapon and as usual everything was going wrong. I finally threw the rifle on the floor in disgust and ran out of the barracks. I made my way to the edge of the camp, looked out at the trees beyond the fence, and decided that I was nothing more or less than a prisoner. A prisoner in a jail operated by cruel and insane jailers. I heard someone call my name and I turned. Sheera, the girl who had given me the gold locket, came up to me. She handed me my weapon, but as if it were something else—a birthday present, or a lovely sweater. "You're smarter than everyone here," she said. I noticed her long brown hands, her long slender fingers and perfectly curved fingernails. She had beautiful hands. "I'm not, I'm stupid," I said. "Well," she conceded, "you are a little obstinate. But you'll grow out of it. Come, the army needs you." She took my hand and led me back to the barracks, and for once, thanks to her and to my good luck, I didn't get caught.

The third memory dated back to the second year of my marriage. I had dragged Daniel to a lecture about civil rights in some remote town in the north; he had not wanted to go but gave in for my sake. When we arrived we found that the lecture had been canceled. The people there invited us to stay for supper, but Daniel was too angry to accept. As we headed home a downpour hit us and our car got stuck in the mud. There was no one around, so we had to abandon the car and start walking. Neither of us was adequately dressed, and the rain chilled us as we trudged through the shallow puddles on the dirt road. By this time Daniel was in such a bad mood that I sat down in the mud and cried. Daniel began laughing, and then we both laughed and he sat down next to me and we kissed. Eventually a Druze came by in a truck. He tied a rope to the fender of our car and pulled us out.

These memories were wonderfully dense and heavy, like an imaginary object that can't be lifted even though it's the size of a pea. They began to merge as I grew drowsy: I was in the mud, sand was blowing around me, Sheera was handing me my weapon, Daniel was kissing me but we couldn't kiss properly because there was sand in my mouth. Sheera's long brown fingers, the rope the Druze tied to our car . . . The pleasant confusion of near-sleep—the last stage before drifting off—took over and I yielded to it.

❂

Daniel and I quarreled again, about a month after our first fight. We quarreled about the mess in the house, and it was a conflict we never resolved, it came up again and again, and we argued about it again and again. My father had been neater than my mother, but it never seemed to bother them. Sometimes my father tidied up after my mother and sometimes he didn't.

But in our case the clash between Daniel's approach to his environment and mine was a problem we didn't know how to solve. Daniel was calm, usually; he felt that keeping one's cool was a national duty. He said that if people became nervous and irritable about everything that was wrong with the country, they became part of what was wrong, because one of the main things wrong with the country was that everyone was nervous and irritable. He either joked about things that bothered him or tackled problems pragmatically. Sometimes he had an outburst—when our tires were slashed, for example, because I'd put a sticker on the car that said AIDS KILLS: WEAR CONDOMS / THE OCCUPATION KILLS: WITHDRAW, but there was something theatrical and innocuous about his anger, as if even he didn't take it seriously.

At first he tried to understand me. "How can you live like this?" he'd ask, truly baffled. "How can it not bother you? It's so ugly. It's so ugly and disgusting. Don't you care whether you step on apple peels at night on your way to the bathroom? How can you not be grossed out by gobs of hair in the sink? Disembodied hair . . . it's like seeing a corpse. Beauty matters. How can someone not care about beauty?"

"I don't mind if you clean up," I offered generously.

"I can't spend my life cleaning up after you, and I resent it. And I just hate coming home from work to this; it makes me think you don't care about me or about how I feel. Why is it so hard for you, Dana, to put a cup in the sink, or hang up a shirt?"

"I feel as nervous when things are neat as you do when they aren't," I said.

"You're just lazy."

"I feel more at home, cozier, if there's a mess. This isn't a museum, it's a place where we live. I like having our stuff all over the place. I get scared when things are too orderly, it makes me think of being forced to do things. Besides, if I put things away I'll forget about them. I need to be reminded that there are bills to pay, and activities coming up."

"Look," he'd say, pulling an empty box of tissues out of a tiny garbage pail. "Even when you put things in the garbage you don't really bother. This box is bigger than the pail, what's the point?"

"It's a reminder. A reminder that it's on the way to that great big garbage dump in the sky."

"I don't think it's funny. I think you're being selfish."

"But why aren't you the one who's selfish, wanting me to conform?"

"I can't believe anyone can prefer ugliness to beauty."

"You have a very narrow definition of beauty, Daniel."

That would hurt him. He felt then that I was attacking the most essential thing about him, the thing that defined him: his passion for architecture. And I would feel remorseful and penitent. I'd start cleaning up, but Daniel's mood would be ruined; the evening would be ruined. And I had no talent for cleaning up. "I don't know how to organize stuff," I said. "This place is too small. There's no room for anything."

So Daniel built all sorts of clever shelves and cupboards for me. But nothing helped. I never reformed, and he never got used to my slovenly habits. We hired a woman to come two afternoons a week and bring order to chaos, but her good work never lasted. "Like the sand in *Woman of the Dunes,*" Daniel said when he was in a good mood and trying to joke about it. But most of the time he wasn't amused and every now and then he walked out of the house in protest, leaving me to sit in the squalor and sulk.

# Sunday

✸

I WAS WORKING ON MY NOVEL when the phone rang. I ignored it, and continued writing.

*He took her in his strong arms and murmured in her ear, "Angela, Angela. Why did I read that letter before I left for St. Petersburg? If Sir Anthony returns tomorrow, nay, if he returns tonight—*

Fifteen minutes later it rang again. I answered this time, though I knew it would be Rafi.

"Hello, is Dana there, please?" he joked.

"Don't call," I said.

"I'm right outside the hotel. Come have coffee with me."

"No, I can't," I said. "I'm busy."

"What building are you in?"

Instinctively I looked out of my living room window, and there was Rafi, standing next to Marik the guard, talking into his cell phone. He waved at me.

"Why? Why are you here?" I asked.

"That's what it says I have to do on my list. Call Dana."

He raised his arm with the white sheet of paper, like a soldier waving a flag of surrender. "You don't believe me," he said. He crossed the street, came up to the window, which was only slightly higher than the top of his head, and tried to show me the paper with the green handwritten notes.

"I'll meet you in the hallway," I said.

I came out to the hall and took the list from his hands.

It was true, my name was there: *Pick up bread, pickles, bananas, rolled oats, vitamin E. Give glasses in for repair. Stain remover for sofa. Call Eve about piano tuner. Pick up Naomi at 16:15, remind Yolande about Thursday. Call Dana.*

I was the last item.

"Call Dana, why?"

"My wife wants to meet you. She knows you—she saw you on television talking about your husband. You're famous, Dana. Anyhow, she wants to invite you over for dinner."

"No."

"Why?"

"You know why."

"Because I'm attracted to you?"

"Yes."

"Let's have coffee at the hotel. It's air-conditioned and my old buddy Coby says it's on the house."

"The manager?"

"Yes."

"I have to save what I have on my computer."

"I'll wait."

"Wait for me there. Don't wait here."

I sat down at my computer and stared at the screen. *Sir Anthony may have the letter Martha sent about the inheritance,* I wrote. *If the Countess sees the letter, her sweet, innocent daughter will be banished from the palace at once and her life will be in grave danger. Bandits roaming the countryside had already—*

I gave up. I closed the file and made my way across the street.

Rafi was waiting for me in the lobby of the City Beach Hotel. He rose when he saw me and smiled. I didn't smile back. I followed him to the dining room: pink and blue flowers in slender vases on each table, four or five foreign journalists stuffing themselves with food from the breakfast buffet.

We sat in the corner and drank coffee. Rafi watched me with his black eyes. I remembered reading somewhere that irises couldn't really be black, only very dark brown.

He produced a pack of cigarettes from his back pocket and with the casual urgency of an addict placed a cigarette in his mouth while looking around for matches. I stared at his hands, his mouth, and remembered Daniel's hands turning the key to his grandmother's flat.

"You smoke."

"Less than I used to. Does it bother you?"

"No, I just hate it when people smoke. I had a friend who died of lung cancer, someone I met in the army. She gave me this locket when our sergeant hurt my feelings." I showed him the tiny gold heart, my mother's smiling face nestled inside. "It's a miserable way to die."

"You're right," Rafi said, inhaling deeply. "What happened with the sergeant?"

"She said it was a good thing my mother was dead, so she wouldn't have to see what a loser her daughter was."

"I guess since she couldn't make you dig a hole."

"I did clean a lot of toilets."

"Toilets plus insults."

"But at least no holes. Did you dig holes?"

"No, not even once. I was a model soldier."

"Daniel was a dysfunctional soldier. They got so mad at him they almost killed him."

"They were so happy with me they almost killed me," Rafi said, laughing.

"I realize now that I've seen you lots of times," I said. "I just got confused because you didn't have hair back then. You used to shave your head and you wore sunglasses."

"I still wear sunglasses."

"Also the red baseball cap is new."

"It was lost. I just found it the other day. It was lost for years."

"Where did you find it?"

"My brother had it all along. I left it at his place once, and it got stuck in a drawer. For several years."

I said, "I don't know why you asked me here."

"This is not what you think," Rafi replied. "Things aren't always what they appear to be. As you of all people know."

"Don't confuse me."

"But you're not easily confused."

"No, so don't try, it's a waste of time."

He laughed again. He was in a good mood.

"I don't know why you're here," I repeated. "I'm married, I love my husband, I'm loyal to him."

"I'm married, too," Rafi said.

"I shouldn't be sitting here with you."

"I guess I'm going to have to report you. I don't want to, but I really have no choice. It's my duty."

"I don't know anything about you. I'm afraid of you."

He said, "Don't be afraid, because I'll protect you and I won't let anything or anyone harm you, not my wife, not myself, no one. And this fear of yours, fear of your own vulnerability, this is one of the things that's making you so unhappy."

"I *am* vulnerable. It's not an irrational fear. But I believe you. Say it again."

"I wouldn't let anyone hurt you. I wouldn't allow it."

"Are you so protective of everyone?"

"I do have a bit of a maternal streak. And you could use some cheering up. Come over for dinner tonight, and we'll invite a few more friends."

"I don't know. I don't know what to say."

"Say yes."

"My life is fine as it is."

"Yes, I can see that."

"I can't tell whether you're being ironic."

"Both ironic and not ironic. Because your life is both fine and not fine."

"Well it's not perfect, of course! I'm waiting for Daniel, I miss him. I miss him all the time. But things could be a lot worse. For example, you could make things worse."

"How, Dana?"

"I don't know."

"I'm not going to make things worse for you, that's not my style at all. I like happy endings as much as you do. We're very similar that way."

"Why do they use camouflage?"

"What?"

"It's something I've always wondered about. That weird camouflage stuff you see all over the place—you know, those rubbery leaves on army shelters, cabins . . . what's it for? Do you have any idea?"

He stared at me.

"What?" I asked.

"Oh, nothing. Pardon me. It's just that I thought I was having coffee with Dana. And now it turns out I'm having coffee with Bana, her twin sister from outer space. My mistake."

"I can't know everything!"

"Her sister from outer space, who is visiting this part of the world for the first time."

"Come on, tell me."

"Well now, let's see. Keeps out the wind, gives our sheds a nice fashionable touch, it's the latest in military deco and you know we like to keep up to date with world fashions. What else? I guess it makes it a bit hard to see what's going on inside."

"I thought of that. I thought it might be for privacy. But sometimes you see it just thrown over blocks of stone."

"That's when the word *camouflage* can come in useful."

"You don't understand. You don't understand what I'm saying. I'm saying it isn't logical. Because sometimes you see that stuff in places where no one's trying to hide anything. Not a rock and not soldiers beating someone up."

"Relax, Dana."

"Sorry. I just get frustrated when no one understands."

"You must live in a perpetual state of frustration."

"No, not at all."

"I think most of the time it's there for privacy, and sometimes it's there so things don't stand out at night, and sometimes it's probably part of the overall chaos that reigns in the army. Someone fills in an order, we need blocks here, and sandbags, and throw in some camouflage for good measure. Then those things arrive, and no one really knows what the camouflage is for and they just throw it on something and no one thinks about it ever again, not the Palestinians, not the army, not civilians, no one in this entire country gives it a moment's thought, except for Dana Hillman, who spends five years wondering about it."

I smiled. "Thank you."

"There's something truly naïve about you, Dana. I can't really explain it, you're not clued out, you know what's what, but you're naïve in some way I can't put my finger on. It's as if you were looking for the pure essence in everything. You believe it's there, and you're determined to find it."

"Daniel said my problem was that I never want to think the

worst. He was right. I hate thinking the worst about people. It's a terrible way to live."

"Really! I'm the exact opposite. I always think the worst." Rafi took one last drag on his cigarette and stubbed it out in the ashtray.

"Are you thinking the worst about me?"

"Yes."

"What's the worst?"

"You have a rip in your T-shirt. You don't brush your hair. You hide behind your camera. That's it."

"I don't like buying clothes Daniel won't get to see. I do brush my hair, but it gets tangled right away. I take photos because I like shapes and textures and contrasts. I like capturing things people might miss or forget otherwise. I like all the strange things that happen all the time, everywhere."

"How did you get into photography?"

"It's a long story."

"I like long stories."

"Well, right after Daniel vanished I began having trouble with my eyes. I couldn't see properly. I had blurry vision, I had trouble seeing distances and also up close—they thought I had a brain tumor. I went to all sorts of specialists but nothing helped. Finally they said I needed a shrink. They made an appointment for me with this old religious guy. At first I thought it wouldn't work out, because he was religious—I thought the barrier between us would be too great. But since I wasn't the one paying I didn't have a choice, I had to take whoever they gave me. As it turned out, we got along really well. He said the country was cursed at the moment. He called it the curse of the golem, when people can no longer think and see and understand. He said Daniel would come back to me when he was ready, and not before, and that in the meantime I should just go on helping other people. He said that in the Bible, Daniel was associated with all sorts of miracles, and that maybe there would be a miracle in this case too, but until then I had to look after myself and after people who were suffering, because I would understand them. I told him about my eyes, and he asked me to bring in photos of different people so we could look at them and see whether looking at them and thinking certain thoughts would help. And when he saw my photographs he said I was talented, and that I should take a photography course, and he also had a feeling that photography would cure me. Maybe it was a coincidence, but the problem did go away soon afterward. I wanted to continue seeing him, but he said he'd done all he could for me. I loved him, and he loved me too."

"That story wasn't too long. Do you just photograph people?"

"No, but when I photograph the landscape I try to show the things people have done to it, the clues it gives you about who lives there and what's going on. Just like clothes. Clothes are clues, too. The Palestinians are incredibly neat. I was at a checkpoint, the new one in Oreif, and the kids were waiting to go to school. They were so neat. Every hair in place, even the knapsacks didn't have a speck of dust on them. They looked scrubbed, their clothes looked scrubbed."

"Yes, they have a lot of self-respect. That's probably why they're constantly worried that they've hurt your feelings. They assume the other person has the same self-respect."

"Do you speak Arabic?"

"A little."

"I've always wondered how they feel when they watch American sitcoms—all the rules are different, the whole family structure, the relationships. Are they shocked?"

"Of course not. They just find it funny. Everyone can relate to those feelings, even if you're not allowed to express them yourself. Probably the more repressed you are in your own life, the more you like watching people on television act goofy.

And as you know, not all Palestinians are traditional."

"I can't come over. I can't come for dinner. Please thank your wife for me."

"Enjoying this conversation too much, Dana?"

"That's a mean thing to say. You said you wouldn't hurt me and already you're being mean."

"I'd apologize if I believed you."

"Oh, fine, fine. You win," I said.

"Great. I'll pick you up at seven."

"Can I bring my neighbor?"

"Of course."

"He's very, very crabby and unpleasant."

"We don't mind."

"He's in a wheelchair, with his leg stumps exposed."

"Sure, bring him. Why not?"

"We can't discuss politics or any of our activities in front of him, it would hurt him."

"Okay."

"Will that be a problem for your wife?"

"I sometimes wonder whether she knows who the prime minister is. She lives in her own world, Dana."

"All right, I'll come. We'll come. But no other guests, please."

"Here's my phone number in case there's a change of plan." He wrote his number on the back of his matchbook and handed it to me. "Does that guy need special transportation?"

"We'll manage. As long as you have an elevator."

"Yes, we do," he said.

❖

Like all couples, we discussed cheating. "What would you do if I cheated on you?" Daniel asked one evening, as we relaxed on the sofa.

"I don't know. I can't imagine it. What would you do?"

"I'd leave you."

"Really?"

"Yes. It would ruin things forever, I'd never be able to trust you, there wouldn't be any point."

"Are you warning me?" I asked, curious.

"Of course not. If you sleep with someone else it's because I've failed you somehow. I hope you'll tell me first if you're ever that unhappy—not that I can imagine it. But if you sleep with another man it will be my fault."

"But you'd still leave me?"

"Yes, because there wouldn't be a way to fix things."

"It won't happen, of course."

"I know . . . Both my parents had lovers," Daniel said.

"Really! You never told me."

"It's no big deal. But I hated it. I hated that whole scene, and I almost lost my respect for them."

"Why? Why did they do it?"

"I don't know. They got along, but they were attracted to other people and they gave in to their attraction, I guess. They didn't talk about it, of course, but we knew. My mother would come home with her eyes red from chlorine; she must have had a rich lover with a swimming pool in the building. My father would come home and go straight to the shower with this guilty look on his face. Then there were phone calls, private calls, which they would take in the bedroom, and they'd shut the door and put on the radio so no one could hear. They must have thought they had retarded kids. I think they really had no idea how obvious they were."

"But did they know about one another?"

"I don't know. They must have. I mean, I can't imagine them not knowing, if it was so obvious to us, but maybe they were so absorbed in their own affairs that they didn't notice that their spouse was cheating too. They were bored, I think. They were bored with their lives, with their horrible clerical jobs."

"My parents were the exact opposite. They had this twosome that was almost impenetrable, because they felt they had shared so much that other people didn't understand. As if everyone was an outsider, except maybe for my uncle and his wife. For one thing, their experiences in South Africa bound them together, what they went through there when they were fighting apartheid."

"What exactly did they go through?"

"I don't really know. They never told me about it, except for hints here and there. They risked their lives and they were in prison for a while. They had a rough time in prison, but it was only for a few months, I think. I should ask my father one of these days. And then when they got here, most of the people they knew weren't as radical as they were. They were a good match."

"I trust you, Dana."

"I trust you, of course."

"Well, you—you trust a lot of people."

"It makes life more pleasant," I said.

"Riskier."

"No, less risky. You'd see that if you tried it."

"I can't."

"Try it sometime. Try trusting people more. You'll see, it works out. It protects you. You think it makes you more vulnerable but it doesn't."

"No, I just can't see that. I think you have to be on the lookout or you'll get stabbed in the back."

"I don't believe that. Most people are nice."

Daniel burst out laughing. "Yes, and history proves it."

"People just get led astray."

"I suppose that's one way of looking at it," Daniel said.

✵

On the way back to my flat I knocked on Volvo's door. "Anyone home?" I called out.

"Enter."

I opened his door and peeked in. He was still in bed, lying on his back. He had been over six feet tall when he had his legs and now he lifted weights to keep his torso and arms in shape. He looked solid and sturdy, lying there on the bed, his stumps protruding from pajama shorts. I had painted the walls of his little room sand white and had decorated them with prints of van Gogh's *Sidewalk Café* and Matisse's *Window*: the café was a compromise, gently suggesting to Volvo an alternative to his rigid outlook while relenting partially on the question of sorrow, but the window, with its dazzling optimism, left no room for discussion. Volvo complained that I was being manipulative; nevertheless, I often caught him staring at Matisse's multiple rectangles of happy light. The room contained only a narrow bed and a chair: Volvo kept his clothes in a suitcase under the bed and his books stacked in tall, precarious piles against the wall. He didn't want to feel settled, he said. "I'll end up in Siberia anyhow," he added. I had no idea what he meant, and didn't bother asking.

"Volvo, do you want to come with me to dinner tonight? Someone I met invited me. A guy, Rafi, and his wife."

"Yeah, all right. Who's favoring me with his or her presence today?" he asked, referring to the volunteers. He always pretended not to know the volunteer schedule, even though there were only four and they always came on the same days: Rosa on Sundays and Thursdays, Joshua on Mondays, Miss (or rather, Sister) Fitzpatrick on Wednesdays, and Daniel's old friend Alex, the albino musician who had played in their band, on either Friday or Saturday, depending on his availability.

"Rosa's coming today, as I'm sure you know." Rosa was a very devoted volunteer, and though she had innumerable health problems of her own, she cleaned Volvo's flat, went shopping for him, and did most of his cooking. She was a widow and extremely talkative; she never noticed Volvo's bad moods because she was too busy telling him about her own tragedy-filled life, past and present.

"God help me."

"Do you need anything?"

"If Rosa lost forty pounds and had a brain transplant she would actually be tolerable."

"She's fine as she is. You're the one who's always sulking."

"If Rosa lost her legs at least she'd weigh less." He began laughing hysterically.

"Very witty."

"Where were you yesterday? That taxi driver waited for you for hours."

"I was just out with friends," I lied. I never had the courage to tell Volvo about my activities. I was afraid he would never speak to me again.

"And then as soon as you got home, you sent him away. So he waited for nothing, unless it was a real quickie."

"Volvo, I've told you a million times, there's nothing sexual between me and Benny, not that it's any of your business. I sent him away because I was tired."

"Pass me my tray, Dana. And get the hell out. What time is this dinner?"

"Rafi's going to pick us up at seven."

"I hope there's room for my chair in his trunk."

"He has a van. We'll manage."

"Who is this guy?"

"Just a friend."

I went out to drop off my film for developing and on the

way I picked up some groceries: potato salad, hummus, bread. Then I returned to my novel. I noticed that I'd made several mistakes the previous night. I'd forgotten that my character's name was Angeline and at some point I started calling her Angela. Then I forgot that Pierre was a count and I made him a prince, and his wicked cousin Martha accidentally turned into his aunt. I wasted a lot of time fixing these mistakes.

I was still writing when Rafi knocked on the door. I didn't hear him at first, or rather, I didn't think the sound I'd heard was a knock. "Were you asleep?" he asked, when I opened the door.

"No, I was at the computer. I'm ready, we just have to get Volvo. He's in the flat next door." I was very nervous.

"Relax, Dana," he said. "There isn't even going to be tear gas."

We knocked on Volvo's door but he didn't answer. "I know you're in there, Volvo. We're ready, Rafi's here. I'm coming in."

I opened the door. Volvo was sitting in his chair reading the newspaper. I could tell he'd been waiting impatiently, but he tried to look bored.

"Volvo, this is Rafi."

"Hi," Rafi said.

"Do you know that when you lose your legs people assume you're also retarded?" Volvo asked, embarking on one of his favorite subjects.

"Yes," Rafi said. "I've seen it many times. They speak to you as if you're deaf, and they use simple words as if your brain's been damaged as well. People are idiots."

Volvo was delighted. "Absolutely true," he said. We wheeled Volvo to the van and Rafi lifted him onto the front seat. I folded the wheelchair and climbed in back with it. "You can't imagine what fun it is to be carried like a sack of potatoes," Volvo said. He held on to the door for balance and buckled himself in.

"You can't imagine what my back is going to feel like tomorrow morning," Rafi said. "Why don't you get yourself some prosthetic legs, for goodness' sake?"

"Ha! Ha ha ha. Very good, very good. A true understanding of anatomy. I see a Nobel Prize in your future, young man."

Rafi looked embarrassed. "You're right, I hadn't really thought it out . . . I guess it wouldn't work . . . Unless you combined legs with crutches maybe?"

"So you can feel better when you see me? So you won't have to feel so bad? For your sake?" he said, embarking on his second favorite subject.

"Well, why shouldn't I want to feel less bad?" Rafi said defensively. "What's good about feeling bad? And if there's nothing good about it, why endorse it?"

Volvo ignored this question. Instead he said, "Nice van. You're obviously filthy rich."

"My wife's rich," Rafi said.

"Yeah, what is she, a drug pusher?"

"She's a pianist, Volvo, and I resent that comment. And if you want to come to my house I'd like an apology."

Volvo grunted. "Very touchy."

"I don't like racist stereotyping."

"I don't even know your wife!"

"You assume she's Sephardi like me."

"You're totally paranoid," Volvo said. "I have no idea what your background is and I couldn't care less."

"Good," Rafi said. "I'm glad to hear it."

"So, how *did* she get rich?"

"Her parents are rich. They own a bathing suit company, they export to Europe and the States."

"Obviously *they're* not Sephardi," he said wickedly. "Just kidding!"

Rafi decided not to respond.

"I used to like to swim," Volvo said glumly. "Well, those days are gone."

"I forgot to ask the two of you if there's any food you don't eat or don't like."

"I eat everything except shrimp, brain, tongue, belly button," I said. "Or liver. I don't want to recognize anything I'm eating, that's the general rule."

"I'm a strict vegetarian," Volvo said. "I don't eat vegetables." He began to laugh in his crazy, hysterical way.

"I did make a lot of vegetable dishes," Rafi said in a worried voice.

"He's just joking," I said.

"I am present," Volvo said imperiously.

"Yes, how could we possibly forget?" Rafi smiled.

It didn't take us long to reach Rafi's building. He pulled the van in front of a luxury apartment building and helped Volvo into his chair. I wheeled Volvo into the lobby and we waited while Rafi parked the van. I felt sorry for the lobby. The building was striving to look like one of the newer five-star hotels along the beach and there was something rather desperate about the little water fountain with its blue and green lights, and the black leather sofas set carefully around it. Daniel used to say I was the only person in the world who felt sorry for places.

In the elevator Rafi pressed the button to the penthouse floor.

"Penthouse!" Volvo said. "How pretentious can you get?"

"Those are the largest flats," Rafi said. "My wife needs room for her piano."

Rafi's wife met us at the door. Her name was Graciela. She had fair skin, a high forehead, and long black hair braided in back. She was taller than Rafi and she was untouchable.

Graciela's shiny piano took up half the living room. The flat was beautiful: thick beige carpets, a panoramic view of the sea, simple Danish furniture, framed paintings and prints on the walls. An inviting place, elegant and sophisticated and at the same time bohemian. It matched Graciela's outfit: a top made of dark crimson velvet and lace, with flowers in relief on the dark velvet, and a matching skirt. The velvet changed color with every movement or change of light, like the sea.

"Hello, Dana," she said. "I'm glad you could come. Our daughter just fell asleep, too bad you missed her. She doesn't usually go to bed so early, but she had a birthday party in the afternoon and she was tired."

I couldn't answer. "Excuse me, I don't feel well," I said, and escaped to the bathroom. There I sat on the edge of the bath and tried to find a way to resurface. I wanted everything Graciela had, except maybe for the flat, because I loved our place, and when we moved it would be into a house Daniel designed. It would be as elegant, as sophisticated, as this apartment. But the rest hurt me. Once, a long time ago, I too wore beautiful clothes. And their daughter, their daughter! I was thirty-seven.

Rafi knocked on the door. "Dana? Everything okay?"

"Yes."

He'd lied to me. He said he would protect me and he did the opposite. He flaunted it all.

"Can I come in?"

"If you want."

Rafi came into the washroom, leaned against the sink.

"It's not what you think," he said.

"I don't think anything."

Graciela joined him in the washroom. She was holding an open box of chocolates. She ignored Rafi and sat down next to me, offered me a chocolate. "These are very special," she said. "Handmade, from France. My parents bring me a box every time they go to Europe. I'm sure you'll like them. What's your favorite flavor? Do you like coconut?"

"Yes, thank you."

"We mix up all our courses here. Chocolates first, then dessert, then the main course . . ."

I couldn't tell whether she was joking because her voice was so controlled and careful. Her movements were controlled too. She was as unhappy as I was.

The meal was in fact a little chaotic—not because the courses were served in reverse order, but because Rafi and Graciela were both so frantically solicitous toward me. They fussed and fretted as though I were an honored but fragile guest. Volvo was stunned into silence for the first time since I had known him; he was wondering whether he'd missed something, because wasn't he the one without legs, wasn't he the one who deserved attention and pity and love? And so he sat there quietly, puzzling it out. And he ate voraciously. He loved food.

They were both solicitous, but each one separately, as though they were not connected in any way and had not been introduced. They never spoke to one another, only to me. There was a routine: Graciela in charge of serving, Rafi in charge of salad and washing up; they didn't negotiate anything.

"Where do you live?" Graciela asked me.

"Opposite the City Beach Hotel."

"I know that hotel. Friends of my parents often stay there. It must be nice to be so close to the sea."

"Yes, and we're all friends in the building."

"Really! That's very nice. How many are you?"

"Me and Volvo on the first floor. Tanya and her mother and Jacky on the second. Benny's on the top floor. Tanya used to be a prostitute but now she's a fortune-teller. Benny drives a taxi."

"And Jacky?"

"You know him, Jacky Davidson. The rock singer."

"Really! I heard he went crazy."

"Yes, he's pretty crazy. But he manages. We all help him out."

"Who looks after his money? He could get ripped off."

"No, his sister looks after all that, though there isn't much, you know. Rock stars don't get rich in this country."

"That's true. Still, there would be royalties . . . What about Tanya, is she good?"

"She has lots of clients."

"I would like to have my fortune told. But I'm always afraid. I'm afraid they'll see something bad."

"They don't tell you the bad things."

"I'd be able to tell, all the same, by the look on their faces."

"Do you perform?" I asked.

She smiled for the first time since I'd arrived. "Yes. I guess you don't follow classical music very much."

"No, I don't like going to hear music alone. Sorry, are you famous?"

"Well, not internationally. I only perform here, and we're such a small country that it's not hard to become well known."

"Do you think you'll have an international career one day?"

"Who knows? I'm getting better all the time, but I never go to competitions, that's the problem."

"Why not?"

"I hate them."

"When's your next concert?"

"I have a recital coming up in February that I'm working on now."

"What pieces will you be playing?"

"Mendelssohn, *Songs Without Words*. Chopin, Nocturne in E-flat, Ballades One and Four. Beethoven's *Appassionata*."

"A romantic program," I said.

"Yes. I'm doing a Bach concerto in the spring, though. The D Minor."

She ate very little. "I'm on a special diet," she explained. "For my joints. There are all these foods I can't eat. But please don't pay attention to me."

"My husband is very musical," I said. "He can play jazz on the piano, even though he never had lessons and he can't read music. He just likes improvising. But music is only a hobby for him. I wish I were musical."

"I don't understand why you can't find him," she said. "Surely the police know where every citizen lives."

"He was clever, he rented a tiny room in the city. And the police said, Well, this is his address, what more do you want? But it was just a cover—he wasn't living there, he was living somewhere else. Someone was collecting his mail at this place, and someone also left notes on the door: *Back soon, gone to the supermarket,* things like that. Someone was in on it, I don't know who. I never found out. Someone in this country knows where he is."

"Did you try writing to him at that address?"

"Yes, of course, but my letters were never picked up. His other mail was picked up, but not my letters. That really hurt me. I stopped trying."

"Is the room still rented?"

"Someone else lives there now. I stopped going after a few months—I saw it was hopeless. A year later I looked in again, and an old couple was living in the flat. I've been back a few times, but it's always the same story: the old couple, wondering what I want."

"Did you try the police again?"

"I tried everything: the government, the army, the police. I didn't get anywhere. They all had that address, the fake one, and that's the one they kept giving me. That's where his disability checks go. But the old couple doesn't know anything about it. They're immigrants, they barely seem to know where they are."

"Have you tried someone higher up in the army?"

"Yes. I mean, I meet all sorts of army people, and once this woman really tried to help me. She looked Daniel up on her computer and I could tell she wasn't really supposed to, that she was doing it because she thought I should know and that he shouldn't be hiding from me. Maybe she just liked me. She looked and looked and typed in all sorts of things, but she couldn't find anything apart from his fake address."

"Maybe you just need someone higher up than that woman."

"She was very high up. Or rather she was the secretary of someone high up. She could have got into trouble probably, but she went ahead. And she couldn't find anything."

"Please have more to eat," Graciela said, handing Volvo a bowl of breaded zucchini. "Rafi made all this especially for you."

"Thank you," I said. "Everything's delicious, really exceptional."

"His mother's recipes."

"Not bad," Volvo admitted.

Rafi didn't say anything. He looked at me and Volvo and his wife, and he seemed slightly worried, as if the three of us were floating in space and he was wondering whether we would eventually land and whether the landing would go smoothly.

We didn't stay long because Volvo began complaining that his hemorrhoids were bothering him. I didn't realize until I was in Rafi's van how tense I'd been all evening. It was a strain, talking to Graciela; it was like talking to someone through a screen, or through water. It made me think of dreams in which I tried to phone someone but the phone wasn't working properly and I kept getting wrong numbers or operator interference.

Rafi drove through the quiet streets. He parked in front of our building, carried Volvo into his flat, and lowered him gently onto the bed. I organized Volvo's tray for the night: sunflower seeds, the newspaper, vitamins, his emergency beeper, an ice pack. He watched me with a look of disdain, but in fact he liked it when people did things for him.

"Have fun," Volvo said bitterly as we were leaving. "As for me, I may as well have had my cock blown off as well."

"Did you? Did you lose your cock?" Rafi asked.

"His cock is perfectly fine," I said. "Trust me."

"In theory," Volvo said.

"Good night, Volvo."

"Who's coming tomorrow?" he asked.

"Joshua."

"God help me. Joshua—one foot in the grave, totally senile, drool constantly hanging from the left side of his mouth. This is what I'm stuck with. Well, have fun. She has lots of lovers, by the way," he told Rafi. "Including a woman."

"Thanks for letting me know," Rafi said.

"Well, two or three anyhow."

"Glad you're keeping count."

"I'm not keeping count. If I were, I'd know whether it was two or three. Or maybe more."

We left Volvo and entered my flat.

"Dana! What happened here?"

"What do you mean?"

"It looks as if someone was here looking for your heroin stash."

"I'm just messy. Sorry."

"No you're not. You're not sorry at all."

"I am. I wish I were neater. I try, but somehow I can never manage it."

"Dana, do you want me to ask our cleaning woman to pay you a visit? Mercedes, she's really good."

"Okay. We had someone when Daniel was here, but I let her go after he vanished because I was broke for a while. Then I started making money, but I never rehired her. It isn't dusty, at least."

"How can you possibly tell?" Rafi laughed.

He began inspecting the flat, like a cat sniffing a new place. He started with the living room, then moved to the kitchen, stared at the wall painting of the two train windows.

"Who did this?"

"Someone from Daniel's firm—I never met her, she did it while I was at work."

He kept staring at the painting. "The letters of his name are hidden everywhere," he said.

"Whose name?"

"Daniel's."

"Really?"

"Yes, look. The legs of the cows, and here, on the barn door, and all over the window curtains. And the grass."

"I never noticed! And neither did Daniel . . . maybe she had a crush on him."

"That would explain all the little hearts."

"Hearts? Where?"

"Here, among the flowers."

"Maybe that's just the way she paints flowers."

"This flower is broken," Rafi said. "That must be her broken heart."

"You might be reading too much into this. But I guess it's possible. Lots of women liked Daniel, I think. Funny that we never noticed!"

"At least you didn't."

"Daniel didn't either."

Rafi didn't say anything. Instead, he moved to the next stop on his inspection tour, the bedroom.

"I spend most of my time here," I said. "We used to watch television in the living room but now I watch in bed."

"Don't you find it claustrophobic, all these leaves?"

"I guess it's getting a bit out of hand, but they're all tangled up, I don't know what to do."

"Just take a scissors and snip some of the stalks. They can be replanted, if they're put in water first. I'm sure you'd find takers . . . What's this?" he asked, noticing my dream notebook with its conspicuous *Madonna and the Fish* cover.

"I write down my dreams. I like to remember them."

"Even the bad ones?"

"I rarely have bad dreams."

"That's unusual."

"Or maybe I don't think of them as bad dreams because they interest me. What's the story with you and Graciela?" I asked. "Are you fighting?"

"No, what made you think that?"

"You didn't speak to each other."

"We don't speak much."

"Why?"

"Graciela isn't talkative."

"That's a stupid answer."

"I don't know what else to say."

"You must talk sometimes. You told her about me."

"No, she saw you before the demonstration, when she dropped me off at the park. And she recognized you, she remembered seeing you on some show about deserted wives."

"Why do you have separate bedrooms?"

"She has problems sleeping. She can't sleep with anyone in her bed, or even in the room, every small sound wakes her up."

"Since always?"

"I think so. Since I've known her, at least."

"When did you meet?"

"A long time ago. Ten years ago. When I was twenty-one."

"You're thirty-one?"

"Yes. I was twenty-one and she was twenty-three."

"And she told you to invite me?"

"She suggested it."

"What were her words exactly?"

"She said, 'That woman, Dana, she's the one with the missing husband. Why not invite her to dinner, if you can get hold of her?'"

"Do you have people over often?"

He slid down to the floor and crouched Arab-style with his knees up.

"Yes, we have people over. Not during the day, during the day she plays. Unless she's having one of her migraines."

"You don't have sex."

"Why do you say that?"

"That's why people get migraines. Women especially. When they don't come."

"You can have sex without orgasm."

"Well, the studies aren't conclusive. I want you to get up now and leave and not come back. Do you think this is what I deserve, to be some sort of voyeur?" I threw myself on the bed and burst into tears. I hadn't cried in years.

Rafi made tea and brought it to the bed and we drank in silence.

Then he left.

❖

Daniel managed to avoid reserve duty five years in a row, but in the sixth year they insisted. He was a hopelessly incompetent soldier. In one of his favorite movies two armies march pompously toward each other, raise their rifles, fire, and fall down dead—all of them, on the spot. Daniel laughed very hard at that scene and he laughed every time he remembered it. He saw fighting as absurd and he refused to take his training seriously: several times he sabotaged practice operations by clowning around. His punishments were much worse than mine. I had to clean toilets, but one time he almost died when he was disciplined. He'd marched backward during an ambush drill, and the sergeant made him march backward around the camp for several hours with all his equipment, until he finally collapsed. Daniel was very entertaining when he told people the story: vomiting on the medic's shoes, reciting Bialik in semi-delirium, being stripped and washed down by a ninety-year-old nurse. But in fact the doctor had filed a complaint, and Daniel later found out that his condition had been critical. Only once did he confess, after we'd been particularly intimate one night, that he'd suffered and cried, and that everyone had seen him crying.

When notices for reserve duty arrived in the mail, Daniel always replied that he was in the middle of a crucial project at work; they had a deadline and he couldn't possibly get away. But this last time the army checked up on him, and found out that he was dispensable after all. He didn't mind all that much. The laundry job itself didn't bother him, but he hated being part of what he called auto-genocide. The government was killing its citizens by the thousands, he said, finishing off the job the Nazis had started. Why should he provide clean uniforms for the pathetic slobs who were being sent to their deaths by heartless politicians? Nevertheless, he was in a good mood when he left. He called me every evening, and described in great detail what he was going to do to me when he got back.

# MONDAY

MONDAYS AND THURSDAYS WERE MY DAYS at the insurance office. I kept the job after Daniel left, but they downsized me to two days a week. This meant I could no longer water the plants, all of which had different watering schedules; my employer had to do it himself. In fact, the only thing I did now was look after correspondence in English; I would have lost the job altogether had they not needed a bilingual typist. The letters I wrote were sometimes cruel, but my employer allowed me to insert mitigating phrases, for whatever they were worth. *We deeply regret, in this time of great difficulty and stress, to inform you, much to our sorrow, that we are unable to cover . . .*

The day passed quickly.

In the evening, Rafi called. "I spoke to Mercedes. She can come tomorrow, is that okay?"

"Yes, thank you."

"How are you?"

"Fine. Boring day at the office where I work."

"What do you do there?"

"Tell people they can't get compensation for the various disasters in their lives. It's not very exciting."

"Will you be at the demo tomorrow?"

"The one at the Defense Ministry? Yes."

"Okay, I'll see you there, I'm bringing some of the signs. Do you need anything?"

"Like what?"

"I don't know. You tell me."

"I don't need anything. How's Graciela?"

"She's working hard."

"How's your daughter?"

"Naomi is fine."

"Yes. Well."

"I'll see you tomorrow. You'll know me by my red hat."

"Your long-lost hat."

"My finally found hat."

"We're talking about hats."

"Yes."

"The characters in the books I write never talk about hats. I think I'll try it out tonight. This conversation is inspiring me."

"You write books?"

I paused. Then I said, "Not real books, just junk romance. I have to go now," I said.

"You all right?"

"I have to go," I said, and hung up. I sat at the kitchen counter and stared at the fridge, which was covered with snapshots of Daniel. Daniel sitting on a chair with our cat in his lap, Daniel and me at a party, Daniel with his friend Alex in Venice. I had not meant to tell Rafi about the romance books. This was the first time anyone other than my father knew something about me that Daniel did not know. In my interviews I always updated Daniel: I talked about all my adventures and misadventures, and about the people around me. That way, if Daniel read or heard the interview, he'd have some idea of what my life was like. But I didn't want to discuss my romance novels in those interviews, so I didn't tell anyone else about them either. Only my father knew. I had to tell him, because he couldn't figure out how I was managing financially, and he was worried. My father was my biggest fan. He bought all my books and he said they were a blast.

I stared at the snapshots and the pain of Daniel's absence stirred inside me. Usually the pain was like a little boy sitting on a little chair in a darkened corner—like Little Jack Horner: it was there, but it stayed in its assigned place, quietly recalcitrant. At other times, without warning, the pain rose and expanded and threatened to suffocate me.

At those times I longed for the drug Vronsky had prescribed when I broke my ankle. I was on an excursion to see new settlement outposts and I found myself near Be'er Shalom, an old settlement deep inside Palestine. Over the years I'd taken a few good photographs of settlers, but never of settlements. I managed that day to sneak away from the group without the army noticing, and I made my way toward Be'er Shalom. I knew it would be fenced in, but I was hoping to take some photographs of the fence, its guards, and of the settlement itself, viewed through the wires. Maybe the guards would even let me inside.

Before I reached the fence I came across a cabin someone had built just outside Be'er Shalom, a cabin surrounded by newly planted trees. Whoever had built the cabin had also constructed an elaborate doghouse next to it. Most likely an eccentric lived here, someone who refused to hide behind a fence, who saw himself perhaps as some sort of prophet.

I went up to the door and knocked. There was no answer. I tried the handle and the door slid open. The room inside was very still, its contents petrified under a thin layer of dust and cobwebs; no one had lived here for some time. And yet nothing had been disturbed or moved, as if the owner were expected back: the effect was spooky, but also intriguing. In one corner a plank of wood set on two cement blocks served as a makeshift bookshelf: it held about thirty books, all in English and all on the same subject, more or less: firearms, war technology, nuclear terrorism.

In the center of the room stood a table covered with black oilcloth. Newspaper clippings, also in English, were spread out on the table. Seemingly random words had been circled and there were indecipherable numbers and symbols in the margins. The clippings were held down by a bottle of transparent glue and a paperweight that appeared to be the skull of a small animal. There was a mattress on the floor, and next to it sticks of incense, an oversized book on the Kabbalah, and a pamphlet of poems written by children in Theresienstadt. I took a photograph of the little animal skull, and I was going to take a few more, but I must have been on edge, because when I heard a noise outside the cabin I panicked and ran out.

I was so flustered I didn't look where I was going, and I tripped on a metal rod protruding from a large uprooted sign that was lying on the ground. Two soldiers were hovering over me, half-smiling. "Seen a ghost?" they asked. I looked at the sign; it was trilingual, and it said, in English, DANGER / FIRING RANGE / ENTRANCE FORBIDDEN / ENTRY REQUIRES PRIOR APPROVAL AND COORDINATION WITH THE ARMY CENTRAL COMMAND COORDINATOR / 02-5305252 / CENTER OPERATES 24 HOURS A DAY / EXCLUDING SATURDAYS AND HOLIDAYS. Its two metal supports had been set in large cement blocks, which now hung helplessly from the rods like Frankenstein's feet.

"Everyone was worried about you," one of the soldiers said. "Next time don't leave the group without permission. We have enough to think about."

"Sorry," I said. I took a photograph of the sign from where I was sitting. Then I discovered that I couldn't get up, and I had to be carried piggyback to the bus. "Who lives in that cabin?" I asked the soldier who was carrying me. "Lived," he said. "Some guy, he was killed a couple of months ago. Are you single?" "I'm in too much pain to remember right now," I said.

Vronsky was on duty at the hospital when Odelia, who had also been at the outpost-tracking activity, brought me to the emergency ward. I used her shoulder as a crutch; the pain was excruciating, but I was stoic and didn't let on. As a result, the nurses didn't think I had more than a sprain, and I had to wait several hours for a doctor to see me.

The doctor was Vronsky. While he was examining me he noticed the flyer in my hand. It was a glossy fund-raising flyer from Be'er Shalom asking Americans to help them fulfill God's promise by sending tax-deductible donations. I'd found it on the rented bus. "What's that?" Vronsky asked. I told him about the illegal outposts and the deserted house of the dead prophet. He seemed interested, though he didn't say much. At midnight he sent me home with a cast and a bottle of painkillers. They were stronger than was usual because Vronsky felt bad that I'd waited so long, and also because by the time he saw me I was no longer stoic, and I told him I'd pass out if I didn't get something strong soon.

I became madly addicted to the pills and when they were finished I begged Vronsky for more. At first he yielded, but after my cast came off he refused to renew the prescription. I was sorry then that my anklebone, which had apparently broken in an unusual manner, healed inexplicably within two weeks. Vronsky discovered by chance that the fracture had healed: the cast was causing me all sorts of problems and had to be removed and replaced. As it turned out, though, the cast wasn't replaced, because Vronsky took another X-ray and found, to his astonishment, that I was cured. "Remarkable," he said. "Most unusual. Two weeks—I've never come across such a case before."

"I still need those pills for pain," I said hopefully, but Vronsky assured me I wouldn't be experiencing any further discomfort. My body never forgot the pleasure of the drug, which had spread inside me like a gentle breeze on a lazy summer day, a day filled with cyclamens sweetly trembling under blue skies. Every now and then a deep craving for the remembered sensation would take hold of me, and one night I was so desperate I tried to find the drug on the street, but no one had heard of it.

Now the familiar desire came back. I needed to narrow the pain of my longing for Daniel, send it back to its corner, but it was stubborn and didn't want to budge. I decided to go out for dinner with Volvo and then walk with him by the sea. The sea at dusk was my best bet.

We ate at a falafel stand down the street and then we strolled along the boardwalk. Some people smiled at Volvo and others averted their eyes. No one was indifferent. When I grew tired of pushing the wheelchair, I parked Volvo at one of the semi-circular shelters scattered along the walk and sat beside him on the curved bench. The sun was setting behind us and the sea turned gray with streaks of orange and white. Then it was dark green and the orange changed to scarlet. And then slowly blue came back, blue with specks of gold.

"You're very distracted," he said. "Are you premenstrual?"

"What's the connection? Or were you just looking for an opportunity to say that word?"

"What form of contraception do you use, if I may ask?"

"You may not ask. Volvo, look how nice the sea is. Look how nice it is here, and everyone's relaxed—why don't you try to relax too? How can you be cranky near the sea?"

"I'm not a happy man, in case you haven't noticed."

"Well, I'm not happy either, but it's still possible to appreciate some things. I was incredibly sad this afternoon, but I feel better now, thanks to this walk, and the sea, and having a falafel with you."

"The difference between us, Dana," he said, "is that you have hope. I, on the other hand, will never wake up one morning to find that this was all just a bad dream."

"Why don't you try to meet someone? If you weren't so grumpy and negative, you could fall in love, you know."

"Brilliant idea," Volvo said. "The best idea I've heard all week. A plan for my rehabilitation. My *spiritual* rehabilitation."

"Why don't you give your family another chance? I'm sure they miss you."

"I already told you. We've been through this."

"Yes, you said they were religious, but—"

"Not religious, fanatic. We no longer have anything in common," he said with self-satisfaction. "I have liberated myself from the chains of superstition and zealotry. I am a free man."

"That's no reason not to see them."

"Their interpretation of my personal disaster fills me with dismay and revulsion," Volvo said. "I will never forgive them for giving God the credit."

"Yes, I know that's frustrating."

"Frustrating! Try twisted, pathological, and betraying a degree of imbecility that staggers the mind."

"You know, Volvo, you're intelligent, you have a lot of talent, why not use it? Why not see a therapist? Or go back to school?"

"I'm too depressed to see a therapist and too smart to go to school," he said, bursting into his wild hyena laugh.

"What exactly did your parents say?"

"I'd rather not dwell on it."

"Come on, tell me."

"I don't want to get into it. But I'll tell you this: they got a perverse pleasure out of what happened to me. They took a graphic photograph of me while I was still unconscious and they made a big poster, until I threatened to sue them if they used it. I hired a lawyer, he sent them a letter."

"Well, who cares? Who cares what they think? It's not important. Anyhow, I can't believe your entire family all feel the same way."

"You're right, it's really only my parents, siblings, six aunts, eight uncles, and forty-seven cousins."

"You must have one person you feel a bit closer to."

"I do have one sister I miss," he admitted. "She's fourteen by now. Just turned fourteen. In August. Sara."

"Why not see her?"

"First, she'd never be allowed to come see me on her own. Secondly, the less she travels, the better. Those roads from the settlements are too dangerous."

"Write her a letter. I'm sure she'd be delighted to hear from you."

"Let's drop this subject. It's kind of you to bring it up, but I'd rather move on to a more stimulating topic. So what's that Rafi guy like in bed? And does his wife know?"

"There's no point trying to annoy me. You'll never succeed."

"I was only asking. He seems nice, actually, if a bit on the touchy side."

"We have to head home, I have to get back to work."

"Ah yes, Dana and her mysterious job. Do you write pornography?"

"No, but you're not that far off."

"Seen Vronsky lately?"

"You know I see him Wednesdays."

"I thought you might be off-schedule just for once. Why always Wednesdays?"

"I told you, Vronsky likes it that way."

"Where do the two of you do it, in his car? That must be awkward, and a bit public."

"We do it right there on the table, in the restaurant. Between courses."

"Yeah, well. He's probably too old to get it up anyhow."

❖

The hospital waiting room. Flowers. The nurses intimidate me. Daniel's parents are spending the summer in Greece, and we can't reach them. They left the name of a hotel, but the hotel doesn't exist, they must have spelled it wrong. The travel agent can't be reached either; she's even farther away, in India. We keep trying hotels with similar-sounding names, but we can't track them down. Nina joins me and starts chanting, *Wa-heh guru, wa-heh guru* until the nurses ask her to leave. She doesn't return, she only phones. My father flies in from Belgium, keeps me company. More flowers, lots of flowers. Daniel's friend Alex brings them. My father is reading Nadine Gordimer. I am happy, happy, I want to dance in the waiting room. Daniel is alive, and every day the news is better. No internal damage, he's going to pull through, and soon I'll be able to see him. In the meantime he's asked not to have visitors and anyhow he's all drugged up. I stand by his closed door until they chase me away. Finally they tell me I can see him the following day. I go home to shower and change and then I look for a gift. And while I'm gone Daniel slips through my fingers.

❖

I had now reached the hardest part of my novel: the obligatory sex scenes. I always left those for last, because they were the only passages that required concentration: the publisher's rules were stringent and you had to get it just right. Apart from that, the sex scenes involved a catastrophic collapse of logic, because

I had to convey the man's thoughts without switching to his point of view. Entering the hero's mind was strictly taboo. I braced myself, and started writing.

*She felt his strong, confident fingers tracing the outline of her exquisite throat and sublime exposed shoulders. He held her well-proportioned body to his and his lips brushed her divine skin. She was resplendent in her brilliant blue gown and dazzling sapphire necklace, which glinted enticingly on her swan-like, curvaceous throat. She shivered as his hands slowly, boldly, caressed her back and the gown fell in a heap around her dainty ankles. Her excitement rose to soaring heights as she stood before him, trembling in her modest lace underslip.*

I needed six sex scenes, but I was exhausted by the time I'd finished the first two. I called it a day and went out for my evening walk. The man from the special unit was waiting for me.

"I was hoping you'd be here. *I sought her, but found her not,*" he said, slightly altering the quote.

"Well, you've found me. You can walk with me, if you like. But please don't ask me to sleep with you. It's not something I do. Besides, I'm very busy. I can't take on anything else."

"Why? Why isn't it something you do? A young woman like you . . ."

"I seem to remember that you're married."

"Married . . ." he said vaguely, as though he wasn't sure what the word meant. "Funny, you supporting the Palestinians, me in a special unit. If you knew the things I know . . . but I can't tell you. If you knew what they think of us, how much they hate us."

"We do know the things you know. We just interpret them differently. Or we see their feelings as natural, and temporary. Or irrelevant to ending the occupation."

"Irrelevant! No, no, you don't know. You don't know and I can't tell you, and it's too bad. Because if you knew . . . you wouldn't do the work you do. You would know that the things they say are not what they really think. They're lying to you when they say they want to live in peace with us. They don't. They want to destroy us. If you saw the things they write."

"Maybe they're lying when they write. Why do you think you're the one who knows what's real and what isn't?"

"Why! Because I see the consequences! I see the plans and I see them carried out!"

"You don't know what would happen if we stopped tormenting them."

"I do know. I do know, and I wish I could tell you."

"It's not that simple. You simplify things. It's dangerous to simplify, it's the basis of every war. Simplification."

"You aren't realistic."

"I'm just more optimistic than you are, that's all. I trust the Palestinians—they're exactly like us. Just people. People without a home or anything else, and if we were in their situation we'd be just as desperate, and some of us would be just as militant as some of them are."

He sighed. "Maybe the next generation will be able to do something. It's too late for this generation, there's too much hatred. Nothing will change for the next thirty years."

"People who were slaughtering each other in Lebanon are now drinking coffee together. One of my Palestinian friends told me that. 'That's the Middle East, my friend,' she said. I agree with her. It can happen, people don't stay angry once they get what they need."

"Why aren't you married, by the way? Why don't you have a family?"

"I am married, but my husband is in hiding. I'm waiting for him to come back. He thinks I won't like him, because he was burned."

"Burned?"

"Yes, his face and arms and parts of his body. He tried to help a soldier who was on fire, and he caught fire too. He's alive, but he lives in hiding somewhere."

"You don't know where?"

"No. He won't let me or anyone else see him. It wouldn't bother me, what he looks like, but he thinks it would."

"What a story!"

"Yes. I miss him."

"Maybe you should forget him."

"No, I'm not going to forget him."

"Such a devoted wife . . . and he gave you up. Still, I can sort of understand it."

"I can't."

"How did the two of them catch fire?"

"Just a stupid accident. My husband was delivering laundry. That's what he did in the army, laundry."

"Laundry! Did he have a low profile?"

"No, he just hated the army. He wanted to do something as unrelated to combat as possible."

"Yeah, okay. Laundry!" He shook his head incredulously. It was hard for him to grasp. "So what happened?"

"He was delivering laundry somewhere, and there was a young conscript there who was fooling around with a smoke grenade. His sleeve caught fire and someone next to him doused him with the contents of a jerrican he thought was full of water, one of those black plastic jerricans, you know the kind. But the can didn't have water in it, it had gasoline. Everyone ran away except my husband. He tried to wrap the guy up in a blanket, but there was gasoline on the floor too."

"What sort of idiot puts gasoline in a black plastic jerrican!" he said. He was furious, as though he'd been there and had witnessed the disaster himself.

"It was a mistake," I said.

"A mistake," he guffawed. "Yeah. I'll bet. Some joker, some joker who should be rotting in prison for several centuries."

"I don't want to think it was on purpose. It could have been an absentminded mistake."

"Yes, to mistake black plastic for metal, that would take a special kind of talent. Well, did your husband save the guy's life?"

"No, he died. It was all for nothing."

"Not really for nothing. He tried."

"No, it was for nothing. A complete waste. He got a citation, but I had to go receive it. He'd vanished by then."

"What a country. The crazy things that happen here. You know, when I was a kid, one afternoon a boulder fell on a boy, and killed him on the spot. Right in our backyard. We all shared a backyard, all these buildings shared one backyard, and there was a slope running along the edge of it, like a hill, with stones and boulders. And the boulder fell on this poor kid and killed him. One minute he was there, the next . . . I was eight. I sometimes think there's a reason for all these freak accidents. Some message. A message from above."

"What message?"

"I don't know. That the place is dangerous. That we need to be stronger, more aware. Another guy I know got eaten alive by bees. In my high school two kids drowned, and one girl died when a branch fell on her during a hike. I swear, it's weird."

"Those sorts of things happen everywhere, you just don't hear about them. We're a small country, so we hear about every death. We hear, and we also remember. We feel bad, and we remember."

"Yes, that's true. We remember."

"Also people here are careless. They drive like they're homicidal and on amphetamines. They think they have to be tough, so they aren't self-protective. They don't avoid bees and they swim where there aren't any lifeguards. The city doesn't clear boulders. We don't look after ourselves, that's the problem. We're too arrogant and vain and we're obsessed with being tough. Maybe we're also suicidal."

"That doesn't seem to describe you."

"You're right, I do try to protect myself. I don't care if people think I'm a coward."

"I do. I would hate that. I would hate it if anyone thought I was a coward."

"People don't distinguish between real bravery and just showing off. Are you going to be here every night I come and walk?"

"Do you want me to be here?"

"No, I need to be alone."

"Who wants to be alone? Isn't it bad enough you haven't got your husband?" He placed his arm around my shoulder.

I slipped away from him. "Yes, it is bad enough. That's why I need to be alone. I like to walk here and think about him."

He was silent for a few minutes. Then he said, "All right, I won't bother you again. But if you ever need anything, call me. Here's my number." He handed me his business card.

But he didn't want to leave; he had something more to say, and he wasn't sure whether he should say it or not. I waited while he deliberated. Finally he decided. "Listen, I can find your husband's address, if you want," he said.

"What do you mean?"

"I told you, I'm in a special unit. I have access to everything. I can look him up on our computer."

"I already tried that. I mean they checked their computers at all the offices I went to. He has a fake address, but it's not where he lives."

"Those weren't the right computers," he said.

"Are you sure?"

"Yes, I'm sure. If he was a soldier, and he's wounded, I can find out where he is."

"When can you try? How soon?" My heart began to beat faster.

"I can do it tomorrow, it's not a problem."

"You mean you can look anyone up?"

"Yes. You deserve to know. Why shouldn't you know? Just don't tell anyone it was me, okay? You have to promise. And I mean no one. Promise."

"I won't tell anyone."

"I just need his ID."

"Do you have a pen?"

"I'll remember. I have a good memory."

"Five-three-two-two-six-four-nine."

"Five-three-two-two-six-four-nine. Call me tomorrow evening around six."

"Yes," I said.

He began jogging along the beach. He turned around once and waved good-bye, jogging backward, then continued on his way.

❖

Daniel's parents returned from Greece two days after he vanished. At that time we were still convinced that Daniel would be back in a day or two. We thought he just wanted some time alone; Nina said he needed "to reestablish his aura" and the doctors said he hadn't finished his treatment, and his health problems would bring him back. In the meantime Nina was practicing a Japanese method of long-distance healing and she asked me to join her, but I was too anxious about Daniel to think about energy currents. I was certain he would contact me soon, but I also sensed that something was wrong.

Nina and I drove down to the airport and waited restlessly

for the plane from Greece. Finally, we saw Daniel's parents striding cheerfully toward us. Daniel's mother was a slim, determined woman who wore her hair in a bun. She was closely tied to national traditions: biking trips across the country, evenings devoted to folk dancing, public sing-alongs of robust pioneer songs and lachrymose ballads. Her husband was tanned and blue-eyed, and seemed to have drunk from the fountain of youth. They were a good-looking couple, hardy and self-assured.

As soon as Nina saw her parents, she began to cry. I had not slept in two days, and probably looked pale and disheveled. When Daniel's parents saw the two of us standing there without Daniel, their daughter weeping, their daughter-in-law pale, they assumed the worst, and Daniel's mother fainted next to her suitcase. There was a great deal of confusion, as everyone around us also thought we'd come with dire news, and none of our explanations seemed to have any effect. An ambulance was called and arrived within seconds; Daniel's mother was lifted onto a stretcher. We tried to explain the situation to his father, but his mind had gone blank and he didn't hear our reassurances, or else didn't believe them. In the end we had no choice but to climb inside the ambulance, and only then were we able to explain to Daniel's mother, who had revived from all the commotion, that Daniel was alive, and not in danger—that though he'd been badly burned and we were not sure exactly where he was at the moment, he was all right.

Daniel's mother began to laugh hysterically at the news of her son's resurrection, and was given a pill to calm her down. It seems that being too happy is also a disorder. We then stepped out of the ambulance, and everyone looked at us with pity. "Terrible, terrible," they murmured. "Be strong." We thanked them and made our way to the car, where we all burst into tears and laughter. Daniel's parents hugged each other and began to kiss passionately; Nina was embarrassed and told them to control themselves.

We gave Daniel's parents a detailed account of what had happened. They didn't seem at all surprised by Daniel's disappearance. "He'll contact us in a few days," I said. "Don't be so sure," Daniel's mother replied placidly, and I never forgave her, especially since she was right.

I never forgave her, and I never forgave their happiness. It didn't matter to them that they could no longer see their son. They knew he was alive; he was collecting his checks and had even rented a flat, which meant that he had a plan and knew what he was doing. I concluded that they didn't like me, had never liked me, and were secretly glad that Daniel had left me. Later I realized that I was wrong, but somehow our relationship disintegrated. Maybe I envied them.

Daniel's grandmother died a few months later, and Nina opened a school for spiritual healing with Elena, the woman who had read *The Possessed* to her grandmother. I lost touch with Nina as well, though I'm still on her mailing list and occasionally I receive brochures inviting me to study various therapeutic arts.

# TUESDAY

I WOKE WITH A START AT FOUR IN THE MORNING. I had no idea how I'd make it through the next fourteen hours. If Aaron really had the address, I might see Daniel this very day; no matter where he was in our small country, I could reach him within a few hours. The idea was almost impossible to fathom. I had read *The Count of Monte Cristo* when I was twelve or thirteen, and I thought of it now. I remembered Edmund's unlikely escape from the dungeon in a canvas bag—in reality he would have certainly drowned—but in the story he managed to cut himself loose, swim in turbulent waters to another island (after all those years in the dungeon he was still fit, with strong lungs), be rescued by sailors on a boat, find a great treasure (the drawing in my edition showed glorious jewels spilling out of a chest), and dispense justice. It was everyone's fantasy. If Aaron know where Daniel was, if it was that simple, I would feel as fortunate as Edmund. On the other hand, I didn't want to get my hopes up; it was possible that Aaron would only find the fake address, like everyone else.

At six in the morning I went out to buy the papers. When I returned to the building I ran into my neighbor Tanya, who was on her way to get cigarettes. She looked chic, as always, in a silky, silver-and-blue-striped dress, with a vermilion scarf around her throat, and her dyed blond hair fashionably styled. She often urged me to try Hair Rave, where the latest cuts were available from pierced men with tattoos on their arms. She felt I didn't care enough about my appearance and often chided me. "At least brush your hair, dear," she'd say. "And why always the same clothes? What about an attractive belt? You're too young to give up, my love. There's no crime in being sought after." She herself was sought after by women and men across the country for her fortune-telling skills, which she practiced, according to the sign on her door, by means of tarot cards, palm reading, and something called "the Chinese method, learned firsthand from a Chinese master in Beijing." I couldn't picture Tanya in Beijing.

I was surprised to see her up so early; Tanya considered eleven in the morning the crack of dawn. She read my mind and said, "I had such a nightmare, I just had to get up. That's the only thing to do when you have a nightmare like that."

"What was it about?"

"Oh, it's hard to describe. I was in some sort of medieval hell, I couldn't get back to the present . . . nothing made sense. Absolutely terrifying, though."

Impulsively I said, "Tanya, can you read my fortune?" I had never asked her before; the idea hadn't occurred to me. No one could predict the future, not even Tanya.

Tanya wasn't in the least surprised. "Of course, my darling one," she said. "As soon as I get back."

"I'll wait upstairs."

I waited in front of Tanya's door. When she returned with her cigarettes she said, "Why did you wait outside! It isn't locked. Come in, dear."

Her flat was tidy but slightly dusty, possibly because she was myopic and too vain to wear glasses. The walls were covered with wallpaper on which delicate pink flowers hovered against a white background. There was a kitchenette in the corner and a door on the left that opened onto a tiny pink-and-white-flowered bedroom. In the middle of the living room stood a round polished mahogany table and four matching chairs. Embroidered cushions leaned precariously against the backs of the chairs. The cushions were new; I hadn't seen them on previous visits. Each one bore the name of a different bird, which was represented in enlarged form at the center of the square. The birds looked immobile and rather aloof, as if they'd decided they had better things to do in life than fly. "Lovely," I said, picking one up. "Where did you get them?"

"My mother made them, poor thing," Tanya sighed. Tanya always referred to her mother as "poor thing" because she'd had a hard life, but in fact her mother seemed content. She was a bulky woman with a few missing teeth, and she always greeted me with a smile when I passed her in the hallway. But she didn't go out much; she had arthritic knees. She liked to bake, and she often left plastic bags filled with cookies or cakes on my doorknob. Or rather, three plastic bags, one inside the other, each knotted tightly. I rarely ate these desserts; they were too sweet for me. I gave them to the octogenarian taxi drivers who sat idly in patio chairs at the taxi stand around the corner, waiting for customers.

"How's your mother?"

"Fine, fine. Have a seat, dear." She reached across the table, took my hands in hers, shut her eyes, and meditated. Then she told me to fold my arms on the table, rest my head on them, and shut my eyes. She came round to where I was sitting and began massaging my shoulders. I had not had a massage since Daniel left, and I'd forgotten how blissful it was. I lost all sense of time and nearly dozed off.

Finally she returned to her seat and I lifted my head. I was sure my eyes were red and swollen. Tanya smiled. Her smile was slightly crooked, and for a brief second I was afraid of her, but then it passed.

"I don't need cards in your case," she said. "Your case is simple. You'll lose your job at that office, either because they'll fire you or because they're going to go bankrupt and shut down, I can't tell. Don't make any large purchases, you're going to need whatever money you have. Try to focus on paying back your debts right away. You're in good health. A new person is going to come into your life, with good results. That's it for now, my darling."

"Thanks, Tanya.. How much do I owe you?"

"Usually I charge two hundred for the first reading, but I'll only charge you fifty, because you're going to lose your job. If you come again, I'll give you ten percent off."

I was impressed. Tanya had found a way to support herself without sex but with the same reliance on our need and desire for comfort, physical pleasure, and hope. Her pessimistic prognosis was hopeful in the sense that it offered the illusion of control; even if you were going to be fired, it helped if you knew it all along. In fact getting fired really had nothing to do with your own failure because, here, it was already in the stars.

But I wasn't ready to leave: I was having an attack of credulousness. "You said a new person was coming into my life. A totally new person, or just new because it's been a long time since I saw him?"

"Wait, I'll try to answer your question." She shut her eyes again. "It's not clear, sweetheart. Maybe next time I'll have more luck with that one."

"Thank you, Tanya. I feel better."

"Anytime," she said, lighting a cigarette.

I paid her and she stuffed the money into her little change

purse, a yellow beaded pouch with a reliable bronze clasp. Two rows of green and red oval beads interrupted the yellow theme for additional decorative potency. Tanya's change purse was the most optimistic personal item I could ever hope to encounter.

I had only slept a few hours during the night, but I was too anxious to nap. I stretched out on the living room sofa with an Anita Brookner novel my father had sent me, and tried to concentrate on the excursions her sentences took into casual revelation. Reading relaxed me, and with the open paperback lying on my chest like a protective talisman, I shut my eyes and drifted off. I dreamed Rafi was trying on different outfits, and asking me what I thought of each one. Some of the outfits were casual and some were formal, and I was upset because I didn't know the price or what he needed them for, so how could I judge?

I woke up shivering. There was a woman in the room, staring down at me.

"Sorry, there was no answer, so I let myself in. I'm Mercedes. Are you sick?"

It took me a few seconds to decipher what she was saying. Then I remembered: Mercedes, the cleaning woman Rafi had promised to send my way. I was still not entirely awake and in my confusion I was surprised that she was a real person, and not someone Rafi had invented in order to make me feel better, the way parents invented tooth fairies for their children.

"Are you sick?" she asked again. She was a small woman with lovely slanted eyes and perfect, delicate features. She seemed to be on bad terms with her beauty, though, and did her best to ignore it: her black hair was held in back with an office worker's rubber band, a shapeless print dress hung limply on her small body as if uncertain of its incarnation as female clothing, and her brown loafers looked like shriveled pumpkins. It was hard to guess her age because she was so sturdy, but I thought she might be in her late forties.

"This place really *is* a mess, Rafi wasn't kidding. Don't worry, you won't recognize it when I'm through. But maybe you'd like tea first? If I can find a clean cup here . . ."

"Yes, thank you. Thank you, Mercedes. Tea would be very nice."

"You're shivering. I think you may have a fever."

"No, it's nothing. It's nothing, I'm fine. I'm just not awake yet."

"Don't worry, I'll look after everything."

I lay back on the sofa. Under ordinary circumstances I would not have wanted a garrulous, overbearing stranger in the house, but Mercedes' certainty about her world and its offerings was exactly what I needed at the moment.

I heard her moving things around in the Dining Car. "Nice mural," she called out to me. "If you don't have detergent and stuff I'll go buy. Oh . . . here's some."

She brought me a glass of sweet tea on a dinner plate. "I didn't know whether you had a tray. Here, sit up, I'll fix your pillow."

I let her fuss over me. Then I watched as she began collecting garbage, dirty dishes, newspapers, and crumpled clothes with brisk, energetic movements. I felt I should get up and help her, but I stayed where I was.

"Would you like to watch television while I work?" she suggested. "You can lie in bed and relax."

I moved obediently to the bedroom and switched on the television. An old movie, *Sunday, Bloody Sunday,* was on. I'd seen it years ago, when I was still in high school. I hadn't understood it then; I had no idea what it was about or why people liked it. Now it was transparent to me, and even though some parts were a little clumsy, I liked it. Once I had wondered what it would be like to be an adult. I thought, like all children, that adulthood was accompanied by esoteric secrets, complicated insights, mysteriously acquired skills. But it turned out to be very simple: you were exactly the same, you were still a child, but you had to find a way to look after yourself. And trying to look after yourself was a full-time job. Sometimes it worked and sometimes it didn't. And that was it.

When the movie ended I watched a talk show. I watched it for half an hour before I realized that I had no idea what anyone was saying or even what the topic of discussion was. I picked up the remote and began flipping channels. I stopped at a music video in which a store-window mannequin was singing. After a few seconds she turned into a beautiful woman and broke out of the store. *You thought you could control me, but you see that you were wrong.*

"Ready for a snack?" Mercedes asked me. "I'm just about finished, I only have the bedroom and bathroom left. I scrubbed every corner. You won't recognize your own flat."

"Thank you," I said.

"I've prepared something for you, come. I had to buy a few things, your fridge was empty."

I joined her in the kitchen. She'd made salad and a spicy bean and vegetable stew. "Are you feeling better?" she asked, serving me and then herself. "I didn't buy any meat—I don't trust the stores around here."

"I'm not really sick, I'm just anxious. My husband's been missing for eleven years and yesterday I met someone who said he can get me his address. I have to call at six. I'm just nervous, that's all."

"Really! After eleven years, no wonder you're excited. But if he ran away, he may not want to be found."

"He didn't really run away."

"That's what we all tell ourselves. Men are men, though. They run away all the time."

"He was burned in a fire. He thought I wouldn't love him anymore."

"Oh! Jeez, men are dumb. They think we're like them. They care about looks, so they think we do. They care about women going gray, so they get all upset when they go gray. As if something like that mattered to us! Still, I can understand you. I'd wait too, for a man I loved. In fact, I'm still waiting, in a way. Not really, but in a way."

"Someone who left you?"

"Not exactly. Just someone I met when I was fourteen. We only spent one afternoon together. I'll tell you the truth, but please don't judge me."

"I won't."

"Yes, I can tell you're not the type to judge. The truth is, I was doing a bit of prostitution. I had no choice, believe me. Anyhow, I only did it very part-time. We were really poor, and I just couldn't bear not having money for anything. So I met this guy. When I think about it now, he was just a kid, not even in the army yet. But I still think of him as a lot older than me. I can't think of him as young, you know what I mean?"

"Yes, it's the same when I think about my kindergarten teacher. She was only twenty, but she'll always seem old to me."

"Well, he was so nice. He bought me ice cream, and I fell in love with him, because he was so incredibly nice and also very good-looking. He refused to sleep with me, he made up an excuse and I pretended to believe him. At first I thought he was turned off by me but then I saw that it wasn't that at all. I just wasn't special enough for him. He wanted someone who was special, even if he was paying for it. He told me I had a lot of talent as an actress, he said he could tell, because he was in acting himself, and he had a good sense for who was talented. I said to myself, One day I'll be a famous star, and I'll invite him to my opening show, and maybe then he'll like me. I also wanted to pay him back. He gave me a loan, and he said I could pay him back when I became a star. For years I kept hoping I'd run into him, and I still keep hoping. In '67 and '73 and '82 I checked every single casualty, I looked at the names and I checked all the photos, so I know he didn't fall. Two of my brothers fell, and my favorite cousin, but he made it. Anyhow, it was ages ago, but I'm pretty sure I'd recognize him. He's probably married and has kids, but I'd still like to meet him, just to tell him that I had a few parts, here and there. I was Honey in *Who's Afraid of Virginia Woolf?* When I said 'Violence! Violence!' everyone had hysterics. I was almost the star of that show. We were just an amateur group, but we got a review and they said I was a natural. Too bad I married the guy who played George. The director had this idea that George and I should be Sephardi and Martha and Nick would be Ashkenazi. Anyhow, me and George, I mean Victor, we started going out during rehearsals, and by the time the show was over, we were engaged. But all Victor wanted me to do was have kids, one after another. I don't mind, I love kids. Still, I wish I could meet that guy, and tell him about Honey. He's the one who gave me the courage to audition. I was in love with him for years, and I still am, a bit."

"What about your husband? Did he go on acting?"

She laughed. "No, unless you call having affairs and then lying about it a form of acting. No, he's had all sorts of jobs, but acting isn't one of them. He's all right. Considering what's out there, he's okay. Well, back to work. I'm almost finished. I'll just fix the bedroom. What do you think so far?"

"It's great, Mercedes. I really appreciate it. I have to go check on my neighbor, and then I might take a little walk. You can let yourself out, you don't have to lock the door. What do I owe you?"

"Rafi already paid me. I'm here instead of at his place. I don't think his wife likes me very much. I hope I can come here again."

I went to check on Volvo, even though it was the last thing I felt like doing. I knocked on his door softly. Luckily, he wasn't answering, and I didn't persist. Possibly he was out: Tuesday was his day alone, without volunteers, and he often went for long strolls down the most crowded streets of the city, hoping to upset as many people as he could, and perhaps also secretly hoping to be hit by a car as he wheeled himself carelessly into heavy traffic. On the other hand, maybe he was secretly hoping to find love. It was hard to tell with Volvo.

I still had an hour until six. I walked along the shore, my phone tucked in my front pocket. At a quarter to six I sat down on the sand, pulled out the phone, and dialed Aaron's number. I couldn't wait any longer.

"Hi," he said. He didn't sound very happy to hear from me.

"Hi, did you get it?"

"No. I don't have anything for you. Dana, listen to me, I'm telling you this as a friend. You have to forget your husband. I know it's hard, but you have to forget him."

"What are you saying? Oh God, is he dead?"

"No, he's not dead. I can't tell you anything. I wish I could, but I can't."

"You don't know, or you don't want to tell me?"

He didn't reply. He was an honest person, he found it hard to lie, and I could tell he was trying to decide what to say. But just the fact that he was hesitating was in itself an answer.

"So you know, you know where he is, but you don't want to tell me, is that it?" My voice was trembling but I was trying to stay calm; I was afraid he'd hang up on me if I became hysterical. Besides, there were people on the beach and I didn't want them listening in on my conversation.

"You have to forget him. That's all I can say. You have to move on, find someone else."

"Has he? Has he found someone else?"

"No, he's alone. Please don't ask any more questions, because that's all I can say."

"Why? Why can't you tell me? Why?"

"I have to go now," he said. "I'm very sorry. I wish I could help you, but I can't."

"It's okay," I said. "It's okay, thank you, you did your best. At least now I know that everyone's lying to me. That's something."

"Well, bye for now. Take care of yourself, Dana." He hung up.

I had told Rafi I would be at the demonstration in front of the Ministry of Defense, but I couldn't move. I held the phone in my hand, stared at the waves, and tried to understand what had just happened. I couldn't think straight: I was in some sort of trance. I shut my eyes and remembered a veiled and bangled belly dancer I'd once seen at a party, long ago. The chiming gold bangles had hypnotized me, and Daniel had laughed as he called my name to bring me back to the real world. I roused myself and phoned Rafi.

"It's me, Dana," I said.

"Dana who, please?" he teased.

"I'm on the beach."

"What's going on?"

"I found out something about Daniel."

"Really?"

"I can't tell you on the phone. Are you going to the demo?"

"I have to, I'm bringing the signs, remember? We can meet after."

"No, okay, I'll come. I can't just sit here staring at the sea. I'll be there soon."

Usually I enjoyed walking and it was only on rare occasions that I took the bus. The entire city had an unsettled look to it, as if the small angular apartment houses and the people walking puposefully through the streets and the cages filled with empty plastic bottles for recycling were all aware that they were part of a theatrical production—though whether farce or Greek tragedy, nobody knew. This was a world that made no effort to seduce you, for it was too caught up in its own satisfied, uncertain presence. I was particularly attached to the little stores and kiosks that sold newspapers and snacks. They never changed, the kiosks and small stores; the world advanced around them, but they adhered to their own time zone. It was hard to believe that these bottles of grapefruit juice and rows of salted bagels could keep these enterprises going, but so far they had. Lately, though, the kiosk operators and store owners had been looking very depressed, and I wondered whether they would finally cave in and vanish.

But now as I walked down the familiar streets, the city could have been invisible, I could have been sleepwalking through it.

The Ministry of Defense was inside a military complex surrounded by a tall wall and barbed wire. Demonstrations against the ministry were held on a small raised lot facing the entrance to the complex. A few bored soldiers were stationed on the sidewalk in order to protect us from ruffians, though if a drive-by shooter decided to target us, there was nothing they'd be able to do. The odds were against a violent attack, though. Most of the lunatics lived in the territories and they spent their energy tormenting Palestinians.

Rafi was already at the lot, standing next to a stack of signs. Sixty or seventy protesters had come to demonstrate, and they were milling around in their usual bewildered way, holding signs that condemned the latest bombing attack on a Palestinian town.

I climbed up to the lot and approached Rafi. I noticed when I stood next to him that we were exactly the same height. He didn't have his hat on, and he wasn't wearing sunglasses.

"What did you find out?" he asked, as though we were in the middle of a conversation.

"I'm not sure. It's very strange."

"Do you want to go for supper after the demonstration? You can tell me about it then."

"Yes."

Down below, on the sidewalk, a few women dressed in black had wrapped their heads in kaffiyehs and were holding stones in their hands, to show solidarity with the Palestinians. Not everyone approved of the women and some demonstrators grumbled, but there wasn't much they could do. One of the women had a can of orange spray paint. She came up to us and offered to spray our IDs orange; she also handed out little stickers for the inside flaps that said MY DEATH MAY NOT BE USED FOR ACTS OF REVENGE. My ID was already half orange (some of the paint had come off) but I took a sticker and so did Rafi.

A soldier from Army Radio came over to Rafi and asked him to say something about why people were demonstrating. She had round puffy cheeks and bangs that reached her eyebrows. I took several photos of her young, open face; she was gazing at Rafi like someone caught in limbo, on the verge of entering either heaven or hell: it wasn't clear to her which one it was likely to be, so she was hedging her bets. When Rafi was through, she thanked him and moved on to someone else.

The demonstration lasted an hour. Cars passed by on the street and the drivers looked at us with interest. Some of them shouted out insults, and some honked. A long honk meant they were angry and a few short honks meant they agreed with us—at least that was my interpretation.

At eight o'clock everyone piled the signs in a heap and went home. Rafi carried them to his van, which was parked nearby. I followed him and helped load the signs in back. Then we left the van where it was and began walking toward a street with a lot of restaurants. As we walked, Rafi phoned Graciela on his mobile phone.

"I met Dana at the demonstration and we're going to have a bite," he said. "I don't know how long I'll be. Do you need anything?"

But Graciela didn't need anything.

"She doesn't mind?" I asked.

"Not at all. She likes having the place to herself in the evening. She takes a long bath, listens to requiems and operas. She's a solitary person."

"How did you meet?"

"At the supermarket. Do you want to eat here?" He stopped at a sidewalk restaurant. We bought sandwiches and french fries at the counter and sat down with our trays at one of the tables. The metal lattice tabletops had tiny diamond-shaped gaps between the strips and I ran my fingers along the pattern.

"Mercedes came over," I said. "She cleaned up. And I had my fortune told by Tanya, who lives upstairs."

"What did she tell you?"

"It was a scam. She gives massages."

"Well, at least you got something for your money."

"I dreamed you were trying on outfits," I said.

"Did I find one?"

"You asked me for advice, but I didn't have all the facts, so I couldn't decide. You're acting like it's no big deal that we're here," I said. "You're acting like it's okay that you're here with me at this restaurant and it doesn't matter and no one cares and so what?"

"It does matter. It matters a lot. And it's okay, for me. I can't speak for you."

"It isn't okay. I love my husband."

"You can love more than one person," he said.

"No, no you can't. That's not love. Love means that the person you love is enough for you, and you don't want or need anyone else and no one else interests you."

"Love means you are completely helpless and there's nothing you can do about it except duck or plunge. But you can't change it, you can't change the way you feel."

"You're making things worse, letting this happen between us. You said you wouldn't hurt me."

"There are some things even I can't control. I'd like to control my appearance in your dreams, for example, but I can't."

"You could have stayed away from me."

"You could have stayed away from me, Dana. What did you find out about Daniel?"

"I met a guy in Intelligence. Just by chance, on the beach. And when he heard about Daniel he said all he had to do was look him up on his special computer and he'd be able to tell me where he was really living. Not his fake address, the real one. I didn't think he'd find anything, but he seemed so sure. He told me to call him today at six in the evening. But when I called he said he couldn't tell me anything and I'd just have to forget Daniel. But he didn't say he didn't have the address. He *did* have it, but for some reason he couldn't tell me. I don't understand it. On the beach he said I had a right to know. But now that he has the information, he's changed his mind. So he must have found out something he didn't expect. But what?"

"That's strange. It's strange that Daniel managed to hide in the first place. Such a small country, surely someone would find out and tell you."

"No one knows what he looks like now. And he probably uses another name. Maybe he never goes out. Maybe he's in an attic somewhere, and someone brings him food and whatever he needs. Maybe a friend of his is hiding him, the one who used to leave those notes on the door. I've thought of everything. I even thought he might be living in a tent somewhere in the desert. Daniel Daniel Daniel Daniel Daniel Daniel Daniel Daniel."

"Do you think what that Intelligence guy found out is that Daniel is living with another woman?"

"No, I asked him that. He said Daniel is alive and he lives alone. And that's all he would tell me. He's the sort of person who can't lie. You know the type?"

"Yes. They're rare enough. Well, maybe he's in some sort of institution?"

"No, I checked every single institution when he first vanished. I hired a private detective, she checked every place like that. Resorts, rest homes, mental institutions, everything. And she still checks them once a year. Besides, why wouldn't this guy want to tell me something like that? He wouldn't hide that sort of information. No, it's something else."

"What would you do if you got his address?"

"Knock on his door. And I wouldn't move or eat until he came out. I'd go on strike. He'd have no choice but to relent."

We didn't say anything more after that. When we finished our meal he said, "I'll drive you home."

"I want to walk. I like walking."

"I'll come with you."

"All right."

As we walked toward the sea, I had a fantasy of the city rising like a floating island and soaring away. I held Raffi's arm for balance, but only for a few seconds, until the sensation passed.

"Looks habitable now," Rafi said as he entered my flat. He sat down on the faded pink and green Turkish carpet. I made coffee and handed him the mug, then settled on the sofa closest to him, my legs curled under me. He said, "I finished my training one month before the uprising broke out. I spent the next two and a half years fighting the riots. Then I was released, and they gave me a big chunk of money. I didn't go back to my parents. I rented a room and every night I went to a bar and drank until I couldn't see straight and usually I woke up with someone in my room and I couldn't remember who she was or how she got there. Then the money ran out. I lay in bed and took my penknife and considered slashing my wrists, but I decided my penknife was too blunt. Basically I didn't have the courage to do it. I got out of bed and showered and went to the supermarket to buy a bottle of vodka—I figured I'd get drunk and then maybe I'd have more courage. But I didn't have enough money for vodka, so I bought fruit juice. That's when I met Graciela. I was having trouble holding the bottle of juice, it almost slipped from my hands, and she caught it. She was well dressed and clean and orderly. I followed her home, to her clean orderly flat—she already had her own place, the one we still live in. She played the piano for me, a piece by Erik Satie. I was in very bad shape, and that piece almost did me in. I stayed there, I didn't leave. We decided to marry. Her parents were against it, they'd been hoping for someone with a better background, someone with money and a profession and fair skin. But they didn't want her to be unhappy. They didn't want anything to interfere with her music, and they were afraid that if they put up a big fuss she'd be upset. She started getting migraines, and she couldn't sleep. Other things started bothering her too. She'd always hated dirt, but her cleaning became obsessive. She felt sick if she saw dirt, and she couldn't go out for long periods of time because she wouldn't use public toilets, or even toilets in other people's houses. She tried seeing a psychiatrist, but nothing came of it. She wouldn't let me touch her when we fucked, she couldn't bear to look at my cock or touch it, and I had to find ways of getting inside without touching any other part of her and without her having to see anything. After Naomi was born, even that stopped. I left her before I knew she was pregnant. Then I heard that she was pregnant—someone who had seen her on the street called me and told me, and I came back. I didn't trust her alone with Naomi. And I was right, she didn't want to touch her, she carried her in a plastic carrier, she never held her or stroked her or touched her. She placed her on a pillow when she wanted to give her a bottle. I suggested we divorce and I take the baby, but she was horrified. She loves Naomi. She loves her, but she can't touch her. I look after Naomi and Graciela plays the piano and gives recitals and concerts and we manage that way. I had a few one-nighters, but I stopped, it was pointless. We have an income from a fund her parents set up for her, and I also work at an after-school program with teens in distress, but there's no money in that, our budget keeps getting cut, we're almost volunteers at this point. I can't leave because the kids depend on me. That's my story, Dana."

"Why? Why did you want to kill yourself?"

"The usual: guilt, remorse. You can get over killing people, there are ways to think about it. You can say it was self-defense, it was war, that's what you're trained to do in a war, you're trained to think it's me or them, and you're defending your country, it's your highest duty. So you can say, well, I had no choice, and that's what the interpretation was then, that's how it looked and felt. You can say, I was attacked, I fought back. I didn't think about whether we should be there in the first place. That wasn't something we thought about. But if you beat people up in front of their kids or watch your friends shoot someone's balls off, you can't justify that sort of thing. And since you can't justify it, you have to face that this is who you are, this is the sort of person you are. I didn't think I could live with that in constant replay another forty or fifty years, day in, day out, night in, night out."

"You really shot someone's balls off? I never heard that one before."

"We caught some guy who'd just killed a couple of soldiers, and these two guys in my unit, who were friends of the soldiers who were killed, more or less lynched him. They started with his balls. Coby was there, too."

"Coby from the hotel?"

"Yes."

"What about now? Are things in constant replay?"

"No, it's different now. I have perspective now about what was going on then, and I can do something about it."

"Is your daughter waiting for you?"

"She's probably in bed by now. She's a very easy child. She never puts up a fuss about anything. It worries me, sometimes."

I said, "I met my husband at a wedding, he was the singer—even though the band was just a hobby he had, a way of earning extra cash. His real passion was architecture, and that's what he was doing, designing houses and buildings. I was nineteen, in the army, and he was a lot older, ten years older than me, but we didn't feel any sort of gap. We were like one person. We even had our own language that we invented. We had a name for each other, Daneli, we were both Daneli, we were almost one person. We told each other everything, and whenever he went out of the house he left me a note with a cartoon—he was very talented, his cartoons were so brilliant, and he did them in just two seconds. We couldn't stay away from each other, we had sex every day, we invented things no one ever heard of or did before. He said he was going to move into my cunt. We laughed because he was very funny, he did imitations of people and he was witty and cracked jokes all the time. Sometimes his humor was very dark, and we fought because I didn't like it. I thought there were some things you shouldn't laugh about, but now I think he was right and I was wrong, but he was older than me, and he knew more about life. We used to go out and everyone would smile at us. We'd wear matching clothes and I was a female version of him and he was a male version of me. I wore sexy clothes, sexier than people wore in those days. After the accident, at the hospital, they wouldn't let me see him, but I thought it was temporary, so I didn't insist. They told me he didn't want visitors and that he was in a lot of pain and on a lot of drugs and that we should give him time. So we did, we gave him time. Now of course I really regret doing that, I should have gone in right away, every day, until it became natural for him. And then they told me he was much better, he was out of danger, they said he was very lucky and there was no infection or internal damage. They said I could see him the next morning and I went out to get him a present, I bought a silk dressing gown, wine-colored with a black collar. But that night he vanished from the hospital. I got there and they said he'd escaped. They were very upset. He hadn't filled in the forms, he just sneaked out. He sent me a letter a few weeks later. And in the letter he said that it was over between us, and he was going to start a new life, a different life—he didn't know yet how or what it would be, but that I had to find a way to forget him because he was no longer the same person, the person I had known was no longer him."

"What about his family?"

"They were upset, but for them, for his parents and sister, the main thing was that he was alive. They didn't understand me, and I was angry so I stopped visiting them. Maybe I was just jealous that they had a consolation I didn't have. He didn't even leave me a child. If only I had got pregnant! I tried, we tried, and I did get pregnant once, but I had a miscarriage in my sixth month. Maybe something went wrong when I miscarried. After that we kept trying but nothing happened."

"How long were you together?"

"Seven years and two months. We had a cat, but she died last year."

"When did you get pregnant?"

"When I was twenty-two."

"You were nineteen when you married?"

"Yes."

"If it took you three or four years the first time, even though you had sex every day, you aren't infertile, it probably just takes you longer."

"Not every day, we did something every day, but he didn't always come inside me, there were other things we liked. But you're right, in the middle of the month we always tried."

"Maybe that was your mistake. My mother always told me the magic number was ten, ten days after your period starts, she said that was the fertile day, not the middle. She has to be an expert, she had nine kids."

"Nine . . . "

"Two died at birth, but she did have nine."

"Which were you?"

"Second. What will you do about Daniel?"

"I just have to find someone else in Intelligence. At least now I know that the army knows where he is—all I have to do is find someone who will tell me. Such a fluke! This could really be it; this could finally be the key. After so many dead ends. Do you know anyone I could ask?"

"No, but it shouldn't be too hard to find someone."

"I just don't understand it. Why aren't they telling me? Do

they want to protect me, or him, or themselves? It doesn't make sense."

"My guess is they want to protect you from something, but I can't figure out what it is."

"You know, now that I think back to that secretary who spent a lot of time trying to get the information for me, I think she also saw what this guy Aaron saw. I remember she was reading the screen, and I was sure she'd finally found something, but then she shook her head. But I remember wondering what she'd read, why it had taken her so long. She wasn't even supposed to be going into those files—she was doing it because she hated her boss, I think, and also she wanted to help me. But then when she found the information, she changed her mind."

"Maybe he's more handicapped than you think."

"But he was fine when he left the hospital."

"Maybe something happened to him afterward."

"No, it can't be that, that wouldn't stop them from telling me. It's something else. This is so crazy! But I'm excited, too. I think I'm getting close; I mean, if I just find the right person now, I'll know. I'll know! I might be seeing Daniel soon. I might be seeing him in a few days, even. I can hardly believe it. This is the first real lead I've had!"

He looked at me and laughed.

"What's so funny?"

"You look like Joan of Arc."

"Well, imagine. Imagine. I've been waiting eleven years. I've been waiting eleven years for a lead. Such a fluke. Such a fluke that I met this guy. He was trying to pick me up."

"Did he succeed? Not that it's my business at all, so you don't have to answer. Forget I asked, in fact."

"He didn't succeed. I think I'm even a bit insulted by the question."

"No one expects you to live like a nun."

"Yeah, well. It's not my style. And usually I wouldn't even talk to him, but I just felt like it, I don't know why. And he asked about Daniel. Imagine if I hadn't met him. On the other hand, imagine if I'd met him ten years ago! I don't even want to think about that."

"You know what the Buddhists say."

"No, what do they say?"

"Things happen when they happen."

"I read the exact opposite somewhere," I said. "I read that the devil is in charge of timing."

"Yes, I guess that's the opposite approach."

"Nothing can make this long wait a good thing. There aren't any advantages. None, none, none."

"Let's go to the sea—do you want to?"

We walked to the sea and sat on the sand and stared at the black waves. The white foam crescents along the edge of the waves rolled toward us and then vanished, like the smiles of ghosts. We sat side by side and watched the waves rising and falling, but we didn't touch.

# WEDNESDAY

I DREAMED I FOUND DANIEL, and he was living with another woman, a tall woman who was young and beautiful. Then I realized that she was blind. And I thought, *I can be blind too, if that's what it takes. I can wear a blindfold.* And I began thinking about all the things I'd have to learn to do while wearing the blindfold. It wouldn't be so hard, I thought. In the dream it seemed like a simple thing, being blind.

When I woke I remembered that my photographs were ready and I went to pick them up. I walked home slowly, made myself *café et lait,* sat down at the kitchen counter, and stared at the envelope. Finally I opened it.

The one of the donkey was very good. The photos of the children were lovely as always, though not because of anything I'd done. There was also a good one from the upper story of the warehouse: a young woman I didn't really remember, with both hands on her ears, and a terrified young man next to her. I captured that second when the sound grenade explodes, the fear in their faces and bodies. The photographs of the soldiers, on the other hand, were static, the angles weren't good, and you couldn't really see their faces. I threw those out. Unfortunately, the photo of the woman who had the seizure didn't come out either. The tear gas had prevented me from focusing or framing properly. I kept it, though; I added it to a shoe box marked *not good but can't throw out*.

The photographs of the two friends were my favorite of this lot. I noticed things about them which I hadn't seen at the time: for example, the man who had given up hope had delicate hands with long slender fingers, and his more optimistic friend was much more depressed than I'd realized when I'd spoken to him. In fact, it was no longer clear which one of them was ready to keep trying and which one wasn't. The man who seemed to have given up on the future looked thoughtful and wise in the photograph, while his friend's shoulders were slumped forward in defeat.

There was one photo of Rafi. I had caught him in profile, looking down at the soldier. His expression was serious and angry, but his body was completely calm, as if he were enjoying an outing at a vacation resort.

I couldn't decide what to do with the photograph. I wanted to hide it, but I knew it was already too late. It had always been too late; from the moment I saw Rafi in the warehouse it was too late. I couldn't bear the thought of concealing something from Daniel when I saw him, and now it seemed I might be closer than ever to finding him. Daniel was moving away from me just when I was closest to reaching him. I wanted to stop his retreat, but I didn't know how to do it. It wasn't Rafi's fault. It wasn't anyone's fault. I placed all the photographs, including the one of Rafi, in a shoe box marked *September* and slid it under my bed.

I returned to the counter and made a list of activists I knew who might have a link to someone in Intelligence. I wondered whether I should also contact Daniel's family and tell them what had happened, but I didn't really have any news for them yet. Besides, if I found out where he was, I had to go see him first, before anyone else. Before he had a chance to escape again.

I began phoning the people on my list. No one asked why I needed information; they assumed I was trying to help a Palestinian in trouble. One had a brother in Intelligence, but he was "a stickler." Another had a brother-in-law with a lot of power, but "he'd open a file on you." The others didn't have any connections.

It was too soon to feel discouraged. Possibly I would have to try old friends of my parents. The problem was that they'd want to see me. I'd have to invest an entire evening in each one, just to get information they might not have; they would also want to know why I needed to talk to an officer in the upper military echelons. I would try my coworkers at the insurance office first. I'd also ask Tanya; more than once I'd seen extremely distinguished-looking men walk confidently up the stairs to her flat.

I decided to finish my novel in the meantime; I was very close to the end. I wrote the last few sex scenes and sent the file to my publishers. Then I signed a form relinquishing copyright and crossed the street to the City Beach Hotel to fax it.

Working on the novel had exhausted me and I lay down for a nap on the sofa, but I had a crabby sleep, as my mother used to say, crowded with distressing dreams. I dreamed, among other things, that Volvo had his legs back, thanks to a miracle drug that rejuvenated cells. But when he tried to walk, he couldn't. He'd forgotten how.

Despite the bad dreams, I didn't really want to wake up. I tried to pull myself out of sleep because I knew that something very important and wonderful had happened in my waking life, something which required my attention. I was also aware that it was Wednesday and that I had to get ready for my weekly dinner with Vronsky. But another part of me seemed to be stuck deep inside the disjointed, garbled images. Only with the greatest effort was I able to break loose. I sat up groggily on the sofa and checked my watch: I had to meet Vronsky at seven. I had just enough time for a quick shower.

The first time Vronsky phoned I was very surprised. It happened a few weeks after our medical relationship had come to an end; he called and asked whether I wanted to go out to dinner with him.

"You know I'm married," I said right away, to avoid any misunderstanding.

"Oh no, nothing like that, I mean . . . I didn't mean . . ." He was very flustered.

"Sure, I'd enjoy it very much."

"I'll show you the article I wrote about you. Not that it will interest you much, it's quite technical. Still, yours was a most unusual case. At seven, then?"

We settled on an Italian restaurant a few blocks from my building, near the American embassy.

After that we ate at the same restaurant every Wednesday, from seven to eight-thirty or nine.

Vronsky was meticulous. He liked everything to be in its place, at the right time, in the right way, and it would have driven me crazy had I seen him more often; but since our meetings were limited to two hours a week, his need for order endeared him to me. He was meticulous but at the same time he never seemed to notice anything around him or anything about me. I soon found out that this was only an act, that in fact he took it all in, every detail, and if he didn't comment on what he saw and felt, it was only because he was afraid. Afraid of me, afraid of himself, afraid also of the future, which would inevitably bring change. He was considerate and made an effort to be friendly and there were times when I felt maternal toward him, even though he was fifty-six, nearly twenty years older than me. He had a grown son who lived in Berlin and designed costumes for avant-garde plays. His wife had died years ago, and he lived with his unmarried sister Sonya, a mathematician. Sonya was deaf.

I had wondered, at first, whether Vronsky was courting me. Odelia was convinced that he was interested, but I finally decided this was not the case. The significant looks or gestures or small verbal hints that indicate a desire to move beyond a platonic relationship never made an appearance. He needed the friendship—that was all. And I enjoyed his company. Sometimes I teased him, because he was so formal and reserved.

I was still on the sofa, trying to summon the initiative to get up and shower, when there was a knock on the door, followed by a muted voice: "It's me, Miss Fitzpatrick. Anybody home?"

Miss Fitzpatrick was one of the volunteers who helped with Volvo. When Volvo first moved into the building it quickly became evident that he was more than I could handle alone. He had no visitors; he had broken all ties with the past, he said. I placed an ad in the paper several weeks running; I had wanted the ad to read, *Interesting, intelligent young man, confined to wheelchair, needs volunteer companionship and help*, but Volvo insisted on, *Young man, no legs, needs unpaid assistant*. This sober text no doubt discouraged some potential candidates, but Miss Fitzpatrick was not put off. I was a little surprised when she called, because she lived in the capital. Later I found out that it was a treat for her to come down to the city; she loved the sea, and was thrilled to find that we lived so close to the beach. She had a rosy face, short brown hair, and the hefty body of a dreamy, artless schoolgirl. When Volvo and I first met her, a large silver cross dangled from a chain around her neck, for she was in fact a nun of some sort, though she introduced herself as Miss Fitzpatrick.

Volvo was appallingly rude during the interview. "I hope you are not a proselytizer," he said, in a menacing voice. I was surprised he knew the word in English; possibly he had looked it up before Miss Fitzpatrick arrived. "I hope you are not thinking to save my soul. I am planning to go straight to hell," he added, laughing shrilly. Miss Fitzpatrick laughed with him. "I can see you've got a good sense of humor. We'll get along well. I love a good joke." But Volvo was determined to test her limits right there and then. "And I do not like to have to stare at a cross all day. I am the atheist." She gathered her cross and slid it inside her tunic. "There, all gone," she said, as though humoring a child who was afraid of the shape in the closet. "Do you wear that thing at night?" Volvo asked. "Young man, I will not ask you what you do in your private time, and you will not ask me what I do in my private time, and we can be good friends." Volvo looked somewhat abashed, but he quickly remembered his plight and recovered. "Fine, fine. Whatever Dana wants is fine with me."

I rarely saw her after that because she liked to take Volvo on excursions that lasted the entire day. She drove him to places of interest or to public parks and gardens.

"So sorry to bother you," she said when I opened the door. "We can't go anywhere, the poor car is in the garage. It's been overburdened, I think. And between us, some of the sisters have yet to master the finer art of shifting gears." She smiled, and two dimples appeared on her cheeks like the imprints of a child's fingers in dough. "Volvo wants me to read to him. Have you any appropriate novel I can borrow, in simple English? Hemingway, perhaps? What do you think?"

"I'm just stepping out, but come in and have a look. Borrow

some books for yourself, too, if you see anything that interests you."

"Oh, goody. I do like a novel now and then. Well, this place has been tidied up nicely."

I decided to forgo the shower. I left Miss Fitzpatrick crouching in front of my bookcase and walked to the restaurant. I was a little early, but I didn't mind waiting. The waitress showed me to our usual table, by the window. The view was not very appealing, but Vronsky suffered from mild claustrophobia and we always reserved this table in advance.

"You're late," I said when he entered the restaurant at exactly seven. It was a worn-out joke, but I always liked it. Vronsky was incapable of being late. Or early.

"If I gave you a hundred dollars, would you wear jeans?" I asked him. He always wore a nondescript pair of trousers, and he seemed to have several identical pairs. It was impossible to say what color they were. They negated the concept of color.

"Hi, Dana. How are you?" He sat down opposite me and folded the cloth napkin in four, set it aside. No one I knew used cloth napkins; they were just there for show, or for tourists. "I don't have jeans."

"If I gave you a hundred dollars and bought you a pair of jeans, would you wear them?"

"They wouldn't fit."

"What if you came with me to the store?"

"I wouldn't want to trouble you."

"What if I told you it would be a dream come true?"

"I'd think you were joking around."

"No, you're wrong, Vronsky. It would give me immense pleasure to go shopping with you and buy you real clothes."

"As you know, I don't like new clothes. I know it's silly and irrational, but I feel self-conscious in new clothes. How are you?"

"How do I look?"

"Worried. A bit pale."

"Tell me what else you've noticed."

"Your shirt is a little torn, at the sleeve."

"What else? In the restaurant?"

"Nothing's changed here. The waitress has had a haircut. That's all."

The waitress heard us and came over to take our order. "My friend likes your new hairstyle," I told her. Vronsky was embarrassed, but he smiled.

She smiled back. "Thanks, my boyfriend thinks it's too short. But everyone else likes it. Maybe he doesn't want me to be too pretty!" She took our order. I always had the same thing, spinach cannelloni, but Vronsky went down the menu, dish by dish, and then he'd start at the top again, so that every week he had something else. He was very particular about food, and one reason he liked this restaurant was that he thought the chef was excellent. He once surprised me and the waitress by commenting, at the end of the meal, "I guess the chef's on vacation?" He'd noticed the difference at once.

While we waited for the food to arrive I said, "Tell me about your latest patients." This was one of our favorite topics.

"Well, today a very young child came in with internal injuries. They were rather unusual, and we were baffled, and the parents were baffled too. They couldn't think of anything that had happened. We were all called in to see if anyone had any ideas. Finally, after we quizzed the parents for a very long time, we discovered what it was. Water. They'd held this poor child too long under the tap at the beach. The stream was too strong for him. And apparently he'd screamed his head off, but they thought it was just because he didn't like the water. They decided for that reason to keep him under the jet longer, to desensitize him, so to speak. Get him used to the water, make a man of him. And the pressure of the jet caused some internal damage. I'm surprised a shower jet would be that strong."

"That's really weird."

"Yes, it was an unusual case. A very sensitive child."

"No, that's not what's weird. What's weird is that I know who you mean, I think. I think I saw them. A young couple, immigrants, he has freckles, she has very large breasts?"

"That may be them."

"That's the strangest coincidence! I saw a couple on the beach this morning and they were holding this thin little scrawny kid under the tap—it's not a shower tap, it's one of those low taps for washing your feet. That's why the stream is so strong. And the kid was screaming, that's why I remember it. The more he screamed, the more determined they were. They were in on it together, enjoying it together, it was horrible. I finally went up to them, but I didn't know what to say. I didn't say anything; I guess I was intimidated. I feel so bad that I didn't say anything."

"I'm sure nothing you could have said would have helped. They're quite stupid, the two of them."

"Will he be okay?"

"We're keeping him under observation, we'll see how things develop."

"Why are doctors so vague?"

"Well, diagnosis is not an exact science, you know. The whole field of medicine is fraught with uncertainty. Look at the strange story of your ankle."

"Don't let that kid go back. Vronsky, promise me you'll alert the social workers. If you don't, I will. Those parents are dangerous."

"In fact, the social worker has already opened a file; it's mandatory in such cases."

"Maybe I could adopt him," I said hopelessly.

"Yes, him and all the thousands of other children with imperfect lives. Dana, imperfect lives are the norm. Your childhood was the exception: doting, responsible parents, a degree of affluence—and even in your case tragedy hit when you were only fourteen."

"That reminds me of something that happened a long time ago. Something Daniel and I saw."

"Yes?"

"You know, I've seen a lot of very sad things. Sometimes they're so sad I think I won't be able to bear it. Refugee camps, people at roadblocks, Dar al-Damar . . . But the saddest thing I ever saw, the worst thing, wasn't what you'd expect. It was a long time ago, before Daniel left. We went to pick mushrooms in the forest. It was one of those perfect days—blue sky, sunny, a soft breeze. And there was this other couple there and they had a daughter who was about four. They were lovely parents, very sensitive. They spoke to her in soft, gentle voices. And the daughter—well, I never saw anything like it. You see these ide-alized kids in Renaissance paintings, but they're not meant to be realistic. But she was smiling at everyone, she was glowing, I never saw anything like it. She was the happiest kid, maybe the happiest person, on earth, and she wanted to share her happiness with everyone, she was smiling at everyone in this sweet, happy, trusting way. Daniel and I just couldn't believe it. She was full of love. And we were both heartbroken—because she was on the wrong planet. It was just so horrible to think of what was waiting for her, how life would hurt her. Someone like that, you want them to be on an island somewhere."

"There's a phase in child development that matches what you describe."

"No, this was different. She stood out. I never saw anyone like this. I never saw any kid smiling like that at strangers."

"I don't know. Sounds a bit sentimental to me, Dana."

"You'd know what I meant if you saw her."

"We all manage to survive. We all go from innocence and glory to adulthood. You want a paradise where everyone is happy. It's unrealistic."

"I guess that's true."

"Maybe you and Daniel were saddened by the girl because you wanted a child."

"No, we were sad because she was such a rare and beautiful thing and we knew it wouldn't last, she'd be crushed."

"If she had nice parents, and inner strength, why wouldn't she go on being full of love? Maybe she's one of those lucky people who stay happy all their lives."

"I would like to believe that. But I don't think it's likely."

"You identify with her. I guess I do too, listening to you."

"Did you have a happy childhood, Vronsky?"

"At times," he said elusively. He almost never talked about his personal life.

"I have something important to tell you, Vronsky. A few things happened this week. First, I found out something about my husband. It turns out that people in the army know where he is, but they refuse to tell me."

"Really!" He seemed very surprised.

"You don't happen to know anyone in Intelligence, do you, Vronsky?"

"I'd be happy to know someone *with* intelligence," he said, smiling wryly.

"Something else happened. I met someone."

"You mean a man? That's good news, Dana."

"It's terrible news! I'm married. And so is he."

"Ah," he said, disappointed.

"I feel I'm getting closer to finding my husband. I just need to find someone in Intelligence who can look up the information. I feel I'm really getting close. What timing!"

"You're in love?"

"No, I love my husband. You can only love one person."

"That hasn't been my experience," Vronsky said, but he wouldn't expand.

"Vronsky, how about today after dinner we go for a walk along the boardwalk?"

"I can't, I promised my sister I'd be home."

"You always have an excuse."

"There's a television show she wants to watch, I sign it for her."

"She's lucky she has you."

"I'm lucky I have her."

"What's she like?"

"Sonya? She has a good sense of humor, she's fun to be with."

"Do you think we should go on having dinner?" I asked him suddenly. I didn't plan to say it, the words just came out on their own. They had a color: deep blue, like the sky at night in the middle of a field.

Vronsky nodded. "I understand," he said.

"I was just asking. Because, you know, you don't really open up to me."

He looked stunned, and very hurt. "I didn't know you felt that way."

"I don't. I didn't mean it."

"I thought you enjoyed our meetings. I enjoy them immensely. But if you're getting bored, that's all right."

"No, I love our meetings. I love our meetings, I don't know what's wrong with me today. I'm just a mess!"

"Let's look at this calmly, Dana. I see I was wrong to take this personally. You've just told me that you feel you might find your husband in the near future. And you've told me that you met someone you're attracted to, though unfortunately he's married. So perhaps we can deduce that you want to simplify your life?"

"What's your first name, Vronsky?"

"Konstantin. Kostya for short."

"You never told me."

"You never asked. But as you know, hardly anyone calls me by that name."

"Isn't that a sort of Christian name?"

"My father was Christian."

"It suits you. You're pretty constant . . . Anyhow, it isn't that, Vronsky. It's not that I want to simplify my life—it's not that vague. It's much more specific. I'm worried that Daniel will be jealous. I don't want anything to stand between us."

"That makes perfect sense."

"Even though I made it clear in my interviews that you were just one of the people helping me out, nothing more."

"I remember."

"But he'd be jealous if I went on seeing you. It wouldn't be appropriate."

"Please don't worry, Dana. You're right, of course."

"Thanks, Vronsky. You're very kind. Will you miss me?"

"Of course I'll miss you."

"I'll miss you too. Can I kiss you good-bye today? I don't mean a final good-bye—I mean, we'll stay in touch, by phone. But can I kiss you good-bye just for now?"

"We'll see," he said.

"When our meal's over I'll walk you to the car, and I'll come inside with you and kiss you good-bye, do you agree?"

"I have to think about it."

"You have the whole meal to think."

When we were through at the restaurant, I walked him to his car. He'd parked in a nearly empty parking lot down the street. I sat on the passenger's seat and he let me kiss him, and he kissed me back. We knew it was our last time together. Tears ran down my cheeks and we both tasted the salt. Vronsky gave me a tissue and then we resumed kissing. He stroked my hair. "Take care of yourself, Dana. I hope you find whatever you're looking for."

I didn't answer; I was very sad. I got out of the car and watched Vronsky pull out of the parking lot and drive away. He didn't look back.

❖

Only once did I feel that Daniel was hiding something from me.

One day, impulsively, for no reason at all, I kissed his feet. It was the middle of the week, and we were on the sofa watching a dreary film noir we'd rented from the video store. The overloaded symbols and clever shots were making us both sleepy, and suddenly Daniel's bare feet looked so happy that I had to lean over and kiss them.

Daniel didn't say anything, but I could see that something was wrong. He got up and went to the kitchen, opened the fridge door, and stared inside, his mind clearly on something else. Finally he let the door swing shut. He said, "I'm going to the corner store to get pretzels," and left. He made that up, about the pretzels; he just wanted a few minutes to himself.

I had no idea what was going on, and he never told me. It was the only time Daniel completely mystified me.

# THURSDAY

I ARRIVED AT THE INSURANCE OFFICE an hour late the next day because I'd slept in, but no one noticed or minded. I felt like an actor or a mime as I went about my work: I remembered my lines and the things I had to do, but none of it was related to who I was and what I was feeling. I asked my fellow workers whether they knew anyone in Intelligence. One had an uncle in Intelligence but he was living abroad; another had a retired grandfather who had once worked on some very secret project. Neither of those leads sounded very promising. I asked my employer, too, but he looked at me suspiciously and asked why I wanted to know. His body became hot and tense; he was familiar with my views and seemed to think I was planning to penetrate state secrets and sell them to the enemy. I dropped the subject before he fired me.

The day had a misty quality to it, but sprang into sharp focus as soon as I entered my building: a shocking smell had taken over the hallway, as if a ghoul from the pit of hell were slowly dissolving in some invisible corner. I ran into my flat, grabbed a towel, held it against my nose, and knocked on Volvo's door to see whether he knew anything. But he was out, probably shopping with Rosa.

I climbed the stairs and tried Tanya's flat. Tanya opened the door immediately. She looked like a character in an old Italian movie, with her eyes widening above a delicate white handkerchief which she held dramatically to her nose, and with her equally dramatic outfit: tight black lace dress, red high-heeled shoes, shiny red bead necklace.

"We can't figure out what that smell is," she said. "And we're afraid to find out! It's definitely coming from Jacky's place. What if he's hanged himself! What if he's been rotting away for a few days in there? That already happened to me once, with my poor friend Irenie. I'm not taking a chance like that again! I still have nightmares."

"I'm sure he's alive," I said, though I was beginning to feel a little worried myself. I rang Jacky's bell but there was no answer. I reminded myself that this in itself didn't mean anything; Jacky rarely answered the door.

"Jacky, open up, it's me, Dana!" I shouted. "Are you there?"

Jacky hardly ever left his flat. When he did go out, he draped himself with prayer shawls. He was very gaunt and his shaggy gray beard reached his midriff; he seemed to belong in a Grimm story, except that no one in Grimm walked around with prayer shawls over his shoulders. We never saw him eating and it wasn't clear what he lived on. There was no point bringing him meals because he'd arrange the food neatly on the hallway floor, where it would attract every cockroach in the city. Maybe that was his intention, to feed the cockroaches. One could never be sure with Jacky.

I continued pounding on the door. Finally it opened a crack and two heavy-lidded eyes peered out at us.

"I have nothing more to tell anyone," Jacky said. "There's no point asking me. I've told them all I know."

"Jacky, what's that smell coming from your flat?"

"What smell?" He opened the door and Tanya and I both stepped back, as if pushed forcefully away. This was a smell with kinetic powers.

"I don't smell anything," he said.

"How can you not smell anything!" I exclaimed.

"That's what they asked me when they took me in. I told them all I knew."

Despite the heat, Jacky was wearing a heavy sweater and brown corduroy pants. It was hard associating him with the pop star who'd had such an enthusiastic and devoted following, once upon a time. Daniel had often sung his songs. *I had a dream about angels, they were carrying you out of the tank, and your uniform grew wings, and I wanted you back.*

Jacky returned to the ratty, rust-colored sofa in the center of the room and folded his arms. The sofa was the only piece of furniture that had survived his efforts to remove listening devices from his flat. "I think it's coming from under the sink," he admitted.

I entered his bare flat, opened the cupboard door under the sink, and stifled a scream. There were five dead mice lying on the torn linoleum. They looked like tiny pink fetuses.

"What is it?" Jacky asked.

"Mice. Dead."

"I knew that," Jacky said. "I put poison."

"Well, why didn't you tell us?"

"I thought maybe the government sent you. They have a file on me."

"Yes, I know. Who can blame them?"

"What should we do?" I asked Tanya.

"I'm not touching them," she said. "Find a man."

"Where?"

"They're all over the place," Tanya laughed.

I went downstairs, crossed the street to the City Beach Hotel, and asked to see Coby, the manager. After a few minutes he emerged from his back office. Coby always wore a suit and tie, which I suppose was expected of him, and he was tall and slim, with dark-framed glasses: the cumulative effect was reassuring. He looked like a character in a slick, fast-paced movie about corporate intrigue; he'd be the person who stuck to his principles and didn't give in to temptation.

"Coby?" I said. "I'm a friend of Rafi's."

"You're Dana, of course. I've seen you around. How are you?"

"We have a mouse problem. In Jacky's apartment. There are some dead mice under the sink."

He smiled. "I'll send the guard," he said. He stepped outside and approached Marik. "Go up with this woman, please, and help her get rid of a dead mouse," he said. "You'll need a bag to put it in."

"Thanks, Marik," I said. "I hope you don't mind mice?"

Marik didn't answer, but he got up from his stool and followed me to Jacky's flat.

Jacky looked at Marik calmly and said, "He's a government agent. I can spot them miles away."

"I wish," Marik said. "Then maybe I'd be paid something."

Using the bag itself as a glove, he maneuvred the mice inside it. "This smell could wake the dead," he said. He had a heavy accent, and when he spoke, the words seemed to be colliding against each other in odd rhythms.

"Thanks," I said.

"Uh," he replied.

"Tell them to stop sending mice," Jacky said. "I've told them everything I know."

"Jacky, aren't you hot? It's boiling in here. Let me open a window, get some air in."

"No, no! They're going to listen in!"

"I'll call them and ask them not to listen for the next ten minutes, okay? I know someone, I have connections."

"Oh, all right," Jacky said. "Anyone seen my glasses, by the way? I used to have a hearing aid, but they took it away during the interrogation."

I opened the window. It didn't stay up on its own but I had given Jacky a stick to hold it up. I looked around for the stick, and finally found it under the sofa.

"Jacky, do you have any more poison lying around?"

"No, I used up the box. But I do have some Band-Aids."

"If you poison any more mice, tell us."

"Maybe, maybe not," Jacky said, smiling to himself.

"Jacky, can I get you anything? Do you have food?"

"I'm not that naïve!" Jacky said. He unzipped his fly. "I have to air my penis," he said.

"The treats that await us!" Tanya said. I looked around in alarm to see whether Marik was still there; he'd think our entire building was populated by deviants. But luckily he'd vanished.

"Well, we'd best be going," I said. "Take care, Jacky. And call me if there are more mice."

I left the flat and shut the door behind me. "Why am I familiar with the penises of two of the three men in this building?" I asked.

Tanya smiled. "Poor Volvo. I heard he was the life of the party before his legs went. Do you think we should find some woman for him—you know, pay someone? I still have some friends in the business, I could get a good deal."

"He says he doesn't want sex. But when I help him bathe that's not the impression I get." We both began giggling like schoolgirls. "'A bit more soap,'" I imitated Volvo, keeping my voice down in case he came back just then.

Tanya returned to her flat and I went to the hotel to thank Coby.

Coby was in the lobby, giving instructions about chairs to Hussein, a bony, nervous man of indeterminate age who worked at the hotel. The lobby was filled with well-dressed religious guests; they were honoring some leader or other, and maybe also raising funds for their political party.

"Situation under control?" he asked me when he'd finished explaining seating arrangements to Hussein.

I nodded. "Thanks."

"Anytime you need something, just ask."

"Thank you. Do you know Rafi well?"

"Of course," he said. "We were in the same unit. Come, let's have coffee. Have you had supper?"

"No, but I can't eat so soon after seeing those mice."

"Poor Jacky. Remember him from before?"

"Of course. Who doesn't?"

"It's the drugs that did it." I followed him to the dining room. We sat by the window, next to the table I'd shared with Rafi four days ago. Coby told the waiter to bring us coffee.

"Once you start mixing them together, anything can happen," he said, still on the subject of Jacky's history. "Once you lose a sense of boundaries . . . once you stop saying, this yes, but this no, you've had it. With drugs, that is. Maybe with anything . . ."

"How's business?"

"Well, lousy of course. The war . . . If you ever need a room, let me know. If you and Rafi ever need a room, just say the word."

"Why would we need a room? I have my own room."

"Well, you know, room service, a hotel, everyone likes hotels for a change."

"Anyhow, I'm married. So is Rafi."

"Rafi's been through a lot."

"He's lucky. He has a wife, a steady income, a well-behaved daughter, a penthouse apartment. I don't feel sorry for him."

Coby raised his eyebrows and gave me a deeply skeptical look. He didn't believe I meant what I said, but he let it drop.

"Coby, do you know anyone in Intelligence?"

"In Intelligence? Why?"

"Not just some clerk but an officer, someone with access to files. Do you?"

"I don't know, I have to think. What's this all about?"

"My husband. I found out that information about him is available in army files. I need to find someone who can get into those files."

"Why not just ask them?"

"I've asked them a million times, of course! They don't want to tell me for some reason. I thought they didn't know, but I just found out that they do know. They know, but they don't want to tell me. So I need someone who can go into the computers and tell me."

"If they're not telling you, there's a good reason," Coby said.

"Like what?"

He shrugged. "I have no idea. But there has to be a reason."

"But what? What could it be? I've thought and thought, and I just can't figure it out. He isn't in an institution, he's alive. He's alive and he lives alone."

"Maybe he's left the country?"

"No, the detective checked. He hasn't left."

"Maybe he left without anyone knowing."

"You have to show your passport no matter how you leave. He doesn't even have a passport, he never applied for one."

"Maybe he's working in espionage."

"Espionage! That's a joke. He spent practically his entire training period in jail—for wearing pajamas under his uniform, for talking back—once he even peed on a whole bunch of grenades. He and some other guys, but he was the initiator, they were having a contest. He hated the army. He deliberately shot in the air at target practice, he begged to be put in laundry, and finally he got his way, he got to do laundry. If he were a spy, this country would be in big trouble."

"You never know. People change. Spying isn't the same as fighting."

"I wish you knew him. That's the last thing he'd do. He doesn't have any qualifications."

"Well, that's all I can think of. I can't think of any other reason."

"Do you know anyone who can find out? Please?"

"Let me think for a minute . . . Let's see. I do have a cousin, I'm not sure exactly what he does, but maybe. I'll talk to him. But if the army has a reason, my cousin is going to have the same reason."

"Just try. Please."

"Sure, I'll ask him. Do you have your husband's ID number?"

I wrote down Daniel's ID on a napkin and Coby slid it into his pocket. "All my hope is on that napkin," I said.

Coby smiled. "I won't lose it, I promise. Where do you know Rafi from?"

"We go to the same activities. We've been at the same events lots of times, but we never talked to one another until the demo last Saturday, in Mejwan. Or rather in Ein Mazra'a, they wouldn't let us into Mejwan."

Coby shook his head. "You guys are so clued out, it's hard to fathom."

"We're not clued out."

"Yeah, well. You only see one side."

"Rafi said you lynched a Palestinian," I said.

"I didn't lynch anyone."

"Yeah, but he says you were there."

"I don't know what he's talking about."

"And someone's balls got shot at."

"There were lots of incidents. It was so long ago, you can't possibly expect me to remember. And if they could have, they would have torn us to pieces too. Luckily, we were too strong. What does it matter, anyhow? It's water under the bridge now. We tried peace, we tried negotiating, we tried giving them what they wanted, and now we're under attack again."

"Yes, we gave them what they wanted. You can now be owners of your own house. But meanwhile we're just going to move into another room, and another room, and also we've got the keys and also we're just going to stay in charge of the water, we hope you don't mind. And oh yes, we still need to post a few guards in the kitchen, and if we kill someone who walks in the garden without our permission we'll be fined two shekels, is that okay with you?"

"Yeah, well. Trust takes time. And you see, we were right not to trust them."

"Maybe they were right not to trust us."

"Maybe. Maybe we're both right. Maybe we're just doomed to go on killing each other forever. I personally am planning to move. I've had it."

"Move where?"

"My wife has relatives in Boston. We're thinking of going next year, but we might be able to pull it off sooner. I want my kids to grow up in a seminormal environment."

"Will you do the same thing in Boston? Hotel management?"

"Maybe, or maybe I'll go into business with my wife's uncle. We'll see."

"You'll miss things about this place."

"Yes, but there will be things I won't miss . . . Seen any good films lately?" he asked. He began talking about European and British directors and their best and worst films. He was mad about Mike Leigh. Bertolucci had a bad-movie phase, he said, but *Besieged* was a masterpiece. He said he used to like Kieslowski, but now he thought he was just a voyeur. Some movies aged well, like *Wild Strawberries,* but others lost their appeal with time, as audiences became more sophisticated.

His conversation helped me forget about the mice, and I took him up on his offer to have dinner, though I insisted on paying. By the time I left the dining room it was eight in the evening, time for the sea.

# FRIDAY

Rafi phoned early on Friday morning. "Are you coming to South Lifna?" he asked.

"Yes, of course."

"Do you want a ride? It's lonely going down on my own. I was supposed to take Dudu but Hagari's sick, he can't come."

"I was planning to go with Odelia. But maybe I'll call her—she already has a full car."

"I'll pick you up at noon, then?"

"Fine."

"Have you made any progress with Daniel?"

"I may have something."

"I've been asking around, too."

"Any luck?"

"I'm not sure. My youngest brother's girlfriend, maybe. But I have to talk to her in person. How are you, Dana?"

"I'm restless."

"Well, we have a long day ahead of us. What will you do until noon?"

"Volvo wants me to read to him."

"Can't he read himself?"

"He says his shoulders get tired."

"What will you read?"

"I'm not sure. I think he has something by Appelfeld."

"That should cheer you both up."

"Actually, those books have a calming effect on us. What about you?"

"I'm taking my daughter swimming. See you at noon."

I spent the morning reading to Volvo, as promised. He lay on his bed with his eyes shut, but I could tell he was listening to every word. He would have been happy for me to go on all day.

"That's it, Volvo. I have to go out now," I told him.

"Where to?"

"Just out with some friends."

"You are a person of many mysteries."

"I'm not, really."

"Just one more chapter."

"You can read the rest yourself, Volvo."

"It's not the same."

"You're not blind. You're not paralyzed. I don't know why I read to you."

"I like being read to. Don't you think I deserve some crumbs of pleasure?"

"We all deserve some crumbs of pleasure. I have to go now."

"I've been thinking lately that I might be gay."

"We'll talk about it another time, Volvo."

"I had a very erotic dream last night involving Alex. It took me entirely by surprise."

"Well, Volvo, that would be great. Any change would be good for you. I have to go, though. Rafi's coming to pick me up."

"Does his wife know?"

"Why don't you call and ask her?"

I went to my flat to get my camera ready. Rafi knocked on my door a few minutes before twelve. "I'm looking for Dana," he said when I answered.

"I think I have everything."

"You don't have to bring water, I have a whole crate in my van. Dana, you look as if I've come to arrest you."

"I shouldn't be going down with you. I should be going with Odelia."

"Well."

"Yes, well."

"I'm really happy you're coming down with me," he said.

"We're just friends."

"Friends! Don't exaggerate . . . Aren't you going to lock your door?"

"Oh . . . yes," I said vaguely, and looked for my house key in my knapsack. I often left my door unlocked. "I can't find the key. Hold on."

I went back inside, took a spare key from a glass bowl in the kitchen, and locked my door.

I followed Rafi to his van, climbed up to the passenger seat. "I spoke to Coby yesterday," I told him as we set out. "I've seen him around, but we never talked before. But there was a mouse under Jacky's sink, five mice actually, and Coby sent the guard, Marik, to get the mice. Marik once saw me naked by accident, ages ago, and he's still embarrassed every time he sees me. After he got rid of the mice I had dinner with Coby and he said he has a cousin in Intelligence, he's going to ask him about Daniel."

"How did the guard see you naked? Through the window?"

"No, on the street. The air from the sidewalk grate blew my dress up. As luck would have it, that was the one time in my life I wasn't wearing underwear."

Rafi burst out laughing. "You're full of surprises, Dana."

"Maybe Coby's cousin is the one."

"That would be great, Dana. Seat belt, please."

"But Coby said he isn't optimistic."

"Why?"

"He says if the army has a reason for not telling me where Daniel is, his cousin will have the same reason. He thinks Daniel is a spy. What a laugh."

"That really does seem unlikely. Who could he spy on? He doesn't speak a word of Arabic, and instead of blending in, he stands out. Besides, I don't think we have a lot of spies these days. Espionage is mostly technological now."

"I feel I'm getting closer. I feel I'm really getting close, after all these years. I just have to find the right person . . . Where are we meeting, by the way?"

"The gas station. We're going in through the southern end of Lifna."

"Too bad we're going on Friday instead of Saturday. All the fanatic settlers will be out."

"The rabbis really wanted to come. There's supposed to be a joint prayer session. So we're compromising by starting late, to accommodate people who work Friday morning."

"I'd like to photograph that, the praying. I have some very good photos of the cave-dwellers from the summer."

"I'd like to see your photographs. Where do you keep them?"

"In shoe boxes, under the bed."

"Are they mostly color or black-and-white?"

"Depends. I'm not really that good."

"I think you are."

"How would you know?"

"I have your book."

He was referring to *Seaside,* the book of photographs Beatrice had produced. She had chosen my beach photos for the collection: our families on the beach, Palestinian families on the Coastal Strip beach, back in the days when there were fewer curfews and it seemed there might even be peace. She'd chosen her favorite photograph for the cover: a father with two girls, one in each arm, walking into the sea, the water already up to his knees. The faces of the two girls were turned toward the camera, tiny faces just above their father's shoulders, one under a white sun bonnet, both girls smiling blissfully, as if to say, *Can anything be more perfect than this?* The father can only be seen from the back, a streak of dark fuzz running down his spine. Is he a Palestinian father or one of our fathers? I won't tell.

Rafi said, "I didn't know Palestinians swam with their clothes on. Your book made me realize that I don't know the most basic things about them."

"Some wear bathing suits."

"Hard to believe there was a time you could go to the strip just like that, and take pictures at the beach," Rafi said, shaking his head.

"I had so much fun. You can't imagine how great it was. We got along really well—they were always inviting me to come home with them. I played with the kids, we built sand castles. People were in a good mood back then."

"How did you communicate?"

"That was never a problem. Most of the men knew Hebrew, and some of the women spoke a little English. And there's always sign language to fall back on. I should learn Arabic, but it's such a hard language."

"If you had it in school from first grade you wouldn't find it hard."

"Yes," I said, "compulsory Arabic from first grade. Then we'll know the Messiah has arrived."

"A few years ago we actually had the illusion that things were getting better. There was talk of making Arabic compulsory, and we really believed it might happen."

"I want a child," I said, remembering the little bcobys I had held at the beach. "You're lucky you have a daughter."

"I can give you a child if you want, Dana. My wife wouldn't object."

"Two wives!"

"No, one wife. But I'd help you out as much as I could."

"I feel I'm going to find Daniel soon. I want his child. And I can't believe Graciela wouldn't mind, no matter what she says. She'd mind a lot. Any woman would."

There was an uncomfortable silence in the car. We'd brought up the forbidden topic. "Just an altruistic offer," Rafi joked, trying to break the tension.

"I'll keep it in mind. Free sperm. You're right, you don't get that kind of offer every day."

But we were still embarrassed. I wanted to reach out and touch his hand, but I looked out of the window instead.

At least eighty cars were already parked at the gas station near the border of the South Lifna Hills. People were standing in small groups and talking, or buying coffee and snacks at the little convenience store, or using the washroom. The gas station was on an isolated strip of road; you couldn't see any towns or cities in the distance, only neat, alternating bands of green and taupe, and beyond them the indistinct mauve dunes of the desert. Near the station, scattered randomly as though abandoned or misplaced, were the usual mystifying objects, the exact nature of which no one could guess: some sort of steel tower; a cement cylinder; equipment and machines that appeared to have been designed for complicated engineering feats. I took a photograph of these unidentified bits of civilization; they captured the improvised feeling we all carried within us. We didn't know where we were going and we wondered

how we'd lasted this long on such flimsy foundations and mud-
dled efforts. The myths we grew up on tried to compensate us,
but myths were slippery by nature. In fact we were lost, walking on air, inside air, falling.

The organizers handed out tape and flyers in three languages:
messages of peace printed in bold letters on white sheets of
paper. We taped them to our cars and then we taped numbers on
our fenders. Rafi's van was tenth. Then the organizers gave
instructions, explained the mission. I didn't listen carefully. The
instructions didn't vary much from activity to activity: no violence, no getting into arguments with army or police or anyone
else we encountered. All interactions would be handled by
trained negotiators. A lawyer spoke to the crowd; the cave
dwellers' hearing had been postponed, which meant their evic-
tion was on hold. It was good news, she said, relatively speaking.

I wandered away from the gathering and caught a glimpse of
Ella leaning against her blue car and staring out into the distance.
She was holding a cup of coffee in one hand and tentatively touching her cropped hair with the other. The sign taped to her car window read: *Everyone has a right to a home.* I took a photograph of her
with my zoom lens; she looked as homeless as any cave dweller.

We didn't leave until two o'clock because one of the lawyers
who was involved in the South Lifna trials had been held up in
court; he'd been trying to stop the deportation of foreign
activists. When he finally arrived, we returned to our cars and
headed out across the invisible border between our country
and the occupied territories. The landscape changed at once:
green was replaced by gray and pale brown; there was no irri-
gation here. The hills on both sides of the road rose and fell
gently, as in a child's drawing of mountains. As we neared
South Lifna, we saw distant figures watching our procession
from the mountains, tiny people against the pearl blue afternoon sky. They were not allowed on the road; this was a

restricted highway, built for the settlers, and it was off-limits to Palestinians. Despite the distance between us, we felt their gratitude; you could tell they were happy we'd come from the way they stood there, their bodies very still, as if they were afraid to break the spell of good luck that had brought us here.

The army had been trying for years to get rid of the cave dwellers. They didn't like the idea of Palestinians scattered throughout the hills, three or four families on one hill, five on another. You couldn't enclose them, it was hard to control their movements. And the government wanted the land.

The army tried expelling them: they put them on trucks, blocked wells, destroyed tents. Possibly they found it difficult to understand why anyone would want to live in caves and tents, in such difficult conditions. And at first I wondered, too, when I spent the night in one of the caves the previous summer, in an effort to stop the latest evictions. These were large natural caves, dark mouths on the sides of the hills. I slept just outside the cave, because I couldn't bear the damp and misery inside. I had never seen such poverty up close. I quickly understood that the cave dwellers needed clothes and medical care and better food and more utensils and plastic sheets for the floor of their caves and waterproof mattresses and toys, but they loved their homes, and I could see why. The hills were like huge friendly turtles, turtles you could love as intensely as you loved any human. The cave dwellers had been on these hills for over one hundred years. In court their lawyers explained that the caves were their homes, and they had nowhere to go. The nearby town, Lifna, had no place for them and they didn't fit in there: they were shepherds and farmers.

Apart from their difficulties with the army, the cave dwellers were continually assaulted by the settlers. One cave dweller had already been killed in a dispute over a stolen sheep.

Our caravan of cars was stopped twice by the army, but for less than an hour each time. But three kilometers before the path that would take us to the cave dwellers, the army stopped us again, and this time they said we would have to turn back. The officer in charge had a friendly, worried face and he peered at us apologetically through his round metal-rimmed glasses. He wanted to let us through, he said, but the settlers from Elisha were blocking the road. "They've driven their cars onto the road, and they won't let you through. You'll have to go back. I don't want a mess here."

We could see the settlement of Elisha in the distance, eighty or ninety suburban houses with triangular burgundy roofs arranged in stiff clusters on a hilltop. The houses looked out of place in this ancient landscape, like small Monopoly pieces; houses without a past, without a future, suspended in a fantasy world their inhabitants claimed was God's. Volvo's family lived in a settlement like this one.

"We're not going back, we have permits, we have blankets to deliver," the main organizer said. He was a young man with floppy black hair. Beatrice knew him well; he taught in her department.

"All right, I'll see what I can do," the officer in charge said. "Maybe we can get tow trucks to tow their cars away."

We wandered along the road and waited. The rabbis who had come to pray with the Palestinians began to worry; they had to be home before sunset.

I sat with Rafi by the side of the road. We waved at the Palestinians in the distance but we couldn't see whether they were waving back. They were too far away.

We waited for three hours. We were very hot, and nearly all of us had run out of water. Rafi passed around the extra bottles he'd brought. Some of the women had to pee, and they wandered away from the road in small groups. There were no boul-

ders or trees to hide behind, so they either took turns shelter-
ing each other or else relied on the courtesy of averted eyes.

The rabbis had to leave; they wouldn't be able to have a joint
prayer session with the Muslims after all. I phoned Beatrice on
my mobile phone and left a message. I told her we were
delayed, and that I'd be too tired for a visit tonight.

Finally the army announced that the area had been declared a
closed military zone. The lawyers argued that this was a government road: it couldn't be declared a closed military zone. If there
was no choice, they said, we would just disobey and start walking.

But the army was adamant. So everyone locked arms and we
began to walk past the army trucks and police vehicles. The
police had been called in, just in case, and now they went to
work. They were furious. They hit the marchers at the edge of
the procession and pushed them to the ground. One officer
knocked down Farid, a heavy man in his fifties, and knelt on his
chest. A group of demonstrators pulled him off Farid, and the
officer turned on them, but Farid was able to get back to his feet.

I lost sight of Rafi for a moment; he'd gone to help Shadi,
who had been dragged into one of the police vans. Then he
came back into view. He was trying to enter the van too, but a
police officer pulled him by the collar, slammed him forward
against the front hood of a police car, and twisted his arm
behind him. With one hand the officer held Rafi's head down
on the hood, with the other he twisted Rafi's arm. I saw Rafi's
face contract with pain, but I couldn't reach him, there were
too many people between us. I couldn't photograph him
either, because a wave of nausea came over me, and I thought I
would vomit. And then abruptly the violence ended. The army
announced that they would allow us to proceed through the
mountains and bypass the people from Elisha. But Shadi would
have to remain behind; he was under arrest.

Several demonstrators lay down on the ground around the

police van in which Shadi was being held. As soon as the police dragged one person away, another moved in. Finally they agreed to release Shadi, though he was given a summons. He stepped out of the van, the summons in his hand, his thin red kaffiyeh wrapped stylishly around his neck. He was young and fearless, and his eyes glowed with amused pride. I took a photograph of him emerging from the van, and I wondered whether he was a heartbreaker.

I heard two officers talking. Now that the struggle was over they were relaxed and gregarious. They didn't care one way or another about the convoy. One of them shook his head and said, "All this for some blankets . . . couldn't they just mail them?"

We each took a blanket or bag of clothes, and we began climbing the hill. The ground was dotted with flat white rocks that looked like the roofs of underground houses. Dark green bramble grew between the rocks, and the earth was hard and dry under our feet. The mountains stretched out on all sides; they looked resigned and mournful under the soft gold of dusk. A large area had been expropriated by the military and was cordoned off by barbed wire and spotlights. We had to walk four kilometers to circumnavigate the enclosure. A few soldiers accompanied us.

Rafi walked next to me. He wasn't carrying a blanket. With his left hand he held his right arm against his midriff. We didn't speak.

It took us nearly an hour to reach the other end of the restricted road. But some of the settler children from Elisha, along with three or four men, had moved down the road in anticipation of our descent from the hills, and they were there now, waiting for us. The women and most of the men had returned to the little hamlet with the burgundy roofs to prepare for the Friday night meal. In an hour the sun would set and they'd all be gone. But the Palestinians waiting for us couldn't travel through the mountains at night. If we didn't get there soon, they'd be forced to disperse.

A teenage girl wearing a long navy skirt and a loose white blouse held a sign that said, *The Left is insane, support bin Laden.*

"Why should I support bin Laden, I don't understand," a bald man standing next to me joked. He lit a cigarette, cupping his hand around the flame.

Next to the girl stood a little boy with earlocks. He'd forgotten all about his sign; he was too busy staring at us as we came down from the hills, and he seemed transfixed by our appearance. I felt he was drawn to us on some level, and I wondered whether he would dream about us tonight, two hundred Jews and a few Arab citizens, bare arms hugging gray-blue and salmon pink blankets, shoes covered with dust, descending in haphazard formation from the hills. Then he remembered his sign, and held it up. *Us here, the Palestinians there: transfer.*

"There, where?" the bald man said, to no one in particular. "Antarctica?"

"Don't move," the soldiers told us. They ordered the settlers to go home, but the settlers refused, and when one of the officers tried to herd them along, a puffy-faced teenage boy kicked him fiercely in the shin. The officer swore.

We couldn't wait any longer. We began walking alongside the road, trying to avoid the settlers. Luckily, they didn't follow us or try to block our way. A soldier beside me stopped to urinate. I took a photograph of him, urinating casually in the midst of the turmoil, reduced for a few seconds to an ordinary human who needed to pee. Tomorrow he could be dead.

He saw me photographing him.

"Hope you don't mind," I said.

He shrugged. "I don't know what you guys are doing here," he said, walking next to me. He lit a cigarette.

"I'm here to take pictures. I believe in the cause, though."

"You're a photographer?"

"I take photos of the conflict."

"How? You can't predict where or when there's going to be shooting."

"Well, I don't photograph combat, of course. I just go wherever I can. Checkpoints, demonstrations, all sorts of activities. The closest I came to combat was Dar al-Damar. I managed to get in a day after the battle ended—there were still some bodies lying in the alleys, covered in sheets, waiting to be buried . . . I have thousands of photographs."

"Aren't you afraid of your name ending up in the obituaries?"

"Aren't you afraid of your name ending up in the obituaries?" He shrugged. "Yeah, I'm afraid. Sort of."

"Then refuse to come here."

"What's this, a lesson in politics?"

"Refuse."

"I can't, I need the money. I don't get a salary in jail."

"Say you have a bad back."

"Any more advice?"

"Why risk your life?"

"Look who's talking! Miss War Photographer . . ."

"I go with groups. The Palestinians usually know who we are."

"*Usually* might be the operative word there."

"It's not dangerous. We're careful, everything is arranged in advance. We coordinate our activities with the Palestinians."

He guffawed. "An entire family was killed thirty meters from here last week. Don't you read the papers? You look too smart to be so stupid."

"You look too nice to be killed for nothing," I said.

"It isn't for nothing. It's to protect idiots like you."

"It's to keep control of land that doesn't belong to us. It's to protect those losers from Elisha."

"Talk to the government, not to me."

"Fine, as long as you're dying for something!"

All at once, his body tensed and he was no longer with me: something was happening, and he felt the entire burden of it. The transformation was astonishing; one moment he was smoking and talking easily to me, the next he was afraid, alert, aiming his weapon and ready to shoot. But it turned out to be nothing: five soldiers were running wildly through the crowd, not because of Palestinians, but because of two little boys from Elisha who had decided to sneak up and attack us. I took a photograph of the ludicrous sight: five armed men chasing two little boys, their earlocks bobbing as they ran, wide mischievous grins on their faces. The soldiers caught up with them. "Stop!" an officer ordered, and his voice was so stern that the boys froze. "Home!" he barked at them, and they obediently turned back.

A few minutes later we reached the turnoff. Palestinians with tractors and wagons were waiting for us. "You made it! You made it! Our good friends!" they exclaimed, laughing happily.

We piled the blankets on the wagons and started up a narrow trail toward one of the caves. The trail curled around the hills and the tractor's wheels as it churned along were so precariously close to the edges that I couldn't bear to look. The light was fading, and it was nearly dark by the time we arrived at a small clearing. A group of twenty cave dwellers stood huddled next to three sturdy tents and a donkey. Most had had to leave, but this small group had stayed to greet us.

A boy of five or six came up to us, his arm outstretched. "*Ahlan wa-sahlan,*" he said. Rafi and I shook his tiny brown hand. The cave-dwellers were very small; the adults were not much taller than the ten-year-olds. Two women offered us coffee, and an old man wearing a robe made a speech. "I hope one day we will have real peace," he said, "and not a mock peace. And we will eat together and pray together."

Two Palestinian boys began to giggle. They were looking at the women demonstrators and nudging each other. I wanted to photograph them, but decided against it; they'd be embarrassed.

It took us a long time to get back to our cars. The road was clear now; the settlers had gone home for the Sabbath meal. I imagined the adults sitting around the table and explaining to their children what the word *traitor* meant: we were traitors to the faith, aspirations and dreams of our own people. We helped the enemy. God would punish us; we'd end up dead as dormice.

An army truck gave the organizers lifts to their cars, and the organizers returned to pick up more people. By the time we were all ready to go it had been dark for some time.

Rafi couldn't drive, because of his arm, so I drove. Daniel had insisted I learn to drive when we married, but our car broke down shortly after he vanished and I never bothered getting a new one. Rafi laughed. "I think you may be the worst driver I've ever encountered," he said.

"I'm out of practice."

"Go into fourth," he said.

"I am in fourth."

"You're in second."

"Oh. Yes, that's better. Should we drive to a hospital?"

"No, it's just a sprain. Asshole."

"That was hard to watch."

He smiled. "Did you get a good shot?"

"I couldn't."

"Too chaotic?"

"No, I felt too sick."

"Not very professional," he teased.

I thought for a moment. "You're right. I'm usually more detached. Not exactly detached . . . but in control. Otherwise

I wouldn't be any use. When I first started, what most worried me was that the Palestinians would think it was callous of me to photograph their misery. But it's exactly the opposite. As soon as they see my camera, they take me all over the place, show me what to photograph. They want people to see, to know."

"Why don't you publish your photographs? In newspapers, I mean."

"I have no idea how to go about it."

"Or post them on a website."

"Ditto."

"I can show you how to do that. We can do it together, I have equipment at home."

"Really?"

"Yes, it's very simple."

"That would be great. I'd like that. But I don't want to bother Graciela."

"It's my flat, too," he said, a little offended.

"I didn't mean that. I just meant if she's at the piano . . ."

"It's my flat, too," he repeated, but he smiled this time. "I more than earn my keep."

"Does your arm hurt?"

"I'll live. Watch out!"

I had narrowly missed crashing into a car that had cut in ahead of me.

"No more talking," I said. "I need to concentrate or we'll never make it home."

I parked outside my building and Rafi followed me into my flat. He called Graciela, but there was no answer, so he left a message. He told her he'd just come back from South Lifna and he was with me, he'd be home later.

"She's going to hate me," I said, putting on the kettle for coffee.

"No, she's not like that. Her mind doesn't work that way. I've never known her to be jealous, ever, of anyone. She's too preoccupied. She's too involved with her music, the rest is just peripheral."

"I can't imagine that. I would have died had I found out that Daniel was with someone else. I was very possessive, and he was too. But it never came up. Should you put your arm in a sling or something?"

"No, I'll be fine. But I think I'll lie down, if that's okay. And if you have a couple of painkillers, that might help. Also, Dana, I don't mean to be rude, but I'm famished. I'm going to pass out if I don't eat something."

"I have bread and cheese."

"That's fine."

"There's a bottle of acetaminophen in the bathroom. You can lie down on the bed, it's more comfortable than the sofa."

I heard him rummaging around in the bathroom drawers. He took the pills and stretched out on the bed with a sigh of relief. "Asshole," he repeated. "Fucking asshole. What did they take Shadi in for anyhow? He didn't do a thing. He was walking like everyone else. Then they complain that Arab citizens aren't devoted to the State. Idiots. Bastard idiots. How to make enemies and alienate people in five easy lessons. How to get people to want you dead in one easy lesson. I don't know how much longer this madness can go on. I can't imagine a more suicidal people than us. We love to suffer. And to take everyone else with us."

I brought half a loaf of bread, a few slices of cheese, and a container of hummus to the bed. Eating on the bed with someone else reminded me of Daniel, and I felt happy.

"That's what Daniel used to say. He called it auto-genocide."

Rafi laughed. "Auto-genocide! Well, he might be right, at the rate we're going."

"I had a conversation with one of the soldiers," I said as we ate. "I tried to persuade him to refuse. He admitted he was scared."

"Sitting ducks . . . You know that poem—*Today we come, tomorrow we go / Today we touch the spray of fire / Your love sends our way*."

"Yes, I like that poem," I said.

"I used to wonder what the love was. I never understood that line. Now it's so clear. The country loves us, it wants our love, and the gift it gives us is death."

"*They always walk backwards, they come at me with their backs.*"

"*Up above the birds slow down, they will eat without a cloth.*"

"Everything was so simple," I said. "And now it's so complicated."

"Because we've fallen in love?" he said, dipping his bread into the hummus.

"Yes."

"It's not as complicated as you think. People complicate things that are simple. They get tangled up for nothing."

"How can you say that? This is a terrible mess."

"It isn't a mess. People are allowed to love each other. It doesn't mean you're disloyal to Daniel. I'm sure he wants you to be happy. It doesn't mean you don't love him or that you've forgotten him."

"How did it happen? Between us?"

"I can't answer for you. I've been watching you for two years. I've been wanting to talk to you for two years at least."

"I hardly noticed you."

"You hardly noticed anyone."

"Until you said, *Enough, already, enough.*"

"When did I say that?"

"To the soldier. The soldier who was telling us to come down."

"Oh yeah. Coward."

"He wasn't a coward. He was scared—I'd be too."

He didn't answer, and I went on, "I didn't recognize you right away, because of your afro. Your hair grows in an afro. Can I touch it?"

"If that's what you want. But once you touch my hair, that's it, there's no going back. Now we can still fight it, if you want. We can decide that we won't do this, because I can't leave my daughter and you want to stay loyal to Daniel."

"Would you tell Graciela?"

"Of course not. And she won't ask. She's not interested."

"But she'll know."

"I told you, she doesn't think that way. She knows I've slept with other women. She isn't interested in that part of my life."

"She won't leave you?"

"No, she loves me. She loves me and she loves Naomi. She can't help the way she is. And I need to live with Naomi. I need to live in the same house with her, full-time. I'm lucky Graciela doesn't want a divorce."

"Do you love her?"

"I'm grateful to her, she helped me when things were very bad. I feel bad for her, too. She's suffering. But I can't help her. She's the only one who can get herself out of it, and maybe even she can't. Maybe she doesn't need to, as long as she has her music."

"I never heard of her before."

"I guess you don't follow classical music."

"I worry that my life's become so narrow."

"*Life is a narrow bridge,*" he said, approximately quoting the Bratslav rabbi. He said it ironically, but I liked the quote.

"*And the main thing is not to be afraid.* My therapist had that on his wall, under a print of one of those Monet lily ponds. Someone told me Monet was going blind when he painted all those ponds . . ."

"Life isn't a bridge at all. Life's a ride in an F-16. Blindfolded. And then you find out the pilot is blindfolded, too."

"You say you have to live with your daughter. But you said if we had a child you'd only help out. What's the difference?"

"The difference is that I can't split myself into two people, and my daughter is used to me being there, and I can't leave her alone with Graciela, but you would be a great mother."

"I was just asking. I don't want that. You have your family and I have Daniel."

"I have my family, Dana. I don't know whether you have Daniel. You have your attachment to him, but what if he rejects you?"

"I know he will, I know he'll reject me, that's what he's been doing all these years, but it's because he doesn't know that I don't care what he looks like."

"Maybe he's the one who can't bear what he looks like."

"It won't matter to him if he sees it doesn't matter to me."

"Do you have any idea what his injury is like?"

"His face, his arms, part of his body."

"Do you know what parts?"

"The thing you're asking about, I don't know. I tried to find out, but you know how evasive doctors are. You know how they hate giving you a straight answer. So I don't know."

"If he can't have sex, that might explain why he left."

"There are lots of ways to have sex," I said.

"Do you know what to expect? Have you seen people who've been burned?"

"Oh, who cares!"

"He's lucky his vision wasn't affected."

"Yes, he was wearing sunglasses, maybe that saved him. His burns weren't that bad, in fact. Relatively speaking. That's what they said at the hospital. They said he mostly had second-degree burns on his body. I think his uniform protected him a bit. The problem was how much of his body was burned, that was the real danger. He had third-degree burns only on his face and his hands. I feel so lucky that he's alive."

"I don't really understand why he left. It can't be just because of his appearance. People adjust to that sort of thing."

"You're right, it doesn't make any sense. And it's not like Daniel, he's not a shallow or vain person. Maybe he wants to protect me, because he thinks it would bother me."

"Dana, is it possible that it was just an excuse, that he wanted to leave anyhow?"

"No. We fought, of course. We fought about the mess, and about all sorts of other stupid things. But we got along. He loved me. He definitely loved me."

"Was he sure you loved him?"

"Why wouldn't he be?"

"I don't know. Were you loyal to him?"

"Of course."

"People get wounded and paralyzed, they go blind, they lose limbs, and they don't vanish—on the contrary. They need their families and friends. And men don't care that much about how they look, I mean they care, but it's not all that important, unless they're exceptionally vain."

"You're not the first one who's thought there was another reason. I think most people assume that he's just eccentric, and that the reason he vanished has nothing to do with the accident. But he wasn't eccentric."

"Leaving you was a cruel thing to do. I'm sorry, I have to say that."

"I don't mind. I know it looks that way, but you're wrong. He didn't mean to hurt me. He doesn't believe I love him, he thinks he did me a favor."

"I don't know how I'm holding back from touching your face, Dana."

"You can touch my face."

"Are you sure? You have to be sure. I'm not saying that to cover myself, or to put the responsibility on your shoulders. It's my responsibility as much as yours. And I know that in a way no one can be sure about anything like this. I just don't know if this is the right thing, and you have to help me."

"I don't know either. Not because of your family, but because I love Daniel."

"I told you what I think. I think it's possible to love more than one person. I know it's possible."

"No, he'd see it as a betrayal. I can't have any secrets from him. But it's already too late, I've already betrayed him by falling in love with you. It's too late. I've hurt him."

I reached out and touched his hair, ran my fingers through the soft carpet of tiny black curls. He shut his eyes.

"Let's just hold each other," he said.

I removed the dishes from the bed and stretched out next to him. He placed his left arm around my waist. "I think we're exactly the same height," I said.

"Tell me about yourself. Tell me about your family. I know your mother died in a car crash. What was she like?"

"Bossy, tough, warm, very affectionate. Outspoken. She wasn't afraid of anyone. And she liked deciding how things should be done. She was generous. She would do anything for anyone."

"What did she do?"

"She was a pathologist."

"And your father? What's he like?"

"Quiet, principled, controlled. And smart. He sings in a choir, he used to be a chess champion, he's interested in cryptography . . . He was disappointed that I didn't finish high school. He thought I would go to university, get lots of degrees. What about you?"

"School, you mean? I fucked it up. I had a scholarship because of my high grades, I could have gone for free after I was discharged. But I was too messed up. And then it was too late."

"Why too late?"

"It's hard to go back to school if you wait too long."

"What was it like, getting drunk?"

"I don't remember. It made me sick, most of the time. It's very hazy now, that period . . . Tell me about the books you write."

"Just junk romance. They're all identical."

"How did you get into it?"

"I found one of those books on the beach, some tourist must have left it there. And I took it home and read it and I thought, I can write that. So I wrote to the publisher, and they tried me out. Now they buy all my books. They're ridiculous, the books, but no one cares, not the readers, not the publishers, and not me."

"Can I see one?"

"I don't have any, except on disk. I've never seen my novels in print, I asked them not to send me copies. I don't own the copyright, I sell all the rights for a lump sum. I don't even know what name they use."

"Does it pay well?"

"Yes, that's how I pay my mortgage and all my other expenses. I've even managed to put money away, so Daniel and I can take a trip when he comes back. A cruise, or a trip to Paris or Ireland. Wherever he wants to go. Just the two of us."

"Read me something from one of them."

I got up and turned on the computer, opened the most recent file, and read him a random passage. *From across the room Martha's eyes pierced Angeline to the quick. Martha whispered to her sister, and they both marched out of the room, still whispering.*

*Angeline's heart beat faster. What perfidious machinations were they planning out there in the rose garden? Just then Pierre ran outside with a hurried gait. His footsteps clicked on the patio tiles and his velvet blue cloak blew in the wind."*

"Come back to bed."

I returned to his arms.

"It's sexy to hear you speak English. What are they planning, the sisters?"

"I can't remember. I just make it up as I go along, and then I forget all about it. The plot doesn't matter, it doesn't have to make much sense. The writing's horrible too, but that's because I don't rewrite or edit. I used to, but then I realized it was a waste of time. No one cares if I say things like *hurried gait* or *perfidious machinations*."

"*Perfidious machinations*—sounds like a car problem."

"You have to use some hard words—it flatters the reader. That's one of the instructions we get."

"Is Pierre the hero?"

"He's the love interest. That's what they're called."

"Why is he wearing a cloak?"

"It's a period novel. It takes place in the past. Horse carriages, cloaks, daggers, sweeping dresses."

"Do you have to do research?"

"I had to learn the names of different types of swords and vehicles. Sometimes I watch movies for the visual details and I take notes. That's about it."

"What are the love scenes like?"

"It's interesting. The writers get a list of words they should be using, and they're not allowed to use any others. Well, it's changed over the years. We can use more words now, and we have to include more sex. We now have to have at least one actual intercourse scene, toward the end, on the night before the wedding. But we can only refer to *thighs* and *breasts*. We can't say *nipples*. We can't say *between* or *spread* or *inside*. It all has to be vague and implicit."

"This conversation is turning me on."

"It's hard to believe people like reading these books, but they sell by the millions."

"How long does it take you to write one?"

"Two or three months, because I don't write every day. In theory I could write faster, but I don't want to."

"I've imagined this moment for a long time."

"I had no idea."

"I liked getting your letter in jail. Even if it wasn't personal."

"What was jail like?"

"Just the usual. Nothing special. Lots of disturbed people who should be getting help, not a jail sentence. One guy in particular."

"Remember the vigil we had for you on the hill?"

"Yes, of course."

"Yes, you waved from down below. *We don't shoot, we don't cry, we don't watch children die . . .* Were you bored in jail?"

"A little. We joked a lot, though. We spent a lot of time laughing."

"It's something we have in common with the Palestinians. We both have a good sense of humor, have you noticed?"

"Yes, it always amazes me," he said. "They never lose their sense of humor, no matter what."

"Especially when our soldiers mispronounce their names or the names of their cities."

"Yes."

"The women don't laugh as much."

"Maybe at home they do. They're more restrained in public. And they have enormous burdens."

"I remember one time I was taking a photograph of this journalist from Canada interviewing a Palestinian guy. And he asked her at the end of the interview where she was from, and she told him. He put his hand on her shoulder as though leading her away, and he said in this serious voice, as if he were giving her advice, 'Go, go home,' and he and his friends burst out laughing. They laughed for about five minutes. I have a nice shot of that . . . I can't imagine you in combat," I said.

"I can't imagine it either."

"I hated the army because I was so spoiled by then. I hated being told what to do. My mother also hated anyone telling her what to do, I must have inherited it from her."

"I feel so detached from all that now. Even the images in my mind, it's as if I'm watching the scene from above, from a distance, and I see myself as one of the figures in the scene."

"How's your arm?"

"Better now. Those pills are working . . . What do you take them for?"

"My period, sometimes."

"Can I take off your clothes now?"

"Yes. I've had sex since Daniel left me, but it hasn't felt like this. This is different."

"For me too. Do you want to use a condom?"

"No."

"I'm happy."

"I hope we won't be sorry."

"Of course we'll be sorry. You can't live and not be sorry."

"Yes."

"Yes."

# Saturday

HE LEFT AT FOUR IN THE MORNING.

"What will you tell Graciela?"

"She won't ask. What are you doing today?"

"I'm in a dilemma. There are two events, and I want to go to both, but it's impossible. I wish these things were a little better coordinated. There's the condolence call and the gay thing."

"I haven't heard about any gay event today."

"It wasn't very well publicized. The army is sending these gay and lesbian soldiers to the High School Pride Club to convince the kids that the army is gay-friendly."

"They must really be getting desperate."

"There's going to be a protest outside, a drag carnival, they're going to parody army uniforms and hand out free tickets to the Hague or the military cemetery. So that's going to be colorful. But the condolence call seems more important. Are you going to that?"

"No, I can't, I have a soccer game with my after-school kids.

And I want to spend some time with my daughter today. Call me when you get home."

I walked him to the door.

"Will you be okay?" he asked.

"Yes."

He kissed me one last time, and left. I returned to my flat, our flat, mine and Daniel's, and sat cross-legged on the unmade bed.

Everything had changed: I had betrayed Daniel. I had held someone else, loved someone else. I would not have believed it possible and I still didn't understand exactly how it had happened, or why.

At the start, during the first few seconds of sex, I had not been able to stop thinking of Daniel; it was as if Rafi and Daniel shared one body. I remembered dreams in which people I knew had merged into one person: Daniel and my mother, Tanya and Odelia, Ella and the woman at the photography store. In my dreams the transformations seemed natural, as though all humans had shifting identities and were continually exchanging one for the other. In waking life the confusion was frightening.

But Daniel faded almost immediately, because Rafi's style in bed was very different. Daniel was funny, playful, imaginative. He joked, he entertained me. Rafi was quiet and intense. It was a serious undertaking for him, sex. Serious and complex, an exploration of another person and of himself. Daniel and I talked about what we wanted to do as though discussing some trip we were going to take and what hotels we would stay at. Rafi did say a few things, but they were not in the category of discussion. Remembering those things now made my stomach lurch, and I longed for him to come back.

What would I tell Daniel when I saw him? It was distressing to think that I would have a secret from him, but the idea of hurting him was unbearable. Maybe I could telescope the years of his absence and make them vanish, make them inconsequential; maybe we could start over. But I wanted to know about his life over the past eleven years and I wanted him to know what had happened to me. It occurred to me that maybe this was the reason I'd started taking photographs: I wanted a record of my life for him. I would show him the photographs, and he would know what I'd seen and, if the photo was good, what I'd felt.

What would I say when I reached the one of Rafi?

I quickly pulled out the shoe box that held the photo of Rafi and removed it from the box. I stared at it and wondered what to do; I felt like a fairy-tale hero who has to find a clever way to dispose of a magic object without activating some dreadful curse.

First I would find Daniel, then I'd decide. In the meantime I placed the photograph on my work table.

I showered, slept for two hours, had a container of yogurt, and set out for the condolence call. It would be a lot harder than the drag carnival, but it was more urgent. I took a taxi to our meeting place at the train station. The taxi driver was in a good mood and whistled cheerfully as he sped down the empty streets. "Where are you off to this early?" he asked conversationally.

"A condolence call," I said. "Two children were killed."

"Good for you!" he exclaimed. He'd misunderstood, and I didn't have the energy to correct him and get yelled at. Maybe he wouldn't yell at me, maybe he'd only shake his head and sigh, but I didn't want to take a chance. Once a taxi driver had thrown me out of the car because of my views. That was the only time, though, that I was banished altogether, and it was because the driver had narrowly missed being blown up that afternoon, had seen body parts flying through the air.

"You're an asset to the State," the happy driver told me. "Please give them my condolences, too."

"I will," I said.

He whistled all the way to the train station. He'd probably had sex the night before. Just like me.

There were two minivans at the train station, waiting to collect everyone. We were a small group: sixteen people in all. The condolence call was in Hroush, which normally would have been a short drive from the city, but it took us nearly eight hours to get there because our two vans were stopped and held up so many times. At one point we were told we had to turn back altogether. Desperate, we climbed out of the vans and sat on the road so that other vehicles would not be able to pass either. There were only two soldiers at this isolated road-stop, and they couldn't drag us all away.

A furious taxi driver who was delivering a group of settlers to their burgundy-roofed homes in the territories flew out of his car and started shouting at us. "What have I done to you?" he cried out, his body tense with rage. "I might like you, if you didn't do things like this. Now you're just making me hate you more!" He turned to the soldier. "Why don't you do something! Why don't you make them move?"

"I'm just waiting to hear from the commander, take it easy," the soldier said. He looked very depressed.

"I can't wait! I have a car full of people here. They need to get home. Idiots!" He meant us.

"He's right, just let us through!" shouted a white-haired man who was sitting next to me. I knew him a little; we had spoken several times on buses or marches. His name was Ezra, and though he was in his eighties he never missed an activity. He wore plaid hiking shorts and his thin, muscular legs were covered with white hair. I pictured him on a farm; I pictured him pushing wheelbarrows for several decades. "Just let us through," he repeated, this time calmly.

"I can't, I have to wait for orders," the soldier replied.

"Why are you here in the first place!" a woman behind me cried out at the soldier. She sounded exasperated and plaintive, as if she were his mother and wanted him to clean up his room. "Why are you cooperating with the occupation!"

"Leave him alone," Ezra said. "It isn't his fault. He's just a soldier."

The driver couldn't control himself any longer. He grabbed Ezra and began pulling him unceremoniously by forearm and shirt collar. Some people rushed to protect Ezra, but he shouted at us, "Don't move! Don't get up!"

The soldier came over and announced, "Okay, you can go through, everyone can go through, *yallah,* get a move on."

We reached Hroush in the late afternoon, but we were not immediately permitted to enter the town. A large ditch had been dug on the main road in order to prevent anyone from getting through. We parked the vans near the ditch and negotiated with the army. The negotiations began with phone calls to various army officials, who all said the decision wasn't up to them, and ended with begging, nagging, and harassing the soldiers until they got bored and relented. I wandered a little off the road to photograph the grotesque remains of an uprooted olive orchard. The twisted trunks and amputated arms of the trees looked like mute messengers of some unspeakable doom, the details of which, perhaps fortunately, we were unable to decipher.

The soldiers watched us as we began crossing the ditch; it was hard to tell what they were thinking. We slipped going down and we slipped climbing up the other side. Those who reached the top first helped the others; I was reminded of a hundred scenes of Palestinians pulling their children up over walls, over rocky mounds of earth, up steep hillsides. By the time we reached Hroush our hands and legs were covered with mud, and the feet of people who had worn sandals were no longer visible.

But our appearance was appropriate for Hroush. Hroush wasn't anything like Ein Mazra'a, which had managed to hold itself together. Nor was it in ruins, like Dar al-Damar, which I had seen only once, after an incursion. Militants had holed up in Dar al-Damar several times, and the army had fired at buildings from helicopters and shelled them with tanks; there had also been fighting in the streets. The town had been reduced to heaps of rubble: houses had spewed out their insides as they collapsed, and bits of furniture—cribs, dishes, mattresses, lamps, embroidered pillows—lay in random patterns on the uneven mounds of stone and dust. Some buildings had survived, but they did not seem habitable.

Here the devastation was more subtle. The village was deserted: everyone was indoors because of the curfew, though there were women and children on the balconies and roofs, silent and watchful, as if decorating their houses with their bodies. No two houses were alike because they'd been built at different times by different people, with whatever material was at hand or had struck the fancy of the builder. The result was a genial display of textures and types of stone or concrete or plaster—porous and rough, smooth and symmetrical, each one a different variation on off-white. Hopeful metal rods protruded from the flat roofs and the beginnings of staircases clung to the sides of the houses, stopping Escher-like in midair: they were vestiges of an intention to expand. Poured concrete pillars would cover the rods and support higher floors, which the stairs would then reach.

The stores were all shuttered down: metal shutter after metal shutter, closed and locked. The awning of one of the empty stores had come loose and lay in a tangled heap on the ground. The fabric had Arabic and English print on it, and I could make out the words *Abu-Jiab Optic,* and a drawing of a pair of glasses. Litter clung to the edges of the wide path that ran through the town, and in a corner formed by two crumbling walls I saw what looked like human shit covered with blue-green flies. Some soldier with nowhere to defecate must have used this improvised outhouse in the middle of the night; the soldiers were still there, inside two armored carriers. Three of them sat on the roofs of their carriers and watched us with stony faces. I took a photograph of the crumbling walls, which were covered with graffiti, and of the horrible excrement in the corner. Remarkably, ordinary cars, including a Red Crescent ambulance, were parked here and there: incongruous signs of the outside world in this closed-down paleoscape.

We considered our sorry state and wondered what we could do about it. The mud had clung to our skin and clothes and we did not feel presentable. We walked over to an outdoor water faucet next to the ambulance and turned it on. Yellow, evil-smelling liquid spluttered out, choked, then vanished altogether. We searched our bags for tissues, poured a few drops of bottled water on them, and did our best to wipe our hands. Ezra went up to the soldiers and asked for a thermos of water. The soldiers ignored him.

We followed the organizer, a short, rotund woman who looked even shorter under her wide-brimmed straw hat. She was holding a piece of paper on which she'd printed directions, but she didn't really need to consult her notes, because as we walked sturdy-looking men leaned out of windows, greeted us, and told us which way to go.

Near the center of the village the buildings were closer together and the houses were older, with pretty domes rising from the roofs. It wasn't as eerie here, because the tanks were farther away and people felt freer. Women sat on chairs just outside their houses and children played noisily on the rooftops.

We knocked on the door of the bereaved family, and a young man with almond-shaped cat eyes and a struggling mustache opened the door. "Yes, yes, please, my parents wait. Thank you, we are happy you come," he said in English, but his voice was unconvincing. He sounded tired and very angry.

It was a relief stepping indoors: the house was full of people, and brought us back to reality. The visiting room was spotless and the walls were bare apart from a few framed photographs of family members and an Arabic text in elaborate calligraphy, also framed. The television was on, but the volume was so low that I wasn't sure what language the man on the screen was speaking. Folding chairs had been brought in to accommodate the several generations represented here: older children held bcobys on their laps, the knees of teenagers touched those of the aged. Everyone looked unhappy, but they welcomed us enthusiastically and urged us to sit down. The children gave us their seats and moved to the carpet; one of the bcobys began to cry and her mother, who appeared to be about sixteen, took the baby away to the kitchen to nurse her. We'd brought a few bags of food and diapers and we set them discreetly in the corner. The young man with the cat eyes served us sweetened tea in small glasses. I wondered whether the sixteen-year-old mother was his wife.

When I brought out my camera, the atmosphere in the room became very serious and intent. The bereaved parents stared hard into the camera lens, as if they were pinning their last hopes on these photographs, as if they believed or prayed that maybe, possibly, when people saw the images and knew the story something would be done. I felt guilty and heartbroken.

Then we watched a video of the children being shot—

someone who'd been sitting on a balcony had caught it with a camcorder as he filmed the tanks crawling through the streets. The killing was very distant and small on-screen. Now the children would live forever as video images, their death would be seen again and again, the tiny distant bodies crumpling on the white street. The two boys, Ashraf and Jamil, had misunderstood; they thought the curfew was lifted; that's what their father had told them. He was the one who had misunderstood, he said. The blaring sound of the megaphone, the bad accents of the soldiers—he had misheard. And they were so excited about going out, they ran onto the street, clutching the two coins their father had given them for chocolate. The coins were still in the fist of one of the boys when his body was retrieved.

I stood near the wall and thought about Rafi and wondered what he would do in this room and what he would say to the parents. He would be able to speak to them in Arabic. The mother was crying, and she had to leave the room when the video came on, but the father was quiet.

We left the village in a gloomy mood. The soldiers watched us with the same blank looks. We avoided their eyes.

In the van driving home, one of the men, who was religious, read us a psalm from a pocket Bible. He had sandy hair, gray eyes, and a sensuous, trusting face. *"The Lord looks down from heaven, he sees all the sons of men. A king is not saved by his great army, a warrior is not delivered by his great strength."* The sound of the words was soothing, but no one was comforted by the words themselves, not even the man who read them.

❉

When I came home I called Rafi. He said he'd come over after Naomi was in bed, later in the evening.

I went for a walk on the beach, but for once even the sea

failed to seduce me. A barrier of images blocked my escape: the house full of relatives, the man with the cat eyes and his teenage wife, the folding chairs, the intense faces staring into the camera, the mother running out of the room. The two small bodies crumpling on the street.

A woman in a black-and-ruby swimsuit was sitting on a rented beach chair reading the newspaper. The tanned, blond man who collected payment for the chairs passed her and asked, "So did they kill him in the end, or not?" There had been an assassination attempt in the morning, but it wasn't clear yet whether the targeted man was dead or merely wounded.

"So did they kill him in the end, or not?"

The words had a hollow, metallic quality to them, like a corroded pipe in a deserted factory. "So did they kill him in the end, or not?" The question echoed in the air: small talk between strangers. Maybe I was starting to go mad.

I was glad to find Benny in my flat when I returned; I wanted some company. Benny looked a little more spruced up than usual. He was wearing a clean blue shirt and a pair of trousers instead of his usual denim shorts.

"Going out?" I asked him.

"Yes, to visit you," he said. "Where have you been all day, Dana? I need to talk to you. I brought some wine and stuff." I saw that he'd set a bottle of wine on the kitchen counter along with all sorts of snacks: cheese borekas and salads from the bakery around the corner, and a poppy seed cake.

"What's the occasion?" I asked.

"I have something I need to talk to you about. Where were you today, by the way?" He lit a cigarette.

I wondered what was going on. Benny was a pragmatic person, and he liked things that were plain: plain food and plain songs and plain people. And if people weren't plain, if they were only predictable, that was fine, because he mistook predictability for plainness and he didn't notice complexity or else he pretended it wasn't there. If he came across anything that required a little more effort on his part, some insight or a departure from his usual way of thinking, he looked the other way. At the same time he was a very restless person, and I sometimes felt he'd become a taxi driver because he couldn't sit still, and that he couldn't sit still because something was missing from his life and he was hoping to find it.

"I went to photograph a condolence visit, two Palestinian children who were killed by a tank."

He sighed. "What about our victims, have you paid any condolence visits there?"

"We've had joint condolence visits . . . our families, their families."

"You don't care about our dead . . ."

"People are doing this so we'll all have fewer dead, hopefully." We'd had this conversation many times. We were constantly repeating ourselves, but neither of us minded. Every time we said the same things they seemed new, they were new. "You know how I feel about our dead, Benny."

"Yes, yes . . . I just get fed up with you."

"You've never even been to a refugee camp. Not even once in your life."

"So what? I know what they're like. It's sad, but they have only themselves to blame. Besides, we have poverty too. They don't have the monopoly on bad living conditions."

"What have you been doing?"

"The usual. I had a fare all the way north today. Rich bastards. You wouldn't believe the money some people in this country have, it boggles the mind. The whole time they were talking about their investments. The numbers they were throwing around . . . Wine?"

"Yes, please."

"This is very good wine," he said, opening the bottle and pouring. "Who painted this mural for you?"

"Someone Daniel worked with."

"Some people have talent . . . Look at those cows." He smiled. "Very cute."

"Well, what do you need to talk to me about?"

"I want to marry you."

"Marry me! Benny, you know I'm married."

"I know we can't marry technically, though I think there's a possibility you'd qualify for divorce based on desertion—I don't know what the rules are. I asked around, but no one seems to know. But even if we can't marry technically, we can live as if we're married. And we can have children."

"I don't know what to say." I was sorry for Benny, but at the same time I was a little suspicious of his motives. I thought he might be trying to get back at Miriam; maybe he wanted to even things out so he wouldn't be so tormented by her new relationship.

"I love you, Dana. I can't stop thinking about you. I come into this flat while you're away, I look at everything, and I feel I'm losing my mind. I watch you while you're sleeping, I've even stroked your hair, I know it's wrong but I couldn't help myself. I feel I'll explode if I can't have you. There are a million obstacles, and I keep telling myself over and over that it's impossible. First, your politics. My family would just go through the roof if they found out. And knowing you, they'd find out in the first five minutes of meeting you, you're not the type to keep that sort of thing to yourself. But on the other hand, I'm over forty, I no longer have to listen to my parents. I'm a big boy, I can do what I want. They'd get used to it, and if they didn't, tough. Then there's the problem of children. If I can't marry you, they'd be illegitimate. That would be really hard in this country. But we could look into it, we could see whether there's a way for you to get a divorce. I think you qualify, someone told me that after a certain amount of time if the husband is missing you qualify, I'm not sure. I don't have a lot of money, this divorce and the war have destroyed me. So there are lots of problems, but on the other hand, I'm just going insane. If you say no, I don't know what I'll do. I feel you like me, but I don't know. Everything depends on you, of course. But maybe even if you don't feel you're ready to decide, you could give me a chance. Get to know me, give me a chance to prove myself."

I was a little stunned by this speech, though I tried not to show it. My dreams about Benny crouching by the side of my bed had not been an invention after all; he had really been there. I couldn't help being moved. "I like you, Benny, but don't you think this is just about Miriam? Maybe you're just trying to get away from her."

"If you said yes, I swear to you I'd never let her into this building again, ever. It would be completely over, completely. I hate her anyhow, it wouldn't be any effort. If that's what's bothering you, don't even think about it."

"Benny, I can't marry you for a million reasons."

He looked very downcast when I said that.

"It's nothing to do with you personally. I love my husband, and I know I'm going to see him one day. In fact I'm getting closer to finding out where he is, I've never been this close."

"You can't waste your life like this, Dana. You're going to be thirty-eight, this is your last chance to have a child. Time doesn't move backward. You'll be eighty years old one day and you'll look back and you won't believe you missed the opportunity to have a life with someone, and a family. If we hurry, we could have two children, even. You said you always wanted children."

"Yes, my husband and I wanted children. We wanted a big family."

"Well, here's your chance. Why not just think about it? I know I can make you very, very happy, if you'll just let me. You can't imagine how much I love you."

"Benny, just last week you were telling me you were in love with Miriam."

"No, I said I had a craving for her. It's pure lust, that's all it is. And it would disappear altogether if it had another outlet."

I didn't say anything. We sat in dejected silence like two captured spies waiting for interrogation. I picked at the borekas and Benny poured himself more wine.

"Do you have someone else?" Benny finally asked.

"No."

"I mean, do you sleep with other people?"

"Not really. Beatrice comes over now and then, that doesn't really count."

"That woman with the curly red hair?"

"Yes."

"So, what, I don't get it—are you a lesbian?"

"No, she's just a friend. It's casual."

"I noticed she was staying here nights, but I thought maybe she just didn't have a place to stay in the city."

"She lives near the university. She's really busy, but she likes to drop by sometimes."

"Who else?"

"That's it, Benny, no one else. Even though, really, it's none of your business, you know."

"What about that doctor guy?"

I shook my head.

"So there's no one."

"No. Just my husband."

"What about that new guy I've seen around here?"

"How come everyone watches who comes and goes out of my apartment? What is it with you people?"

"I just happened to run into him as he was leaving, that's all. And it was late at night, so you can't blame me for wondering. But I don't mean to interfere. I was coming back from work, that's all. Don't get all excited."

"He's just someone from one of the peace groups. He's married, he has a daughter."

He sighed. "Think about it, anyhow. Promise me you'll think about it. I know how sad you are," he said, surprising me. He'd never said anything like that before. "But life can be great, too. It's just a question of finding the pearls in the mud, you know. I lost thirty-six friends. Well, friends and acquaintances. In '82, '83, in Lebanon. Thirty-six." He shook his head, as though still incredulous. "My best friend included. He was shot right next to me. Someone threw a smoke grenade and he lifted his head a few inches to see better, and he got shot in the chest. And then his brother went crazy because of it, so I lost them both, I was close to both of them. You have to learn to get over things. You have to go on; otherwise, what's the point of life, you might as well just kill yourself." He began to tremble. He was trembling from head to foot. I knew what that was all about: he was trying to gather the courage to make a pass. I felt bad for him again.

"You're shaking," I said.

"Yes, I'm nervous."

"I can't have sex with you, Benny. I'm sorry. I'm loyal to my husband. Please don't ask. You're very handsome and I'm sure you're a fabulous lover, but I can't betray my husband."

He got up. He was very angry, but he was trying to control himself.

"Well, I guess there's nothing more to say."

"Please don't be angry. Is this the end of our friendship?"

"No, I'm not giving up that easily," he said.

Then he left.

✷

When Rafi came over I told him about Benny's proposal.

"People are picking up that things are changing for you," Rafi said, looking inside my fridge.

"No, it's just a coincidence. That's the way it is, things always happen at once. You come into my life just when I might be close to finding Daniel, so why not add a marriage proposal to the pudding! Poor Benny. Though I don't think he really loves me, it's just an infatuation."

"Do you have rice?" he asked.

"Yes, in the closet on your left. Are you going to cook?"

"I'll make us a meal. You're not very well equipped. What do you live on?"

"It varies . . ."

"I'll bring some spices tomorrow, if that's okay. When will you be home?"

"You can come anytime. I'll give you a key, just take one from the glass bowl. They're all house keys."

"Dana! What are you doing with ten copies of your house key?"

"I don't know. I give them to people, and then they lose them, so I make more copies, then they find them . . ."

"How many people have your key?"

"Well, Volvo and his volunteers, Benny, Tanya, her mother, some friends . . ."

"Why Volvo and the volunteers?"

"Oh, in case they need something . . . he doesn't have anything at his place, he refuses to buy stuff for himself. He doesn't even have a stove, maybe you noticed. Rosa does all his cooking here."

"Aren't you afraid someone's going to steal your photography equipment?"

"People who volunteer to look after someone without legs are not going to steal anything."

"Don't be so naïve, Dana."

"I'm not naïve. If you knew the volunteers, you wouldn't worry. Miss Fitzpatrick is some sort of nun, Alex is Daniel's oldest friend, and Joshua is about ninety years old. And the idea of Rosa stealing is about as plausible as the idea of Rosa deciding to be a porn star."

"If you give your key to everyone, eventually it will get into the wrong hands—don't you see that? Aren't you afraid someone will come in while you're sleeping?"

"I have a chain on the door."

He laughed. "Yes, that chain is really something. We should recommend it to the army. They should come and take a look, they could learn something."

"I guess you're right. I guess I should be more careful. I just don't care, though. I don't care."

"You'd care if you were raped in the middle of the night."

"I feel safe here."

"I want you to get a new lock. I'll pay for it. Call a locksmith tomorrow, get a new lock installed, a decent one. And don't hand out your key to the volunteers. Or to anyone else."

"Okay."

"Do you want me to look after it?"

"Yes, please."

"Have you heard from Coby?"

"Not yet. But I have a good feeling. I feel he might find out for me. I might be seeing Daniel in a few days! What are you making there? It smells good."

"Well, I'm doing my best, with what you have here. I guess I was lucky to find an onion."

"Mercedes bought that. How's Graciela?"

"She's the same. Working hard."

"I'm jealous of her."

"Of what?"

"She's elegant. She has nice clothes. She has your child."

"You can have all those things."

"Coby said you've had a hard life."

"Did he say that?"

"Yes. Have you?"

He put a lid on the pot and lowered the heat. "This has to simmer. Let's wait on the sofa."

He cleared the sofa and stretched out, and I lay down on top of him. "Did you? Have a hard life?" I asked again.

"I don't know. These things are relative. We were poor, it was a tough neighborhood. My father was violent. He broke my arm once, and it lowered my profile. I cried when my profile came in. I wanted a ninety-seven, but I lost over twenty points because of my arm, because I don't have total flexibility. That's why it hurt so much yesterday, when that asshole grabbed it."

"Why did your father break your arm?"

"I was bad, he was frustrated. I set a shack on fire with some of my friends. We were all frustrated, we fed each other's frustrations and made them worse. But some things were pretty good. My father was okay in his calm moments. My older brother's a great guy."

"What did your parents do?"

"My father had a lot of jobs. My mother made pottery. She could have done a lot more with her life, but she never had the opportunity."

"It's sad to think of you living with someone who hurt you."

"I don't think of it that way at all. It all made me who I am. I can't imagine a different past, I have no idea who I'd be or whether I'd like that person."

"Are your parents still alive?"

"My mother died while I was in the army. My father's still around, but he's in poor health—he's in a home. He was forty-five when he married my mother, and she was only twenty. So he's pretty old now."

"How did he break your arm?"

"He pushed me down some stairs. I was bad, too. I kicked him, I bit him. I was totally out of control. But he was bigger, and he had a belt."

"I was so spoiled all my life. My parents were so protective. I was their only child, they really doted on me."

"I can't imagine not having brothers and sisters."

"Yes, I really did want a big family. But on the other hand, I liked getting all the attention."

"How come your parents stopped at one?"

"They waited awhile to have me. And they were busy with their careers by then. They really invested a lot in me—I guess they weren't too keen on doing that more than once."

"Invested, how?"

"Just, you know, trying to give me the best of everything. Getting mad if my teachers weren't perfect. Being involved in my life. My father started reading the newspaper to me when I was four. That continued right through the years, we were always looking at articles together and talking about them. He and his brother used to go to refugee camps, to do volunteer work, and they took me along. I was lucky, I had a great childhood. At least until my mother died."

"Was that hard?"

"The first week was terrible, and I did some pretty crazy stuff. I kept thinking there was an invisible starfish clinging to my chest, this cold, self-satisfied, smirking starfish. I took shower after shower trying to get it off. Then I tried ice cubes, and I can't remember what else. I had to keep my arms against my chest all the time, under my shirt, otherwise the starfish feeling came back. Then I sort of got involved with things again, I got back into life. It was strange . . . People respond in different ways to things. After Daniel left, that's when her death hurt me, years later. I had a delayed response, I think. What about when your mother died?"

"It was hard, but I was in the army—I didn't have time to be sad. I felt guilty, mostly. I wished I'd been nicer to her, more supportive. I wished I hadn't worried her so much."

"This is going to end, between us," I said. "It's going to end as soon as Daniel comes back."

"Okay."

"I'm sorry."

"I'm not free either."

"We'll just enjoy the time we have together, and we'll remember it as something short and sweet that we had together, is that all right? Daniel won't mind. I was loyal to him for eleven years, he won't mind if I loved someone for a few days right at the end. I won't tell him, so as not to hurt him, but I think if he knew he'd forgive me."

"I think you're right. I think he won't mind. I'm sure he wants you to be happy."

"Thank you. Maybe one day I'll tell him, maybe not, it depends on whether I think it would hurt him or not."

"You'll feel what's right. You don't have to plan it."

"Graciela hasn't asked about me?"

"No, but I think she knows."

"I'm sure she hates me!"

"I told you, she's much too preoccupied to hate you or me or anyone else."

"Why is she like that? So closed?"

"I don't know. I was supposed to study psychology, that's what I had a scholarship for, and maybe if I'd gone through with it I'd know. But as it is, I don't know."

"Maybe something happened when she was young."

"Almost certainly something happened when she was young."

"On the other hand, musical genius is often accompanied by eccentricity, maybe it's physiological."

"I don't think so," he said. "Not in her case. But who knows? I think supper's almost ready, I'll go take a peek."

"It smells great."

"I'll be glad if it's edible. How can you live without cooking?"

We sat down to eat, and Rafi had a glass of Benny's wine.

In the middle of the meal I pushed my plate away. "I can't eat this. I can't eat this. This is all wrong. You shouldn't be here. I want you to go."

"Can I finish my food first?"

"No. Yes. Oh God, what a horrible day!" I said. "What a horrible day. The two boys on the video, crumpling on the street over and over, the screen was so white, they were nothing, just alive and then dead on the street, nothing, just dark figures on the screen and their mother had to leave the room and their sister was crying in the corner and sucking her finger and pulling her hair, just pulling her hair out of sheer stress, the whole place is like a ghost town and there's no water, shit in some corner, soldiers with faces like stone, we don't even deserve this stupid country anymore, we don't deserve it! Then you come here and make dinner, you come here and ruin everything and now I have to lie to Daniel. And Benny saw you leaving and every time I see him he's going to look at me and he thinks he wants me and I'm never going to see Vronsky again, and last night I thought I heard a mouse in the walls—can't you see, can't you see what a mess you're making of everything?"

"This rice thing actually came out better than I thought," Rafi said, helping himself to another serving.

"I had another dream about you," I said. "It was very strange. It was the end of days, there was hardly anyone left on the planet. Some people were standing around a huge cauldron, stirring it.

It was hard to get food, and they were waiting impatiently for the food in the cauldron to be ready, even though I knew there wasn't much in there, mostly grass and herbs and dandelions. Then you came and you were carrying a dead rabbit, covered with ants, and I was horrified but all the others were so happy, and they threw the rabbit into the cauldron and they crowned you."

"They crowned me? How?"

"I can't remember. Just some crown they had."

"You know, there's a game I play with my after-school kids, they really love it. We play it all the time, they have a blast."

"What sort of game?"

"I can show you if you want."

"Yes, I'm curious."

"Let's finish supper first."

I had lost my appetite, but Rafi more than made up for it. He finished everything in the pot. We cleared the counter and left the dishes in the sink.

"Do you have any kerchiefs?"

"No."

"Some old clothing I can tear up?"

"Yes, I have some rags. Under the sink."

Rafi rummaged around and pulled out a T-shirt I had bought at a peace event, with a picture of a dove made of our flags and Palestinian flags. I used it for washing up because it was too big on me.

He cut two strips from the bottom of the shirt. Then he turned off all the lights in the house and we sat on the living room floor, on the carpet. Rafi blindfolded himself, and told me to do the same.

"Okay," he said. "We take turns. We say what we're afraid of, and why. I'll go first. I'm afraid of nightmares, because I'm afraid of being afraid."

"I'm afraid of mice."

"You have to say why."

"I'm afraid of mice because they're creepy and ugly."

"I'm afraid of falling from an airplane because there's nothing to hold on to."

"I'm afraid of getting cancer because I don't want to go through chemotherapy."

"I'm afraid of getting cancer because it's painful and I don't want to die."

"I'm afraid of tunnels and narrow places and being stuck somewhere I can't get out of. I'm afraid of being in a car that falls off a bridge and fills with water and I can't get out. Because . . . I'm neurotic."

"You need a better reason," Rafi said.

"Because I don't want to be trapped."

"I'm afraid of my feelings for you because they're so strong and I could lose you."

"I'm afraid of you, because you don't belong in my life."

"I'm afraid of witches because they have magical powers."

"You believe in witches?"

"No questions allowed, but no."

"I'm afraid of pens that don't work, pencils that aren't sharpened, traffic lights that don't work, telephones that don't work, because I need things to go smoothly."

"I'm afraid of getting blown up because I'm too young to die and my daughter needs me and the kids need me and I love you."

"I'm afraid of your love. I'm afraid of loving you. I'm afraid of losing Daniel forever. Because . . . because I'm afraid, that's all."

"I'm afraid of a nuclear war because of the horror."

"I'm afraid of a nuclear war because of the horror."

"I'm afraid of old age and not being able to get it up anymore because I'll be embarrassed and I'll feel like a loser."

"I'm afraid of my breasts sagging and not having my period and not having a child, ever. Because I want a child."

"I'm afraid of my mean side because I don't like it."

"I'm afraid of my mean side because I always regret it afterward."

"I'm afraid of not being a good enough father. Because my daughter deserves the best."

"I'm afraid of this game. I'm afraid of not seeing and not understanding and not knowing. I want to stop."

"I'm afraid of webbed hands and people with tails because they're going to come in the middle of the night to get me."

"I'm afraid of the dark because there could be monsters. I want to stop," I said.

"I'm afraid of good things because of when they end."

"I'm afraid of good things because I don't deserve them. Because I let Daniel slip through my fingers. Because I didn't go into his room right away and I let everyone bully me and I failed him completely. I let him down, it's all my fault. He fought for me, when I had my miscarriage he fought with everyone in the entire hospital, he never gave up, but I didn't fight for him. I was a wimp, I couldn't stand up to them for his sake. It's my fault. When he didn't see me, day after day, he must have thought I'd deserted him, that it was because of how he looked. Or maybe he thought I came in while he was sleeping and that I was so horrified that I stayed away and that I'd decided to leave him and that's why he ran away. And now I'm afraid I'll never find him, I'm afraid he never saw my ads or my interviews and he doesn't know I want him more than anything in the world. I'm afraid of not knowing the future and also of being alone and also of my life, which I hate, I hate it, I hate it."

I tore off my blindfold. "I'm tired of helping everyone," I said.

"I'm tired of helping everyone, too."

"I want to be selfish."

"Me too."

"Let's be selfish," I said.

"Okay."

"Let's be selfish tonight."

"Good idea."

"Tonight nothing else and no one else will exist."

"And tomorrow?"

"Tomorrow we'll go back to real life."

"How about we begin with a bath?" Rafi suggested.

"Yes, I'd like that," I said.

He filled the clawfoot tub and we lay down in the hot water. I felt my body relaxing. "Very stressful day," I said.

"Why not take a break for a while?"

"I can't. I always think about the shots I'll be missing. I never took a bath with Daniel. He didn't like baths."

"People aren't used to baths in this country. I only got into taking baths when I moved in with Graciela, because she could afford it . . . I really think you should consider taking a short vacation from the activities, Dana."

"One time I almost didn't go to this activity. There was going to be a demonstration against the Wall, and I had my period, and a sore throat—I was coming down with something. I really didn't think I could make it but at the last minute I decided to go. And I got one of my best photographs ever on that day. A photograph I would never have had a chance to take anywhere else, because it was such a fluke."

"What of?"

"Blue ribbons. There was this barbed wire coming out of the ground—this was in Palestine. And it couldn't be pulled out, it was stuck, so someone had tied a blue ribbon to it, so that cars and pedestrians would see it and be warned. Well, I focused my camera on it, and right at that second this man from one of the refugee camps, who had come for the demo, stepped into my field of vision, and he had the same blue ribbon wrapped around his shoe. The shoe was falling apart and he couldn't buy new shoes so he'd wrapped the shoe up in blue ribbon to keep it together. I have a shot of that, of the shoe next to the barbed wire. It's a really important photograph for me, it just sums up everything. Anyhow, I'm not usually affected the way I was today. It wasn't just Hroush, it was everything. I didn't know I felt so guilty about Daniel."

"Amazing, the obvious things we can't see."

"What are you hiding from yourself?"

"What is the logical flaw in that question?"

"I mean, was there something you hid from yourself and then figured out and then wondered how you could have not realized?"

"Sure. Lots of things to do with Graciela, for example. When she began seeing me as dirty, I thought that was because I really was dirty, because of everything I'd done. That's ridiculous. It's entirely her problem; in fact, I have very good hygiene."

"You're in a good mood, I see."

"Yes, I am. I'm in a good mood, thanks to you. I may even have another sip of that wine your suitor brought you."

"Poor Benny!"

"He'll survive."

"I didn't only refuse to marry him, I also refused to have sex with him."

"Now I'm really shocked."

"Well, it hurt his feelings."

"Hurt his balls, more like."

"He has sex with Miriam all the time. She sneaks in here almost every second day."

"Dana, how could you refuse such a tempting offer?"

"Don't make fun of him, he's okay."

"Can't you tell how jealous I am?"

"Jealous of Benny!"

"Yes, I always wanted hairy arms."

"You're so mean."

"True."

"Do your after-school kids really like that game?"

"Yes, it makes them laugh, they have hysterics. They like to think of scarier and scarier things, they go wild. It's a good outlet for them."

A knock on the door startled us. "Expecting anyone?" Rafi asked.

"Could be Alex, he sometimes comes on Fridays. Or even Benny! Let's not answer."

"Fine with me."

There were a few more knocks and then the person went away. We had forgotten all about the visitor, but later, when Rafi opened the door to leave, we found a note pinned to the door. It read: *I have Daniel's address. Come to the hotel tomorrow. Coby.*

# SUNDAY

IT SEEMED TO ME THAT I DIDN'T SLEEP all night, though I think I dreamed that I was awake. I know at one point I had a hallucinatory dream: Coby came into the room and told me that Daniel was living in a lighthouse on a rock island in the middle of the sea, and that was why no one could find him.

At five in the morning I went into the hotel and sat on the sofa in the lobby, facing the reception desk. There was no one in the lobby apart from Hussein and the desk clerk. The clerk asked if he could help. "I'm waiting for Coby—it's urgent," I said. He shrugged; working in a hotel must have inured him to strange behavior.

I was lucky; Coby was early that morning. At seven o'clock he walked in.

"I'll be with you in a sec," he said, and disappeared into a back office.

I waited another ten minutes, and finally he emerged. I was so disoriented that for a second I wondered how he could look so composed in his perfectly pressed suit when I was such a wreck. He led the way to the dining room and poured coffee for both of us.

"You look pale."

"Coby, I haven't slept all night, what do you think? I'm so excited I can't breathe."

"But it isn't very good news, Dana."

"Just tell me!"

"Well, he lives in the territories, inside the Coastal Strip. He's in Qal'at al-Maraya."

"Qal'at al-Maraya!"

"I don't know how or why, my cousin wouldn't say more. By the way, my cousin is going to kill us both if anyone finds out he's the one who got the address."

"Do you have his address?"

"Yes, I wrote it down for you." He handed me my napkin, the one on which I'd written Daniel's ID number. Under the number he'd written: *7 al-Ma'arri Street, Qal'at al-Maraya.*

"Qal'at al-Maraya . . . I was there so many times! I used to go to the beach to take photos there almost once a week."

"I have no idea how he managed it—how he got them to trust him. Maybe he's converted?"

"That's even more ridiculous than your spy theory. Oh God, I'm so happy, thank you, thank you, thank you!" I got up and hugged him. "I'm going to see him! I'm going to see Daniel, maybe in only an hour—I'll take a taxi, how do I look? What should I bring? Thank you, thank you, I have to go now."

I turned to leave but Coby caught my arm. "Dana, hold on. Sit down a minute."

"I can't. I can't wait. Sorry, I have to go. I hope I look all right."

"Dana, you can't go, you don't have a permit, you're not going to get in. You're not thinking. Calm down, and come back to the table, we have to figure out what you're going to do."

"I'll get in, don't worry. I'll just beg."

"Yes, begging really works at checkpoints. Or with the army in general."

"They have to let me in."

"Dana, sit down. Here, take one of these."

I sat down at the table because people were looking at us. He pulled a bottle of large green pills out of his pocket.

"What are these?"

"My father's tranquilizers. Have one, you'll feel better."

"I don't *want* to feel tranquil, Coby!"

"Fine. But you can't just go to the Coastal Strip. You won't get in."

"I'll find a way. I can't wait. I can't wait. It seems so unreal, like a dream. What if I wake up?"

"Want me to pinch you?"

"Qal'at al-Maraya . . . he must have learned Arabic . . ."

"I guess so."

"He was always good at languages. He learned Russian so he could talk to his grandmother . . . Thank you, Coby. Thank you. You can't imagine how I feel."

"I'm getting an idea."

"I'm going to see Daniel . . ."

"You need a permit, and it's very dangerous, I have no idea how you'll manage it. I don't think they'll give you a permit."

"Maybe Ella can help me."

"Ella?"

"The journalist. She might be able to help me. Maybe I could go down there with her. Everyone knows her there. I think she even has a flat she rents in Qal'at al-Maraya for occasional use."

"Please be careful."

"I have such butterflies in my stomach now. Can I borrow your phone, please?"

Coby handed me his mobile phone and I called Rafi. I told him that I had Daniel's address, but that I couldn't leave right away. "Do you want me to come over?" he asked.

"Yes, I'm all jittery," I said.

Then I left a message at Odelia's, asking her for Ella's phone number.

"I was there, in Qal'at al-Maraya," I repeated. "And all I had to do was ask someone . . ."

"I hope I did the right thing," Coby said.

"I don't understand why they kept it from me in the first place! So he lives in Qal'at al-Maraya, so what!"

Coby's eyes narrowed and he raised his eyebrows. He looked at me with a mixture of skepticism and reproach, the way he had when I'd said that Rafi had a good life.

"I can't believe I know where he is and I have to wait. I don't know how I'll manage. If only I could just hop in a taxi. People do get in. People do get in and out."

"Just don't try anything stupid, Dana," he said. "Don't even think about trying to sneak in. No one will know who you are, and we have some trigger-happy people in our army."

"I won't."

"Promise. Promise not to try and sneak in."

"Okay."

"If our guys don't shoot you, theirs will."

"Okay."

"Do you know the word for 'foreigner'?"

"No."

"*Ajnabi*. If anything happens, speak English and say you're a foreigner, and you're there to support Palestine. Don't take your ID with you."

"You think everyone in Palestine is a terrorist!"

"No, of course not, but somehow it only takes one bullet to die, not three million."

"I won't go in alone, I'll go with Ella. I'm not going to lie to Palestinians about who I am. And everyone knows Ella. I can't believe I'm going to see my husband. I'm going to see him! Maybe in just a day or two, I don't know how I'll make it through the next few hours. Do I look okay?"

Coby laughed. "Well, you're not as pale as you were earlier this morning."

"I'm so nervous, you can't imagine. Should I bring something? This is boring for you . . ."

"No, not at all. Though I should probably be getting back to work." He yawned and stretched his arms. "Never enough sleep. We had two busloads of tourists yesterday."

"Tourists . . ." I said, barely listening.

"Yes, a Christian group. 'Jesus Is the One,' something like that. At least someone wants to visit the Holy Land."

"Thanks, Coby. Thanks for the address. You don't know what this means to me."

"I'm sorry I didn't have better news."

"This is great news. He isn't dead, he isn't with another woman. I can't wait!"

"I hope it works out. I hope you can convince him to come home."

"Yes. Yes."

"I have to get back to work. Let me know how things turn out. I'm not sure I did the right thing—if anything happens to you, it's on my shoulders."

"Nothing will happen."

"Help yourself to the breakfast buffet, by the way. There's always a lot left over anyhow. Even with the Christians here."

❖

I sat at the table in the hotel dining room and tried to imagine my husband in Qal'at al-Maraya, living in a little flat there, or maybe renting a room in someone's house. How well did he know Arabic? Had he taught himself? He must have hired a teacher. Could he read and write Arabic too? Did he go out? How did he support himself? Maybe the money from the army was enough—things were cheaper there. What were his days like, day in, day out, alone in a Palestinian city? He had probably made some friends. But how did he get them to trust him? He had vanished during the uprising—how had he managed to move in without being killed? And what about now? Everything he loved was here: going to shows and walking down the streets and the crazy people on television, laughing at them and cracking jokes and making all sorts of puns, and the sea . . . well, he still had the sea. I could have sent him a message in a bottle.

From the window of the dining hall I saw a man approach my building. He was carrying a large toolbox and walking very deliberately to the front door. I wondered who he was; it was way too early for Tanya to be prophesying. Maybe she or her mother had some sort of plumbing emergency. Then it hit me: this was probably the locksmith Rafi had promised to send my way, to protect me from evil. I hurried out of the hotel and into the building.

The locksmith was standing at the door to my apartment, knocking loudly. Then he kicked the door. "Open up!" he yelled.

"It's me, I'm here," I said.

"You Dana?"

"Yes."

"Unlock."

"It's open," I said.

He flung the door open and bellowed at me, "Out of my way!" Then he reconsidered. "Money up front or I'm going home."

"Okay. Just tell me how much it is."

"Two hundred."

I gave him the money and he stuffed the bills in his back pocket. I was a little worried about him; I was afraid he was going to have a nervous breakdown in front of my eyes. I could imagine him picking up his hammer and smashing all the walls in the building.

He began taking apart the lock on my door. He was a short, stocky man with a wide face, narrow eyes, and a pursed mouth. His eyes weren't naturally narrow; he was just very tense. He began cursing the door and various other opponents.

"Fuck his fucking mother," he said.

"Who?" I asked.

He looked up at me and tried to decide whether to swear at me or to answer. Finally he said, "Fucking son of a whore who attacked me, I'll rip his fucking heart out and throw it to the dogs. Look what he did—"

I saw that his arm was covered with blood and that in fact he was still bleeding. I wondered how I'd failed to notice: maybe it was because he was hairy, or maybe his anger eclipsed everything else about him.

"I'll get something for that," I said.

"Don't bother."

I went to the kitchen and ran a towel under warm water. I brought it to the locksmith and said, "Here, put this on it."

"What are you, a fucking nurse?"

"You could get an infection. You should really come in and wash your arm."

He took the towel and threw it on the floor. "Screw this," he said.

"What happened?"

"Fucking maniacs. Her husband wasn't supposed to be anywhere around, and what's it my business anyhow, I just do the
locks, I'm not her fucking lover, I don't know this person from
a whore on the street. But I'm the one who gets attacked."

"Why didn't you call the police?"

He guffawed. "Anyhow, I beat him up good. Gave him a run
for his money, damned bastard."

"I guess I'm out of my depth here."

"That's right, baby. Nice place you got here. Who *you* keeping out? I swear if I have any more crazy boyfriends today I'm
not responsible for my actions."

"I'm not keeping anyone out, and I don't have a boyfriend.
And I think everyone's responsible for their actions."

He looked up at me. I stepped back.

He returned to his work, letting out his rage on the lock. I
made coffee while he worked and when it was ready I handed
him a mug. He seemed very surprised.

"Thanks," he said.

"You're welcome. You know, you're very good-looking, but
your face is so strained."

"Yeah, well, life's a bitch."

"I guess you're in a hard line of work."

"Better than fixing people's toilets. Better than being up to
your arms in other people's shit."

"Is that what you used to do?"

"Still do. Why you changing your lock?"

"I gave my key to a lot of people. And the guy who called you
thinks it isn't safe, he wants me to have a new lock. That's all."

"He's right. Everyone's a fucking crook out there."

"Do you want to come in and wash your arm?"

"Yeah, may as well."

He had a strident way of walking and I was afraid he'd bump

into something or accidentally turn over a piece of furniture. He went into the bathroom and rinsed his arm. "Looks like the fucking Taj Mahal in here," he said, as the water from the tap turned red. I gave him another towel. "What are you, Mother Teresa?"

"If I were injured, I'd expect you to do the same for me. And I'll bet you would."

"I'll bet I wouldn't."

"I'll bet you would."

"I'll bet I wouldn't."

"I'll bet you would."

"You're pretty stubborn, in your own quiet way."

"Yes, I am."

He smiled. "You're okay."

"You look very nice when you smile."

"What, are you coming on to me?"

"No, as I'm sure you can tell."

"Yeah, you're a bit of a cold fish, aren't you?"

"Thanks."

"Not really a cold fish, but, I don't know, a mermaid maybe?"

"Yeah, okay."

"I'll just finish up with the door. It's nearly done."

"There's a woman upstairs who tells fortunes. You should try her out." I figured one of Tanya's massages would do him good.

"Why?"

"She's really good."

"I don't believe in that fucking shit."

"She's different."

"What, you getting a cut?"

"I don't care if you go or not. It was just a suggestion."

"Well, maybe. How much does she charge?"

"Around fifty."

"I'll think about it."

When he'd left I knocked on Volvo's door. I was hoping Alex would be there.

Alex was Daniel's oldest friend. In high school he had formed the little band that had played at my cousin's wedding, and when Daniel finished his army service, they traveled together to Italy, Paris, Greece, and South America. Alex had a release from the army because he was albino; there was a military clause somewhere that exempted albinos, for no good reason—but Alex wasn't complaining.

Alex still had white hair, of course, but it was very short now. He was a professional musician, and he'd worked with just about every singer and group in the country. He was also active in Gays Against the Occupation; he was the one who had come up with their slogan, *No Pride in the Occupation*. Alex was the only volunteer Volvo didn't complain about, and the only one who could tease Volvo. He called him "pinup boy," "irresistible," "heartthrob," "sex object." Remarkably, Volvo was amused.

Alex answered the door. "Dana! I'm happy to see you. My handsome friend and I are having a heart-to-heart."

Volvo was sitting in his chair, and I could tell that they really had been having a serious conversation.

"Hi, Volvo."

"Hi, Dana," Volvo said courteously, possibly for the first time since I'd known him.

"Alex, when you have a moment, can I see you? It's about Daniel. You don't mind, Volvo, do you?"

Volvo waved his hand regally to indicate his consent, and Alex followed me to my flat. We sat on the sofa and Alex took my hand and held it in his lap. His transparent blue eyes danced because of his astigmatism, but made him look as if he was concentrating hard on what you were saying and deliberating upon every word.

"Listen, Alex. I've found Daniel."

"You found him! Where? Have you seen him?"

"No, not yet. In the end it was so easy. I could have found him years ago. I don't want to think about that."

"I was sure he was hiding in some cave in India. I never thought we'd find him. Well, where is he?"

"He's in Qal'at al-Maraya."

"Really!"

"Yes. He doesn't know I've found him. And I haven't told anyone. I have to see him first, before I let anyone know."

"How did you find out, after all this time?"

"The army knew all along. Someone high up gave it to me."

"That simple . . . Poor Dana, after all your efforts. Crazy. Qal'at al-Maraya. What was he thinking?"

"I'm going to ask Ella to help me get to him."

"Good idea."

"I should let you get back to Volvo."

"He's fine. Are you?"

"Of course! I've never been happier in my life—I don't know how I'll survive until I see him."

"He's not going to be exactly the same, honey."

"I know. But he's still Daniel."

"Yes, but people change. You have to be prepared for that. People go through things, their lives change, they're not the same people. Look at me. Twenty years ago I was wandering from party to party like some lost minstrel, stoned out of my mind most of the time. Now I'm a member of the bourgeoisie, and I spend my days worrying about my credit rating."

"The basic things stay the same."

"Well, it's true I've always been gay! By the way, our friend Volvo has just decided he's gay, too."

"Oh yes, he mentioned something. Well . . . I guess it's possible."

"He wants me to take him to a gay bar."

"That's great news! Finally, a sign of life. Who knows, he might meet someone."

"For sure he'll meet someone. He's quite good-looking. Dana, be careful. I'm not happy about you wandering around Qal'at al-Maraya."

"I'll go with Ella, everyone knows her."

"That's a good idea, angel. Though you know, our marvelous army shot at Ella's car a few months ago. It was a miracle she wasn't killed."

"Yes, I remember."

He shook his head. "Poor Daniel. Living in what is at the moment one of the planet's hellholes."

"Some parts of Qal'at al-Maraya are really beautiful—it's not like he's living in a refugee camp. But I guess it's bad everywhere on the strip now."

"Good luck, sweetie. Call me if you need anything."

He let himself out, and I stayed on the sofa, motionless, all my emotions on hold.

❖

I was still sitting on the sofa and staring into space when Rafi came over. He brought food: spices in glass jars, vegetables, an interesting assortment of grains. I watched him as he took the items out of plastic bags. We didn't touch; we were both shy today.

"So, where is he?" Rafi asked. "And can I get a cup of coffee around here?"

"Yes, of course. He's in Qal'at al-Maraya."

"Qal'at al-Maraya! Well, that's interesting."

"Yes."

"I wonder how he managed to keep that a secret. Everyone

knows everything in this country. Especially something like that."

"I'm so angry at the army. They knew all along."

"Maybe the people you spoke to didn't know." He lit a cigarette; he seemed very tense.

"I had no help at all. No one wanted to help me find him, not his family, not my friends, no one. Certainly no one in any of the offices I went to. I didn't know who to turn to."

"People think they know what's best for us."

"Why? Why would that be best for me?"

"I don't know. Maybe they thought he'd gone mad. Maybe they didn't want you to go running after him and move there also."

"Why would it be classified information, though? I just don't understand."

"Maybe it isn't classified, just not easily available."

"I'm thinking back to that woman, that woman who spent a lot of time trying to look Daniel up on her computer, just because she was on my side, you know. She probably wasn't even supposed to be going in, but she was alone in the office, and she began checking all sorts of things. She found out that he was in Qal'at al-Maraya. And she just decided not to tell me. Or else she was afraid of getting into trouble. I remember now that when she was reading the screen a weird look came over her face. What right does she have to ruin my life? What right do they have to keep that sort of information from me?"

"What will you do now?"

"He has to see that I still love him. He must be so lonely there."

"You don't know, Dana. You don't know what his life is like. Maybe he's found a way to be happy. Maybe he's made some close friends. I wonder how he managed to get in, though. How he got them to trust him, I can't imagine it."

"Yes, it was right in the middle of the uprising."

"You're right . . . eleven years ago . . . It seems impossible. They would never have trusted him, a former soldier, wounded, I wonder how he did it."

"You're very tense, Rafi."

"That's the first time you've used my name."

"Really?"

"Really."

"I can't believe that. I'm sorry. Rafi. Rafi. I'm sorry."

"I forgive you."

"Are you upset?"

"Let's put on some music." He went over to my CD collection and put on a record that had just come out, various artists singing Jacky's greatest hits. The clear pure voice of one of my favorite female vocalists filled the room. *A carnival of fools, showgirls on the shore, shrapnel in the air, sand on the floor. Come dance with me, dance with me, for the sake of the dream, and we'll both pretend that we can be seen.*

"I have to tell my father," I said. "I have to call him. What time is it in Belgium?"

"I think they're around three or four hours back, I'm not sure."

"I'm calling, I can't wait."

It took me a few minutes to find my father's number; I almost never phoned him. He sounded groggy when he answered.

"Dad? It's me."

"What's happened?" he asked, immediately worried.

"Nothing, nothing, it's good news."

"Ah, the kind I like. Hold on, hold on. Just a second, I can't hear without my glasses. Ah, here . . . Yes."

"I found Daniel's address."

There was a long silence at the other end. "Dad, are you there?"

"Yes, yes, I'm just trying to digest what you said. He's alive?"

"Of course he's alive. Didn't you know that?"

"Yes—no—I mean, I had no idea, honey."

"I told you he's alive, the army still sends him his disability checks."

"Ah, that's right. Have you seen him?"

"Of course not! I just got the address now. It was a fluke. He's in Qal'at al-Maraya, that's why I couldn't find him."

"Qal'at al-Maraya! What's he doing there?"

"Hiding, obviously. What a brilliant hiding place."

"Dana, how do you feel about all this?"

"What do you think, Dad? I've only waited eleven years! I'm so excited I can hardly breathe."

"I'm very happy for you, darling. Very, very happy. But how the hell will you get to him?"

"Ella, maybe."

"Do you think you should write to him first?"

"No, no, I won't let him get away this time. How's Gitte?"

"Fine, fine. She says to send her love."

"Say hi from me, too. Tell her the good news."

"I will. Keep me posted. I hope it goes well, duckie. I'm sure it will. This is like one of your romance novels, isn't it?"

"Well, not exactly. But who knows, maybe I'll write one about a long-lost true love. There's a song about that, isn't there? Mummy used to like it."

"*Well, if he's in some battle slain,*" my father began to sing, "*I'll lie still when the moon doth wane. If he's drowned in the deep salt sea, I'll be true to his memory. And if he's found another love, and he and his love both married be, I wish them health and happiness, where they dwell across the sea.*" He stopped singing and coughed. "Bit early in the morning, my voice isn't quite awake."

"Don't stop there! Sing me the end!"

"*He picked her up all in his arms, and kisses gave her one, two, three, saying weep no more, my own true love, I am your long-lost John Riley.*"

"You're right, it's very romantic."

"This really is wonderful news, Dana. Qal'at al-Maraya, Jesus. Please be careful, duckie. Good idea to go down with Ella. Don't try it on your own."

"I couldn't even if I wanted to. Otherwise I'd be in a taxi right now."

"Yes. Well."

"Dad, can I ask you something?"

"Of course."

"What did you and Mum do back in South Africa?"

He laughed. "In fifty words or less?"

"I mean, were you in prison? You never really told me."

"Why are you asking now?"

"It came up . . . in a conversation. And I realized that I had no idea."

"I'm sure I told you we were in prison, for four months. I was in for four, your mother for three."

"I'd like to know more."

"Why don't you come visit, duckie? I'll be happy to tell you about all our antics."

"Why didn't you tell me when I was younger?"

"To protect you, I suppose. It would have upset you."

"Why?"

"Well, we had a hard time. The bad old days. When are you coming to visit?"

"We'll both come, we'll come together. Me and Daniel. It will be so great!"

"Yes, that really would be a dream come true."

"Bye, Dad."

"Hugs."

Rafi was sitting at the kitchen counter, smoking and looking at a newspaper, but I could tell he wasn't concentrating on what he was reading.

"My father's a bit of a mystery to me," I said.

"Why?"

"He just is. He's quiet, but there's a lot going on inside his brain."

"Have you met his wife?"

"No, she's afraid of flying. They're very happy together. Guess what? Volvo thinks he's gay."

"I can't think about Volvo right now," Rafi said.

"I've never seen you like this. Of course, I've only known you for a week . . ."

Before he could to answer, the phone rang. It was Ella.

"Hi, Dana?" she said. "Odelia told me you were trying to reach me."

"Yes, it's about Daniel. He's living in Qal'at al-Maraya."

"Yes, I know. Do you want to see him?"

"Of course!"

"I can take you tomorrow."

"You mean—you've known all this time?"

"We can talk about it when we meet. I've already spoken to him; I had a feeling that's what you were calling about."

"You spoke to him!"

"Yes, he's expecting you."

"I'm so confused."

"We'll talk on the way there. I really have to run—I have a situation here."

"Okay."

"Meet me at the train station at six in the morning, we'll get an early start. Bring water, your ID, of course, and a sandwich. It can take a bit of time. Bye." She hung up.

"Well," Rafi said.

"I'm so confused!" I repeated. "Ella knows. It sounds as if she knew where Daniel was all along. Why didn't she tell me? She's spoken to him! She told him I'd called her."

"Ella knows a lot of things no one else knows. Don't forget she's there all the time, she knows hundreds of people. Dana, maybe she's the one who's been picking up his mail."

"But now I'm so angry with her. And yet she's my only link . . ."

"Don't blame her. She's a journalist, she has to know how to keep some things secret. It's Daniel who asked her not to tell you. You should be angry with him if anyone."

"You're not really reading that newspaper, are you? Let's talk." We moved to the living room and sat at opposite ends of the sofa.

"No, I'm not angry with him," I said. "Because he has a reason. Ella didn't have a reason."

"What did Daniel say?"

"He said I could come."

"How do you feel?"

"I'm so nervous, you can't imagine. I feel a hundred things. I'm happy, I'm excited."

"You're afraid."

"No. Yes. Not of him."

"Are you afraid he'll reject you in person?"

"No, he won't reject me, not when he sees me, when he sees how much I love him."

"He's forty-seven now, isn't he?"

"Yes, that's true. That's true. I still think of him as thirty-six, but he's older, of course."

"Are you afraid of what you'll feel?"

"No, I'll feel happy, I just want to see him and be with him, it's a dream come true. I know what I'm afraid of. I'm afraid it's a trick. I mean, why would he agree, just because I found him? Is it some kind of game? 'You can't see me until you find me?'"

"He probably figured there wasn't anything he could do at this point. You'd found him, and now you'd have to see him."

"I don't believe this is happening. I'm afraid something will ruin it. That's what I'm afraid of. That he'll dodge me again."

"There's nowhere left for him to go."

"I'll bring him the silk dressing gown I bought when he was in the hospital, just before he escaped. I've kept it for him, it's still in perfect condition. What else? Should I bring some photographs? No . . . I'll wait with those. I don't want any distraction, I just want us. Maybe just the bird photo, it's my favorite one."

"What bird photo?"

"Remember the demo at Rmeid? On the anniversary of the killings?"

"Yes, I was there."

"Remember how the police and army agreed to stay away? A moment of sanity! They were actually able to see that if they just didn't show up everything would go smoothly. Well, I was right up front, and I saw some of these very religious Muslim guys in their green robes waving their green flags and I admit I was a bit scared. I figured—fundamentalists, who knew what they were up to. Suddenly they all got very excited. They began pointing and shouting and I thought, Oh no, the police are here after all, shit. They were really agitated and I was sure violence was about to break out. And then I saw what they were pointing at. Birds! A whole flock of black birds, hundreds of birds in formation, sweeping across the white sky. I have a shot of that, of the birds and the guys in the robes pointing at the birds and getting all excited. Maybe they thought the birds were the souls of the boys who were killed. The picture came out really good, I'll show it to you later. Maybe I'll just bring that one to show Daniel."

"I wonder whether the army was worried that he'd crossed over."

"Worried about what? He didn't know anything, apart from

how to fold uniforms. But I still can't believe that Ella knew. She let me suffer. She let me suffer all these years. I hate her."

"Maybe it hasn't been years."

"Yes, it must have been, because she's been reporting from there for years, and obviously she'd know about something like that. How could she be so cruel?"

"Maybe it was really hard for her," Rafi said. "Maybe she thought that if Daniel really didn't want to see you, telling you his address wouldn't do anyone any good."

"Don't defend her. Anyhow, who cares. The main thing is that I'm going to see him!"

"I hope it goes well, Dana."

"Yes. I'll bring him back here. I'll bring him back and we can start having a life again, both of us."

"He may not want to come back. Why not wait and see?"

"I wonder how he feels, knowing I'll be coming tomorrow?"

"Probably even more nervous than you."

"I don't know how I'll survive until tomorrow. Yes, I do know. Can you stay? Can you stay with me, or do you have to be home?"

"I can stay."

"I still love you."

"I know."

"But Daniel comes first."

"No one has to come first or second."

"Maybe not in the way people feel, but in what people do they have to make a choice."

"That's true."

"I want to be with you until tomorrow. And then it will be over."

"Don't plan everything, Dana. Life's easier if you don't make too many plans."

"You think it won't work out between me and Daniel, but you're wrong. You don't know how close we were."

"I just think you need to take things a step at a time. It's been eleven years. A lot has happened to Daniel since then. Try to imagine what his life has been like. He must have found a way to integrate into that society. He might be a different person now."

"No, he's not different. His personality was too strong. And our societies aren't that different! We have a lot in common."

"Whatever happens, I'll stand by you."

"Thank you. Let's go somewhere. I don't want to stay here, I want to feel this is his place now."

"We can go to a hotel if you like."

"Yes, I'd like that. You know, Coby offered us a room."

He laughed. "Are you sure that's not too far? We don't want to get carried away."

"It doesn't have to be another part of the country, just another place. Am I being selfish?"

"No, it makes sense, Dana. I'm surprised you haven't asked me to leave altogether."

"I'd like to, but I can't."

"Dana, are you punishing Daniel?"

"What do you mean? That I'm using you? Using you to get back at him for leaving me? Is that what you think?"

"I'm asking."

"I'm not using you." Tears rolled down my cheeks. "That's the second time you've made me cry."

"I'm glad. You haven't been crying enough since Daniel left."

"No, I didn't cry, because I knew I'd see him. I knew we'd be together again. And I was right. Let's go across the street and check in."

"Yes. Good old Coby."

❖

"Nice room."

"Mm."

"That was very moving, the way the two of you said hello."

"Who?"

"You and Coby."

"What do you mean?"

"The way you both looked at each other. As if you were incredibly happy to see one another."

"I guess we were close once. Coby was a sniper, though; so a lot of the time we had different assignments."

"I asked him about the lynching. He said he had no idea what I was talking about."

"Is that what he said?"

"Yes."

"He was standing right next to me. He threw up. A lot of us felt like puking, but he actually did. Then he reported the two guys."

"Is he married?"

"Yes, he has two daughters, he's done well for himself."

"I shouldn't have brought that up."

"I don't mind. Maybe you're trying to get your mind off other things. Or to talk about them in terms of my experiences."

"That's an odd way of looking at it . . . I forgot to tell Volvo I won't be looking in tonight. Oh well, he'll manage."

"I wonder whether he was so aggressive before he lost his legs."

"I met someone who knew him from before—he said Volvo was one of the funniest and most upbeat people he knew. He always had a mind of his own, though. He left his family, became secular, not a lot of people do that. I think they told him that was why he lost his legs, that it was a punishment from God . . . Listen to us! This is what lovers talk about in this country! What a place to live!"

"How about we banish the world for the next twenty hours?"

"What did you tell Graciela?"

"I told her you'd found Daniel. She was very happy for you."

"She's really strange."

"She's pimping for me. It makes her feel in control, she thinks she chose you. You're a safe partner in her eyes, and this way she doesn't feel as bad about not sleeping with me."

"You didn't tell me that before."

"Besides, she really does like you, Dana. Is there anyone who doesn't like you, by the way?"

"Lots of people. My sergeant hated me with a passion. I ran into her a couple of years ago and she still hates me. And one of the journalists who interviewed me about Daniel said I was pathetic, neurotic, self-absorbed. She thought waiting for Daniel was self-indulgence of the first order, and also selfish of me. The woman at the photo shop can't stand me—she's always making snide remarks."

"Did you tell that interviewer to go to hell?"

"No, she was right. She was right about me. Beatrice also thinks it's self-indulgence, and she's my friend."

"Are you and Beatrice close?"

"Not really, though she sometimes stays the night. It's nothing serious. It worked out for me too, it was my way of having sex without betraying Daniel."

"That sort of turns me on."

"It was nothing special. She's not the romantic type. I'm not going to continue seeing her now, of course."

"How old is she?"

"Who knows! Impossible to tell. She lost a son in '89, if that's a clue. But I think she had him very young, he was her eldest. She has a five-year-old, too. I thought we were banishing the outside world."

"Harder than it sounds."

"You understand people better than I do, Rafi."

"I don't understand anyone."

"I love you."

"I love you."

"I love Daniel."

"So one gathers."

"You have a scar here, I didn't notice before."

"Yes, a knife found its way to my thigh. I didn't even feel it when it happened. Guy grabbed my rifle strap, stuck a knife in my leg. I wasn't aware it was happening, I didn't feel a thing. Someone pointed out to me afterward that I was bleeding."

"I guess it's hopeless. We'll never succeed in having the sort of conversation lovers have in Hollywood films. We're doomed."

"We're haunted."

"We're possessed."

"We're horny."

"We're in love."

"We're sexy."

"We're fabulous."

"I love your body. I love your breasts."

"You're handsome. Extremely handsome."

"Yes, everyone always said so. Especially my mother."

"Your eyes are black."

"Dark brown."

"They look black. I love your mouth. Are we doing better now?"

"Much better."

"How come I don't feel guilty, Rafi?"

"Because you're angry at Daniel."

"I'm not. I understand him. I feel bad for him."

"Okay."

"I'm happy I'm here with you. Thank you for coming, thank

you for staying with me until I go. Thank you for not minding that it's the last time. You're very nice to me, Rafi."

"I'm hoping it won't be the last time. I want you to find Daniel, of course. But I hope we can go on being lovers."

"I'm not the type."

"I don't think Daniel's going to come back here, Dana."

"He will."

"He's probably become attached to his home."

"This is his home."

"Well . . . I'm sure he's missed you. I'm sure he still misses you."

"You must have women falling in love with you all the time. You're so cute . . ."

"Some women have come on to me, but whether it's love . . . I have no idea."

"I hope I didn't hurt Benny too much."

"Benny again! What's Benny doing in this room? I'm ready to put up with Daniel, but that's my limit."

"I forget you're not my therapist. Rafi, what do you see in me? I can't figure it out."

"I like your breasts."

"Seriously."

"Well, what do you like about yourself? The things you like are probably the things I like."

"I don't like myself that much. I'm boring."

"Boring . . . is that what you think? What's boring about you?"

"I do the same things all the time."

"Yes, but they're charming things, Dana. But I'm not going to tell you what I like about you, because it's going to make you too vain. Especially since I am possibly on the verge of losing you forever and being heartbroken for the next few years."

"You're just joking around."

"No, I'm not joking around. If you don't see me anymore it's going to hurt me. What do you think?"

"I guess I find it hard to believe you're really attached to me."

"You don't want to believe it, Dana, because it's inconvenient."

"I told you this would be a mess. And you said no. You said you believe in happy endings."

"If only life would cooperate."

"Let's not talk anymore, Rafi. Words ruin things. Let's just love each other."

"Fine with me."

"Do that thing you did last time."

"You mean this?"

# MONDAY

I LEFT THE HOTEL ROOM BEFORE RAFI WOKE. I was glad he was sleeping; I didn't want to say good-bye. I dressed quietly and left him a note, telling him I'd call him from the Coastal Strip to let him know I was all right, and asking him not to phone me. Then I went back to my flat and packed the dressing gown and the photograph of the men and the birds. I decided to take my toothbrush and a change of clothes as well, since I would be staying overnight. I assumed Daniel would need time to get organized, and that I'd stay with him until he was ready to come back.

In the taxi to the train station my heart was pounding, and I was having difficulty breathing. The driver asked me whether I was feeling unwell.

"I'm just excited," I said. "I'm going to see my husband. I haven't seen him in eleven years." Telling a stranger something that was utterly meaningless for him, but of such immense significance to me, was a diversionary tactic. Or maybe I was trying to pull this event out of the realm of the supernatural to the surface of normal life, in order to give it weight and presence.

"He's been out of the country?"

"Yes."

"Why so long?"

"He got lost."

The driver laughed. "You're funny," he said. Then he sighed happily. "I'm laughing, I'm sitting here next to you. And I'm alive. You don't appreciate life until you see death. Two hours ago I was sure it was the end for me . . . I haven't come so close since the fucking war."

"Which war?"

"Take your pick."

"What happened?"

"I swore to myself I wouldn't do drug pickups, but business is so lousy. I have to eat, I have to pay the rent. And drug pickups pay really well, one hundred fifty shekels for a twenty-minute ride, there and back. So I figured, what the hell. Without money you can't stay alive anyhow. That's what I said to myself, but it isn't true. I'd rather be in debt and alive, I know that now. Two hours ago I had a gun pointed at my head, because by mistake I got a look at the dealer."

"Do you think it will last, this feeling of being happy to be alive?"

He shrugged. "Probably not. I'd like to hang on to it, though. I really would."

When we arrived at the train station Ella was already there, waiting in her small blue car and talking on her mobile phone. She motioned me to come inside and with her free hand made room for me by moving junk from the passenger seat to the back. The car was like a large suitcase, stuffed with boxes, papers, food wrappers, batteries, a large flashlight, another mobile phone, a tape recorder, hats, socks, a rain jacket, a ratty cushion, blankets, and a bag of disposable diapers.

I waited for Ella to finish her phone conversation. She was speaking in Arabic, with English words inserted here and there when she didn't know the Arabic word. When she was through, she said, "Hi. Thanks for being on time. There's an envelope in the glove compartment . . . that's your permit. I need to stop somewhere for coffee. Coffee, and I also have to pee. What a night . . . don't ask."

"You've been up all night?"

"Yes." She sighed, and pressed on the gas. She was a bit of a wild driver.

We found a food stand and Ella got out to buy coffee and a bottle of water. Then we drove to the apartment building Daniel had given as his address, where the old couple lived now.

"This is where I pick up his mail," Ella said. "You can give him this month's check."

"I can't believe you never told me," I said.

"He asked me not to."

I stepped out of her car and stared at the building. It was a four-story apartment house, menacing, impenetrable, expelling breaths of invisible pain like smoke. Eleven years ago I had kept watch here. I had stationed myself across the street, on a rock, hidden by a row of dry, hostile bushes. I remembered thinking that this was what it was like to be a fugitive. You hid from the rest of civilization and you tried to look unobtrusive. I was afraid to move or sleep; I was afraid I'd miss Daniel's secret messenger. I thought there was even a chance I would see Daniel himself, late at night; maybe he was the one leaving the notes on the door in disguised, alien handwriting. But in the end I had to sleep and I had to eat. I tried to rent a flat in the building, or in the building facing Daniel's, but nothing was available.

We entered the familiar dark hallway. Ella used a key to open the mailbox and took out an envelope. "His allowance," she said.

"Did you leave those notes on the door?"

"What notes?"

"*Gone to the supermarket, back in five minutes.* I still have those notes, I tore them off the door and kept them."

"No, that wasn't me. A widow lived here—I guess those were her notes. She put an ad in the paper, room for rent, and Daniel took it—that is, he paid the rent so he could collect mail here."

"But I knocked on the door, there was never anyone."

"She was a little paranoid."

"Who lives there now? That old couple, who are they?"

"Her relatives, I think. She died, and they moved in."

"Does he still pay rent?"

"No, not for a long time now. But I still pick up his mail here, no one minds."

I took the envelope from her and stared at the label. "Does he get other mail, too?"

"Not really. His mother writes now and then."

"His mother!"

"Yes, she figured out he was getting his mail. And she was right."

I ran out of the building, ran to the bushes in the back, and retched. Ella held my forehead, as if I were a little child.

"Dana, are you with us?"

Ella had pulled my hair back with her hands. I remembered going to my aunt, Belinda, because I thought I had lice. I was in high school, and I didn't want anyone to know, so I went to Belinda, who was an obstetrician. She sat me down on her little round piano stool, next to the balcony, where the light was best. She lifted strands of hair, looked behind my ears, my neck, and suddenly I realized that she was playing with my hair, just playing with my hair entirely for her own pleasure.

"Dana?"

"I'm okay," I said.

"Have some water." She handed me her bottled water and we walked back to the car.

When we were on the highway, Ella said, "We'll only have two checkpoints, if we're lucky. The one at Selah shouldn't be a problem—no one's allowed out of the Coastal Strip, just about, so it's pretty dead. But the checkpoints inside the strip are total pandemonium. It's going to be a long wait once we're inside."

I was shivering. Ella said, "This is very hard for you."

"Why didn't you tell me I could write? Why didn't his mother tell me?"

"She had no way of knowing whether her letters ever reached Daniel. She never had an answer."

"It's my fault, I stopped seeing his family, I stopped going over."

"Daniel saw you on television, he heard you on the radio—it was very clever, what you did. Better than a letter, don't you think?"

"Yes." I was finding it hard to concentrate. "How did he do it? How did he go into hiding there?"

"I don't know the details. Maybe he'll tell you about it."

"But if the army has his real address, how come they send the checks to that place?"

She shrugged. "Different department, I guess."

"What does he do there?"

"He's a teacher."

"A teacher!"

"Yes, he teaches math and science, and also English."

"Does he have cable?"

"Yes."

"Does he have friends?"

"That's the impression I get."

"You never told me . . ."

"No, I never told you, Dana. When Daniel first asked me to keep his whereabouts a secret he persuaded me that it was for the best, that you didn't love him. But then I decided, later, that he was wrong and we fought about it. I told him he was being unfair and putting me in a horrible position, as if I don't have enough on my shoulders already. I don't want you to talk about this to anyone, but one of my colleagues once got someone killed. He thought he disguised the information enough in his article but he didn't. He nearly had a nervous breakdown, even though he's not the first person it's happened to and he won't be the last."

"He can't assume it was his fault."

"You tell yourself, 'It wasn't necessarily me, it wasn't necessarily my article,' but deep inside, you know it was. I have to keep secrets, I have no choice. I really tried to get him to call you. But Daniel's stubborn, as stubborn as you are. He wouldn't give in."

"Did he say he missed me?"

"He didn't have to say. I think he saw you once on the beach, when you came to photograph. He can see a section of the beach from his window."

"My God."

"It must have been hard for him, too."

"Never mind. It's all over now, I'm going to see him, the nightmare's over."

"How did you find out?"

"Just by fluke."

"It shows you how cut off we are, that no one found out about Daniel. We're worlds apart, even though in half an hour we're going to be at the border."

"I've been to other checkpoints, but never to Selah. This is the first time in years that I've gone somewhere like this without my camera."

"I'd be interested in seeing your photos sometime."

"Usually I take pictures of people, but at the checkpoints I mostly photograph objects, because they tell you a lot. Once the army sent the border guards some breakfast in a cardboard container, but it was just apples and yogurt, and the guards were so disgusted they kicked the container. I took a photo of the smashed apples and the yogurt spilling out. The container stayed there all day, in the middle of the road, cars drove over it, and it kept getting messier and messier. No one cares. Sometimes I get the feeling the guards are high."

"What makes you say that?"

"Well, I don't know for sure, but I've never seen people behaving that way without drugs. Laughing hysterically, hugging each other, I'd guess it's E. Just once or twice, I got that impression. The worst things I've seen, I've seen at checkpoints. Well, I don't have to tell you, you see it every day."

"There's always some new craziness."

"How come you were up all night?"

"Someone had a problem . . ." she said vaguely.

"Will you write about it?"

"Maybe."

"What's Daniel's life like? Does he speak Arabic?"

"Yes, of course."

"Yes, you said he was a teacher. He'd have to anyhow, to get by. It's so hard to imagine, though . . . is he happy?"

"I don't know, Dana. How can I know something like that?"

"What does he look like? Is he very different?"

"You'll see for yourself."

"But he teaches kids."

"Everyone's used to him in the community. He's well liked."

"I can't picture him as a teacher. He's so goofy. How often do you see him? How often do you talk to him?"

"I go over once a month," she said and there was something

in the way she said it that gave me a jolt. I wondered if what I'd heard in her voice was the memory of sex. She must have sensed my suspicion, because she added a little too quickly, as if to cover her tracks, "I bring him his check and things he wants from the city—books, music."

But I refused to be distracted. "Do you fuck?" I asked, and my callousness surprised me. I'd never spoken to anyone that way.

Her phone rang, and when the conversation was over, we both pretended I hadn't asked her the question, or that she hadn't heard me. "We're here," she said, slowing down.

We had reached Selah, the checkpoint at the northern end of the Coastal Strip. The only other vehicles were carrying people to and from the settlements. We were waved through; they didn't even ask to see my permit.

Seeing the Coastal Strip brought back a flood of memories: the beach, the smell of sea salt and falafel, Palestinian families having picnics on the sand, the bossy young men, the daring women who went into the water with their skirts hitched up. Once a man slapped his wife and all the women on the beach surrounded him with shouts and accusations, while he stood there helplessly; it was only with the greatest effort that I restrained myself from photographing them. There was hope back then, even though it turned out to be an illusion.

Then I remembered that I was going to see Daniel very soon, and my heart began pounding hard and fast.

Almost immediately after Selah, we hit another checkpoint. This one was very chaotic.

We joined a very long queue of cars, taxis, transits, and pedestrians. Young, old, male, female, children, families, students. One young woman, slender and dressed in black slacks and a pale blue blouse, was carrying an infant in her arms. The child looked unwell, and the woman, who could have been a university student, was furious. I had never seen such seething rage. The woman wasn't carrying anything else, only the child; not even a bottle for the child. Whatever she had, money or her ID, must have been in the pockets of her slacks. The baby was asleep, and appeared to be feverish. She made her way through the crowd, pushing ahead of the queue, and no one dared to stop her. I wondered whether her fierce desperation would get her through the checkpoint.

The line crawled forward, inch by inch. There was a small white car ahead of us, with two men inside. Finally the white car reached the barrier. The driver handed the border guard his ID but the two other men in the car didn't have theirs. They began to explain, but the soldier wasn't interested. He motioned to his three friends to come over. The guards dragged out the two men and took them to a wall at the side of the road. They cuffed the men's hands behind their backs, blindfolded them, turned them toward the wall and pushed them down to the ground, because you can't stand up when you're blindfolded and your hands are bound, someone had once explained that to me.

It was the first time I had witnessed this sort of arrest. I had seen men in detention or being taken away in a van or being led to a shed. At times they had been handcuffed, but not blindfolded and pushed down facing a wall. Seeing these things in real life was different from seeing it in newspapers or even on television. I wanted to take a photograph of the arrest but I didn't have my camera. It was impossible to sit there and not do anything. I ran out of Ella's car and threw myself on one of the men, wrapped my arms around him. I felt his warm, surprised body next to mine, his head turning quizzically back, and his blindfold touched my cheek.

The soldier who ordered the three men arrested pulled me away and threw me on the ground. He crouched over me and slapped my arm. "Are you crazy?" he shouted at me. I heard Ella's voice saying, "Leave her alone." But the soldier was too angry. He went on hitting my arm again and again. I had never been hit before, except in play. It was hard to believe that this was a human hand was striking me and not a metal bar; I was unfamiliar with the force of a strong body. I was surprised, too, at how hurt my feelings were. The tears that came to my eyes had more to do with insult than pain.

"Are you out of your mind?" he repeated. "What's wrong with you? What's the matter with you?" He was letting out all his frustration on me.

Ella was shouting at him but he ignored her. Finally one of the border guards, a short kid with an earring, came over and said something. The soldier stood up and lit a cigarette.

"You're completely insane," the kid with the earring told me. He used the plural form, as though I represented an entire race.

I dusted myself off and headed back toward the car.

"Hey." The soldier who had hit me pulled me back. "You're not going anywhere. What's she doing with you, anyhow?" he asked Ella.

"We're together. I have a permit for both of us."

"Yeah. Well, she's forfeited her permit. You can go. She's staying."

I looked at him with disgust. His small brown eyes emitted a dull, steady glow of stupidity. Stupidity was overall his most outstanding characteristic. I remembered a female soldier I had seen once at a new checkpoint that had been set up in a Palestinian neighborhood outside the capital. She was quite young, maybe even a teenager. She had round yellow-green eyes and her face was expressionless as she checked the IDs of pedestrians and let them through. Then three women wrapped up in black and white *hijab* came up to her, and for some unknown reason her face came to life. I don't know why; I don't know what it was about these women, two of them young and pretty, one much older, that roused her from her apathy. "Where are you going?" she asked, and her eyes widened and bulged out, so that the whites showed above and below her yellow-green irises. It was a look that challenged them to prove they deserved to stay alive, while asserting at the same time that they did not. I almost laughed, because I remembered the tactic from high school: there were one or two girls who always tried to make you feel small and inconsequential, and they had perfected that bulge. They had no idea how stupid their faces became when they looked at someone that way: like mechanical toys with defective wiring. And now here was this soldier with her uniform and slanted cap and weapon, trying out that look on these three women. The women didn't seem to notice. "We're going to school, to teach," they said calmly. They were impervious to her contempt; she could keep them from getting through, but she couldn't penetrate their equanimity. Their emotional lives were entirely inaccessible to her, and that was their saving grace. Defeated, the soldier had handed back their IDs and let them pass.

"I have to get through," I said. "Someone's expecting me."

That only made it worse, of course. "In your dreams," the soldier said.

"This is completely arbitrary!" Ella stormed at him.

He didn't bother answering her.

She drove her car to the side of the road and made a few phone calls, waited, negotiated, made more phone calls, but nothing helped, and in the end I persuaded her to continue without me. She had an important meeting to get to; people were counting on her.

"Go sit next to your friends," the soldier ordered. "Not too close, though. And no talking."

"I'm older than you," I said.

"Go."

I sat next to the blindfolded men and leaned my back against the wall. I turned my head to them and said, "I'm sorry." Then I repeated it in English.

"You are the brave," the one next to me answered in English.

There was nothing more to say. I watched as cars and people arrived at the barrier and were either let through without a search, or searched and turned away, or searched and let through. Some of those who were not permitted to pass pleaded and argued, but they didn't have a chance with the stupid soldier. I wanted to kick him in the balls.

I sat there for two hours. I tried calling Rafi on my mobile phone, but he didn't answer, so I left a message telling him I was under arrest. My back began to hurt and I was dying of thirst; I'd finished my small bottle of water. I could tell the men next to me were thirsty too and I asked the kid with the earring to give them water. He came over with a plastic bottle and brought it to their mouths as if they were handicapped and he was their nurse. I got up and stretched, then sat down again. The blindfolded men were much more patient than I was; they seemed almost to be in a meditative state. I wondered whether they were in fact praying, or whether they were just very patient. I'd often noticed how patient Palestinians were in general. They didn't get antsy the way we did.

Finally a police car arrived. I said good-bye to the two blindfolded men. "God send you good luck," one of them said.

An officer ushered me into the backseat of the car and drove me to one of the settlements, a closed-off suburban haven in the midst of hell. It was my first time in a settlement and I was terrified of being killed.

The police station was white and new and oddly silent. "This station looks like a sugar cube some giant dropped on the lawn," I told the officer. I could tell he liked the image, but he pretended he hadn't heard me.

The inside of the building was as neat and sterile as the outside. The police officer sat on one side of a desk and I sat facing him. It was a game, a ridiculous game with assigned roles, and I wondered how we hadn't all tired of playing it. I wondered how it was that we weren't bored to death. Well, I was bored. I had finally reached the point where I was bored to death.

"What were you doing here?" the police officer asked me. He was bald and he looked a bit like a toad. He had mild toad eyes and a squat amphibian body. If I kissed him he would turn into a handsome prince.

"I'm a terrorist, can't you tell?"

"Let's start over. What are you doing here?"

"I'm visiting my husband."

"Is this another joke? Don't push me, I'm not in a good mood."

"It's not a joke. I apologize, I'm just frustrated. I'm here to see my husband."

"Your husband, where?"

"My husband lives in Qal'at al-Maraya."

"You're married to an Arab?"

"No. He was wounded in the army and he went into hiding. I just found out. So I've come to see him."

"In the army! I can't make heads or tails of your story."

"Well, that's the story."

"What's he doing in a Palestinian city? Did he have a . . . you know . . . breakdown or something?"

"Yes. He lost his mind, so he went to live in Qal'at al-Maraya, and now I want to see him."

"You're better off without him! How come I never heard about this? An insane former soldier living in a Palestinian town!"

"I don't know. Check your computer. He's there."

"What were you doing trying to free a prisoner?"

"I wasn't trying to free him. Obviously! How could I? I just wanted to . . . I just couldn't bear to watch it."

"Next time stay at home. This isn't a place for the softhearted. Do you think we're here to play Ping-Pong?"

"Aren't you bored? Aren't you sick and tired of all this?"

"Of course I'm sick and tired of it! You think you have a monopoly on that? You think only the left knows what's going on? If you think that, you have even less brains than I gave you credit for."

"This is Palestine. This isn't our land."

"You can say that about the whole country. All right, you can go. I'll get someone to drive you."

"Yes, yes, you *can* say it about the whole country. We don't even deserve the part we have. You can write that in my file."

"Believe it or not, Miss Hillman, this interview has come to an end. Someone will drive you to Selah. You can wait outside."

"A settler?"

"Yes."

"No, I don't want to get into a car with a settler. I want to live a few more years."

"The car is bulletproof."

"Just take me to the gate, I'll take a Palestinian transit. Or I'll walk."

"You don't have a choice. A car is going to take you to Selah. Once you cross over, you can take whatever means of transportation you want. We don't ever want to see you here again."

"You can't keep me out."

"Yes we can."

He told me to wait, and returned a few minutes later with a driver. The driver looked like an ordinary person, someone I might have seen on any city street. But we were enemies: he hated me for supporting the Palestinians and I hated him for living in a settlement. I climbed into the back of his luxurious, air-conditioned limousine; it was the most expensive car I'd ever been in. He drove me to Selah, which was in fact only minutes away from the settlement. Neither of us said anything, not even good-bye; we were both too angry.

Standing before me at Selah was a magnificent man. He had a close white and charcoal beard and small metal-rimmed glasses, very slightly tinted. He wasn't wearing the uniform of a border guard, and he wasn't a soldier; he appeared to be another sort of guard, sent here perhaps to fill in for someone. His navy bulletproof vest lay against his body like a baby carrier. He had broad shoulders and he stood with his hands in his pockets, looking relaxed, casual, and modest; he could have been a crossing guard at a school. His body and his thin mouth suggested a gentle soul, kind and good. He was almost certainly an immigrant, and this was probably the only job he could find in these hard times.

I knew at once that he would help me. I went up to him, showed him my permit, and said, "I need to get to Qal'at al-Maraya." I had no idea whether news of my arrest had reached him. In any case, he nodded and without taking his hands out of his pockets indicated with a movement of his head that I could pass through.

I turned around and began walking down the road toward Qal'at al-Maraya. I had no idea how I would pass the second checkpoint, the one with the violent soldier, but I'd find a way. Nothing could stop me.

❖

A taxi slowed down next to me, and even though I would have preferred to walk, I couldn't refuse. The drive to the checkpoint was very short and the driver wanted to charge me half a shekel. It was a ridiculously low amount, even for a short ride. I gave him ten shekels and he was very grateful. As I stepped out he surprised me by saying, "Thank you for what you did. You were very brave." I wondered by what remarkable system of communication word spread so quickly in the strip.

I joined the long queue of bodies at the checkpoint. Everyone was dusty, miserable and fretful. They clutched documents; they were hot; some of the children were too tired to stand, and their parents held them until the parents were also tired. Many of the people in line were sick. One or two hobbled on crutches, and several sat by the side of the road, pale and feverish. I could have been at some nineteenth-century procession at Lourdes, except that no one here expected a miracle.

Progress was very slow and it took me an hour to reach the barrier. The kid with the earring stared at me in amazement. He couldn't believe I was back. He called over an officer, a huge man with a blank, narrow face and sunglasses that returned your own reflection when you looked at them. The officer kept gulping water from a canteen he held in his left hand.

He said, "Weren't you told that we don't want to see you again?"

"I need to get in. Please. I'm going to see my husband," I said. "He lives here."

The officer was confused. "You're married to a Palestinian?"

"No, he just lives here."

"Wait."

He disappeared into a little hut covered with rubbery camouflage. When he came out a few minutes later, he said, "You can't go in. Especially you. If you don't leave I have instructions to arrest you."

"I have a permit."

"Your permit is void."

"I want to see my husband."

"It isn't up to me."

"I won't leave until you let me through."

"You will leave."

"No I won't." I sat down on the ground.

The officer bent down and lifted me. "You're quite light," he said. He slung me over his shoulders, carried me to a closed army van, and came inside with me. The van smelled of rust, sweat, and rancid food; its floor and walls were filthy and the seats were covered with sticky black dirt. The man seemed much too big for the small compartment. *Fe fi fo fum,* I thought. *I smell the blood of an Englishman.* My father used to read me that story.

"Please let me through. Please. I want to see my husband. I haven't seen him in eleven years." I stared at his sunglasses, at my own distorted face in the silvery lenses.

"Maybe he doesn't want to see you."

"He does. He really does."

"What the hell is he doing living in a Palestinian city?"

"Hiding."

"What did you do to him?" he joked.

"It isn't funny."

"He must be a bit wrong in the head. What do you need that for? You're better off without him, believe me. Smoke?"

"No thanks."

He lit a cigarette and looked at me, or at least I assumed he was looking at me; I couldn't be sure because of his glasses. He smiled cynically. "So, Dana, Dana. What are we going to do with you, Dana?"

"I'm not leaving."

"We'll just have to take you back, then. It may take a while, though."

"Fine. Then I'll come back another time and I'll just sneak in and I'll get shot and it will be your fault," I said. "Because nothing is going to stop me. I've waited eleven years and if I can't see my husband I don't care if I live or die. And it's going to be your fault, yours personally. You'll see my picture in the paper and you'll know I died because of you."

He was upset when I said that. I couldn't tell by looking at his face, but I sensed it in his body, in the air between us.

"You can't sneak in."

"Yes I can. I'll just bypass the roadblock, or run through. And some guard will order me to stop and I won't and he'll think I'm Palestinian and he'll shoot me. Or else some militant will think I'm a settler and kill me. Either way, I'll die."

He paused, and I could see him trying to decide what to do. Finally he made up his mind. "Okay. okay, I'll let you through."

"Thank you."

"How long are you planning to stay?"

"I don't know. Not long."

"I'm trusting you."

"Do I look like a dangerous person?"

"Looks don't mean anything. And your husband—well, he's gone over to the other side. He's obviously dangerous."

"My husband is a recluse. He was burned in an accident in the army, he's disfigured, that's why he's hiding."

"What kind of stupid reason is that?"

"You're right, it's stupid."

"I never heard of such a thing. It's bullshit. He's obviously not telling you everything. Be careful, don't trust him. You're too trusting, I can see that."

"Okay."

"And you . . . eleven years. Why can't you face the fact that he's lost interest in you? You remind me of my girlfriend. Three years she wouldn't get the message—I had to get a court order in the end. What is it with you women?"

"I don't know."

"You can go. Be careful, Dana. Use your head."

❉

I desperately needed a few minutes alone. I ducked behind a tree and tried to make myself very small as I slid to the ground, my back against the trunk. A faint, damp smell of sewage water hung in the air, and the current crop on this patch of land was cigarette butts. My body felt brittle, as if my veins had turned into electric wires. I remembered dreams I'd had when my mother died: I would lift a panel on my skin and discover that I was made not of flesh and bone but of robot parts and batteries. I reached into my bag and touched the soft silk of the dressing gown. It now seemed a very odd thing to do, bringing a silk dressing gown to this place—like clutching at a box of candy during a shipwreck. But I didn't care. Touching the dressing gown comforted me.

I took my phone out of my pocket and called Rafi. This time he answered. "I'm so glad you called. I heard what happened from Ella. Are you all right?"

"Ella called you?"

"I called her, after I got your message."

"Well, I got through. I got past the checkpoint, I'm on my way to Qal'at al-Maraya."

"Where are you?"

"I'm sitting on the side of the road at the moment. Hiding behind a tree."

"Ella said you were arrested. She said some asshole beat you."

"Yeah, but I'm fine now. The main thing is that I got through."

"You're okay?"

"Yes. Rafi?"

"I'm here."

"I love you."

"Thank you for calling, Dana."

"I'll always love you."

"I'll expect that in triplicate, please. By Tuesday at the latest."

"I felt really bad a few minutes ago, but I'm better now."

"Be careful, Dana."

"I'm already a hero here."

"Just be careful. No one trusts anyone, and that includes you."

"I think I'm only about twenty minutes from the city. Oh . . . I've been found." Five teenage boys and two little girls had emerged out of nowhere. They appeared to be brothers and sisters. "I have to go," I said. "I'll call you later. I promise." I rose and smiled at the kids.

"Hi, how are you?" a thin boy wearing black rubber boots asked me in English.

"Fine. How are you?"

"Where from?"

"South Africa."

"Welcome, welcome. Stay with us in house?"

"I can't. I'm on my way to see my husband."

"You want almond?"

"Yes, thank you."

"I go bring," the boy said. He gave the other children instructions, and dashed away.

"Brothers and sisters?" I asked.

The smallest girl nodded. She was a bright little thing, and I was not surprised that she already understood English.

The boy returned almost instantly with almonds wrapped in newspaper. "Thank you," I said. I took out my wallet and gave them five shekels, each. They were delighted, and began debating among themselves in Arabic; my guess was that they were trying to decide whether to ask for more, seeing as I was both a millionaire and generous.

"I have to go now," I said. "Be careful," I added. The boy burst out laughing. He translated what I'd said to the others, and they all laughed.

"Be careful, not die!" the boy echoed. "Be careful!" Then he led his troupe away.

I turned toward the road and an empty transit stopped immediately.

"I have to get to Qal'at al-Maraya." I showed the driver the address.

"I take you," he said. He was a lined, leathery man who looked as though he'd spent his entire life resisting the elements, with only partial success.

My heart began beating fast again as we drove. When we entered the city, I began to tremble.

"Qal'at al-Maraya," the driver announced proudly.

I stared out of the window and tried to calm down. I remembered the first time I saw the city, how surprised I was by its size. High-rises, wide streets, boulevards lined with palm trees, hundreds of new sun-bleached apartment and office buildings, wealthy suburbs that looked like country clubs. The poorer areas were lively and noisy, and seemed shielded by the powerful presence of the sea. At dusk, a soft mauve light enveloped the entire city like a veil.

"It's changed a little since I was last here," I told the transit driver.

He sighed and shook his head. "Yes, many change. Look." He slowed down as we passed a scene of devastation: collapsed buildings, piles of rubble, broken glass everywhere. In big red letters someone had scrawled on the remains of a wall, *Gift from America*. The wall was riddled with holes.

"Here fifteen dead. Four children, one baby."

There were other signs of distress in the city. Stores were closed and there was graffiti everywhere. Litter had accumulated on the sidewalks and several lampposts were bent out of shape. Skinny cats dashed behind cars; a garbage pail had rolled into the middle of the road and the driver had to stop the car and move the pail to the sidewalk. Very few people were out on the streets.

"You visit friend?"

"Husband."

"Yes? Good. Family good."

He drove to the northern end of the city and stopped in front of an unusual house, oval instead of square or rectangular, with three nearly identical sections one on top of the other, a little like a wedding cake.

"This it," the driver said.

"Thank you."

"You want I wait?"

"No thanks, I'm staying for a while. Is twenty shekels okay?"

"God protect you," he said. "You are brave, you help our people. *Ma' salame.*"

I climbed the five stairs leading to the door of the house and knocked. I was barely breathing.

Daniel opened the door and let me in. His eyes had not changed, they were exactly the same. His face was unrecognizable, though. He looked like a wrinkled Martian.

I glanced around me. The room was oblong, with gently curving corners and a spiral wooden staircase at one end. It was filled with sculptures, some life-size and others very small. The large ones were white stone and the small ones were painted clay. They were all of me.

Rage swept through my body like something blind that was looking for a way out. I had never felt such anger before. I began hitting Daniel with my fists. I didn't care where my fists landed. He put his arms up to protect himself, but I didn't stop, and finally he took my wrists in his hands. I pulled away, turned my back to him. I walked over to the nearest table, picked up a brightly painted clay sculpture and smashed it on the floor.

"I liked that one," Daniel said. His voice was also the same: it was the voice I had fallen in love with, loved still.

"I hate you," I said. I was crying.

Daniel said, "I'll make tea."

"No, I don't want anything."

"If you want to leave, it's okay."

"That's what you'd like, isn't it?"

"No, I think we should talk. But if you want to go, I'll understand."

"How could you have done this to me? How could you be so cruel? And what sort of bullshit is that about being another person! You're exactly the same person. What's changed? Nothing! And for some crazy imaginary neurotic insane reason you leave me and hurt me and don't contact me and don't phone me and I have to wonder whether you're still alive and worry about you all the time and long for you and suffer. And not even know that I can write to you and then I find out that someone is picking up your mail, and I have to go around like some desperate beggar, pleading for your address and everyone saying *you have the address, you have it*. And you sit here like some sort of Hunchback of Notre Dame and you make statues of me which I never knew you even knew how to do, suddenly you're a sculptor, and it's creepy, when all along you could have me, and don't try to fool me, I know you're perfectly sane, you don't fool me. You're just a fucking asshole, that's what you are."

Daniel said, "Come upstairs, Dana."

He began climbing up the spiral stairs. I followed him. I noticed that he'd lost weight.

"You're thinner than you were."

"I guess I'm more active."

There was a kitchen area at the far end of the second floor and a double bed near the stairway. Shelves holding neat rows of books and CDs lined the walls.

Daniel lit the stove and put the kettle on.

We both sat at the table and stared at each other. Then Daniel smiled. His face changed completely; he looked like a grinning cat. A grinning Martian cat.

"What are you smiling about?" I asked. I was sulking now.

"You haven't changed at all, Dana. I'm happy to see you."

The kettle whistled and Daniel placed mint leaves in two glass cups with handles and poured water over them and stirred in sugar. He placed the glass cups on the table and sat down facing me.

I didn't drink the tea. Instead, I folded my arms and looked at Daniel defiantly.

"How did you find me?" he asked.

"I met a man on the beach. And he said how come you don't have a family. And I said, I have a husband but he's fucking hiding and he said well I'm in a special fucking unit and I have access to every fucking citizen in this fucking country and if you want I'll get his address for you from my fucking computer. Only he didn't of course. But at least he told me the army knew. So I looked for someone in Intelligence. That's how."

"Ella told me you threw yourself on someone under arrest at the checkpoint."

"Yeah."

"You must have known it would get you into trouble."

"Yes, it's my fault I had trouble getting here. It's my fault I never thought to ask Ella, hey, by the way, do you happen to have my husband's address and are you the one who picks up his mail? And it's my fault that every office I went to they gave me that fake address and said you were there. And it's my fault I spent a year of my life trying to find you, hiring private detectives, running to every office I could, stalking that building so I could see who was putting those signs on the door, sitting in the rain an entire night hoping I'd catch them, it's my fault. What is this, some sort of hide-and-seek game?"

"You know, Dana, that's not what I meant. I meant that it was very brave of you to do that, knowing you'd get into trouble, and given how badly you wanted to see me. I'm sure those men appreciated it. I didn't mean that you planned it in order to avoid seeing me. I know you wanted to see me."

"Why did you agree, all of a sudden?"

"I didn't have a choice. Ella said you'd found me."

"And if you had a choice I wouldn't be sitting here right now?"

"I'm glad you're here."

He brought a bowl of delicious-looking chocolate squares to the table, but I didn't touch them either. I said, "Maybe you fell in love with someone else?"

"No, I haven't been with anyone."

"And now?"

"I still love you."

"No, no—you can't love me. You'd never do this to someone you loved. You didn't even leave me a child!"

"I was sure you'd find someone else."

"I guess you just don't know anything about me."

"Lots of guys wanted you when we were together."

"Who? What are you talking about? What are you saying?"

"I'm saying that I thought you'd have a lot of offers and that you'd take one."

"Yes, and that's all I needed, offers, and I'd accept them,

because anyone will do, after all, what does it matter, one man is as good as another. And by the way I had no offers at all. Because everyone knew how I felt. Because for a year I couldn't even see straight. Literally. I thought I was going blind. Every morning I'd wake up with blurred vision. I thought I had a brain tumor and I didn't care, because I didn't want to go on living without you."

"You were angry."

"No, I wasn't angry. Because I'm an idiot. I should have said to myself, well forget him, because he obviously doesn't love you because if he loved you he wouldn't do this to you. But all I thought about was how you didn't understand and I just had to explain it to you. But now I realize that there's nothing to understand. You knew how I felt and you didn't care. Those statues, they're just lies. And since when are you a sculptor anyhow?"

"I always liked doing that sort of thing, as you know."

"I don't know anything about you, apparently."

"Do you want a different kind of tea? Or maybe some hummus?"

"No thanks." I got up from the table and began inspecting my surroundings. The bed was covered with an elaborate embroidered bedspread.

"Where did you get the bedspread?"

"It was a gift from the mother of one of the kids I taught."

I examined the CDs and books and videos on his shelves. He had all the latest music, along with his old favorites. He had the most recent novels, too.

There were a few books in Arabic. "Was Arabic hard to learn?"

"Pretty hard."

"Ella said you're a teacher now."

"I teach at the local school."

"Well, you always were brainy. I guess you designed this house?"

"Yes."

"Who built it?"

"Local builders."

"Did they think it was weird?"

"No, they liked it. This house isn't mine, technically. I rent the land, and I rent the house. But the plot was vacant, so I designed the house myself. The owners got a good deal."

"How could you afford it?"

"My mother sold Granny's flat and sent me the money. She figured I'd need it, wherever I was."

"I can't believe she never told me she was writing to you."

"One of the things she mentioned in her letters was that you'd stopped going over to see them, or answering their calls. So she probably never had a chance to tell you."

"How could you not answer her letters?"

"She never asked for an answer. She always wrote, *I know that you're receiving my letters, and that's enough for me.*"

"Yes, that's why I was so angry at your family—they thought it should be enough for me, too."

"No, they knew perfectly well that it wasn't. My mother chided me quite a bit about that."

"Really?"

"Yes."

"Why didn't you pick up the letters I wrote you at the start? Do you have any idea how much that hurt me?"

"You would have been even angrier if the letters had been picked up and you never got an answer. But you kept me informed through your interviews."

"That's what Ella said. Well, it would have been a lot easier to write to you! Did you see my ads?"

"Yes."

"How did you get the people here to trust you right in the middle of the riots? How come they didn't kill you?"

"It's a long story."

"Tell me." I leaned against the wall, my arms still folded. Daniel remained sitting at the table, drinking his tea.

"I didn't come here to move in. I got into a taxi outside the hospital and I told the driver to take me to an isolated part of the coast. He lived in a coastal settlement, as it happened. It was just a fluke. He dropped me off at their beach, a little reluctantly, and I walked along the shore, southward. I guess I knew it was dangerous, but I didn't care. Finally I got tired and I sat on the sand, trying to figure out what to do with my life. Some people passed by, but when they saw me they got scared and ran away. I had a bottle of Valium I'd stolen from the hospital and I finally decided that the best thing would be to swallow all the pills. So that's what I did. But some Palestinians found me, maybe the ones who had run away, and they took me home with them. Well, you know how the Palestinians are. They had no idea what was wrong with me, so they just put me to bed, and three days later I woke up. I still don't understand why I didn't die."

"People don't die from too much Valium. It's not toxic enough. I used to volunteer at a suicide hotline, they taught us that stuff."

"Well, anyhow, I woke up, and they were really happy. The family had a retarded boy and I taught him to eat by himself. Then after about two weeks a group of men came to visit me. They were very friendly, apologetic, but they said they needed to know what my plans were. I told them I'd like to stay. It seemed to me that if I had to remain alive, this would be the best place. No one knew me here—I could have a new identity. They wanted to know how I'd been injured, and what my political views were, and what I thought of their struggle and whether I knew any Palestinians. I told them about Isa, the architect who had his keys taken away in that place I worked at, remember him? By coincidence, they knew him—he has some relatives in one of the camps. They spoke to him and I guess he gave me a good reference. I told them I wanted to stay and learn Arabic and that I could be a teacher and help out. I'm making it a lot shorter than it was. It really took longer, and it was more complicated, but that's the essence. After all these years, the people here are still a bit of a mystery to me. Sometimes they all start laughing, and you have no idea what the joke is. They have some sort of collective understanding about things, and you have no idea how they reached it. They rely less on words than we do—they often communicate in more subtle ways. So I don't exactly know why they decided to accept me. Maybe it was just luck."

"Why, Daniel? Why did you leave me? Why?"

"I heard what you told Alex. You thought I was asleep but I wasn't."

"What are you talking about?"

"In the hospital room, when you thought I was sleeping."

"I was never in that room. They wouldn't let me in."

"But I heard you, Dana. You said you were in love with another man, and you had planned to tell me when I came back from reserve duty, but now that I looked like a monster you couldn't do it, and you'd stay with me. I even know the man's name. Leopold."

"Leopold! The only Leopold I know is King Leopold. Or Leopold Bloom. Daniel, you dreamed it. Or you were hallucinating. I can't believe you thought that was real."

"I remember it so vividly."

"Do you think I'd say something like that in your presence? Do you think I'd come when you were asleep but not when you were awake? Daniel, if this is why you left, because of some crazy dream you had, that is the saddest, most ridiculous thing I ever heard in my life. It's like something out of *Wuthering Heights*."

"Well, it doesn't really matter whether it was or wasn't a dream. It would never have worked out between us. If it was a dream, then that's what the dream was telling me."

"What do you mean, 'if'? You think I'm lying to you?"

"I think you might want to protect me, or you might be embarrassed."

"I never lied to you."

"How can I know that?"

"Did you ever catch me lying?"

"Once or twice."

"About what?"

"Well, small things."

"Like what?"

"You said you couldn't find the healthy kind of cat food."

"Cat food! Well, there's a life-and-death issue. Can you have sex, by the way?"

"Yes."

"Have you?"

"Who with? There's no casual sex here, you know."

"I'm even angrier with you now. Angry and insulted. You obviously don't have a shred of trust. And I've waited eleven years to stand here and be called a liar by someone who can't even tell a dream from reality."

"Your tea's getting cold. And you must be hungry."

"I don't want to have tea with someone who has such a low opinion of me."

I continued my inspection of the room. I touched objects, looked inside the wardrobe, opened drawers. I touched his clothes, his sandals. I noticed a few small bowls filled with water on the kitchen floor. "Do you have a cat?"

"Three cats."

"Where are they?"

"Hiding. They're not used to visitors."

"Where's the bathroom?"

"Downstairs."

"What's upstairs?"

"My workshop and the computer."

"Do you have friends?"

"People are friendly to me."

"Are you lonely?"

"Sometimes."

"Do you watch TV?"

"All the time."

"Do you watch Torture TV?"

"Yes."

"Ella said you had cable."

"I did, but it doesn't work now. Everything's messed up here, as you know."

"I brought you a present. Not that you deserve it." I pulled the dressing gown out of my bag. It was creased from being scrunched up all day.

He came over and took the bundle from my hand. "What is this?"

"A dressing gown. It's silk. I bought it for you the day before I was supposed to see you at the hospital. Well, I saved it for you, even though you don't need it anymore. It only got creased today—it was in perfect condition until now. I kept it in plastic."

He unraveled the bundle, held up the gown. "It's beautiful, Dana. Thank you." He slipped it on over his clothes.

"You have to steam it to get the creases out. Is it true that you saw me from your window when I came to photograph?"

"Yes, once. I can only see a tiny part of the beach from my

upstairs window, but suddenly there you were. I was sure you were here because you'd found me. But you never came. Then I found out you'd come to take pictures. I have your book of photographs."

"Good for you."

"I saw the review in the paper and I ordered a copy."

"Hard to believe that it was once easy to come down here, that things were peaceful for a while."

"It was never really peaceful. That was just an illusion everyone was happy to maintain for a short time."

"Actually . . . I do remember a Leopold. Daniel, think. You knew him too. Think for a minute."

"I have thought. I've thought about it a million times, of course."

"Remember the Italian restaurant where we used to eat? Near the embassy? There was a waiter there, his name was Leopold. He had long dark hair, he wore it in a ponytail."

"I think I vaguely remember that waiter. I'm sure I never knew his name."

"You did. We joked about it. That's where that part of your dream came from."

"You did flirt with that waiter, as I recall."

"I didn't."

"You flirted with everyone, Dana. Not deliberately, maybe not even consciously, but you were always flirting. And those sexy clothes . . ."

"Okay, that's it. I'm going. This is obviously hopeless. I'm not going to sit here and be insulted in every possible way you can think of. Go ahead and reinvent the past. I'm leaving."

"Don't go. Please stay a little longer. We can't leave things hanging like this."

"Daniel, you *wanted* me to wear sexy clothes. I did it for you, for us. So you'd be proud of me, so you'd be turned on, and also so I'd be turned on. I haven't worn anything except jeans since you left. Why didn't you ever tell me all these things?"

"You never had anything with that waiter?"

"Of course not. I don't know anything about him except his name and that he had crooked teeth, as I remember. And he was nice. He was probably gay."

"How's Alex?"

"What do you care? You left all of us. You hurt your family, Alex, me. All the people you loved, supposedly, and who loved you."

"I had nothing to offer anyone."

"Why? You're not even handicapped. So what's the big deal?"

"You're just pretending, Dana."

"You know, I never realized what a superficial person you were. I used to say you had a narrow view of aesthetics and I was right. You don't know anything about beauty and you obviously never will. I don't know what I ever saw in you. You're vain, shallow, suspicious, cruel. I don't know why I waited for you all these years."

"When you walked in here, I could tell you had seen me before. Because everyone reacts. And you didn't. You must have seen me in the hospital."

"All I see when I see you is Daniel. I'm sorry if that's not enough for you. *Leopold*. I can't believe it. Leopold, the phantom lover. At least you could have asked me."

"How could I ask you when I heard you tell Alex you were going to lie to me, that you were going to stay with me out of pity? My mother was there too, and she was crying."

"Well, that proves it! Your mother was in Greece!"

"Didn't she come back when she heard?"

"We couldn't track your parents down. Didn't you know that?"

"No."

"Did you think I was just putting on a big act when I put all those ads in the paper?"

"I thought you felt guilty."

"Daniel, I want to touch you."

"I'm out of practice."

"Well, it's like riding a bike. You don't really forget."

"I think we have to talk first about what you want and what I want and where we go from here."

"No, I think we have to touch first, and then talk."

"It's too overwhelming for me."

"Tough. You think you can control everything. Well, for once I'm deciding." I pulled off my clothes and lay naked on the embroidered bedspread.

"Just like that first time," he said.

"Has my body changed?"

"No. Incredibly, it's exactly the same. Your arm is bruised, though."

I looked at my arm. He was right, my upper arm had turned copper brown and blue. "It's that schmuck who hit me. It looks worse than it is, it doesn't hurt."

"Everyone's gone crazy. There's no sanity left. Poor Dana."

"He was angry about other things, and he was letting it out on me . . . Aren't you going to kiss me?"

"No, I can't."

"At least sit next to me."

He walked over to the bed, sat down at the edge, and looked at me, but he didn't touch me.

I took his hand and put it on my midriff. His eyes filled with tears.

"What have you got to cry about?" I said. "I'm the one who should be crying."

"You had your turn, now it's mine. I'm not ready for this," Daniel said. "You're going too fast."

"Maybe because I've waited such a long time. Maybe it makes me impatient."

"A few minutes ago you were ready to strangle me."

"Remember our fights?" I asked.

"Yes."

"I used to get so mad. What did we fight about, apart from the mess?"

"About nothing, really. Once I laughed at something in a movie and you got mad. Sometimes you hated my jokes. Once I woke you in the middle of the night to ask you to remind me to pay some bill or other. It was just an excuse, I wanted to wake you because I missed you. You were pretty mad. Another time we argued about that television interviewer, I didn't like her, you did, or maybe it was the other way around. After your miscarriage we argued about whether I should have been so rude to the hospital staff. You felt it backfired, I was convinced you would have died otherwise. We argued about cat food. That's all I remember, though I'm sure there were a few more I've forgotten. We didn't argue much, if you consider that we were together seven years and two months."

"We always made up pretty fast."

"Not this fast. And anyhow, have we made up?"

"No. I'm still pissed off at you."

"We should wait until you aren't pissed off."

"You're just looking for an excuse."

"You're forcing yourself to overlook how you feel."

"You don't know anything about me or how I feel. You used to be so in tune with me. Why don't you just touch me if you don't believe me?"

I took his hand and placed it between my legs.

"Yes, you're wet."

"You sound surprised."

"I am surprised." He started moving his hand the way I liked, he remembered exactly what I liked. Then suddenly he stopped, got up, and moved away.

"I can't," he said.

I didn't say anything. I lay on the bed, naked and miserable. I pulled off the bedspread and blankets, and slid under the sheets and shut my eyes. In a few minutes I was asleep.

❉

I slept for an hour. I woke up to the sound of purring; there was a black-and-white cat lying at my feet. Daniel was gone. He'd left a note on the table: *Went to buy food, back very soon. Don't go out, it's dangerous.* He underlined *Don't go out* several times and added a tiny drawing to the note, the way he used to do when we lived together. His style had changed a little—it was more abstract. He'd drawn me sleeping and dreaming of a cat pyramid.

I found a dark green T-shirt in one of his drawers and I put it on; it reached my thighs. Then I climbed the spiral stairs to the upper story of the house. The walls of his workshop were covered with postcards, clippings from magazines, cartoons from newspapers. I remembered some of the cartoons, and I remembered thinking that Daniel would like them. One showed a camp counselor who was all dressed up for hiking telling campers in a bunk, *Today, children, we're going to the balcony.* In another, two storekeepers in a mall were laughing hysterically at a robber who was holding them up with a gun. A mock headline about an actual poisoning incident read ARAB POISONED HIMSELF, CUT INTO PIECES, COVERED WITH BREAD CRUMBS, SOLD PIECES TO JEWS. The headline was taped to a fashion advertisement showing a sexy woman suggestively checking another woman for bombs at the entrance to a store. Daniel had drawn a mustache on one of the women.

. I went down to the ground floor and looked at the sculptures. Some were exactly my size, and some were very small, set on tables that matched the kitchen table upstairs. I was shown in various poses, naked or wearing outfits I had once owned. The small clay figures were painted in startling, witty ways. There were at least fifty sculptures in the room. I also found a stack of notebooks Daniel was in the middle of correcting. Student notebooks, compositions in English. *My name is Marwan. I am boy. I go school. Last week I jump from window and break toe. In the end only it was paper bag went boom.*

And Daniel's comments. *Very good work, Marwan.* A new part of him.

I opened another notebook. *My name is Leila. When I grow up I want to die for Palestine.* Daniel had written, *I hope you will live for Palestine, Leila.*

I read all the compositions. *I am Muhammad. I have five big brothers and when they mad at me I run to mother. I am trying to learn brave.* Daniel wrote, *You are already a very brave young man, Muhammad.*

I heard Daniel's key in the lock. I ran to the door and jumped on him when he entered. He was forced to drop his bags and hold me. I wound my legs around his waist and kissed him for a long time.

"See what you've been missing, you stupid idiot," I said.

"Let's make supper," he said.

We went up to the kitchen and cooked in silence. It was just like the old days; we didn't need to talk. We knew exactly what we were making and what to do. We made cabbage croquettes and bean salad and baked potatoes with melted cheese and a huge pot of couscous.

Then we ate. I was very hungry. I felt as if I hadn't eaten in several years, and I kept heaping more and more food onto my plate.

"I'm a vegetarian now," Daniel said.

"How come?"

"I got food poisoning three times from meat here, so I just quit. And I found I didn't miss it. Once you get out of the habit, you lose interest."

"What else has changed about you? Tell me everything."

"I have a good friend, William. He's an American-born Palestinian, and his Arabic is even worse than mine. We see a lot of each other——he comes over for dinner, we play chess. He's a lawyer. He left a cushy life to come here, and he keeps asking himself how long it's going to be before he has a nervous break-down and goes back to Colorado. He's a good guy, you'd like him. He thought I should contact you. So did Ella."

"Do you know any real militants?"

"Such a naïve question, Dana. It just shows how out of touch people on the outside are."

"You don't joke around the way you used to."

"That's true. I joke around with my students, though. They love to laugh."

"Alex said you'd be different."

"Who else knows that you've found me?"

"Just Alex and another friend. I didn't tell your family."

I watched his hands as he helped himself to salad. I took one of his hands in mine and kissed it. "I love your wrinkled hand."

He pulled away. "Don't," he said.

"Okay, that's new, that's not like you . . . But I'll get used to it. I dreamed I could only have you if I was blind. And I was willing to be blind, if that's what it took . . . What's it like teaching here?"

"It's hard, of course. Sometimes it's more about just making it through the day. Tension and fighting inside the classroom, incursion hell outside the classroom, more tension and fighting at home . . . the kids are under unimaginable stress. You have to get used to compromising."

"That reminds me of something. I was at a checkpoint, and you know how these Palestinian men just hang around all day, hands in pockets, just trapped with nowhere to go. I went over to take some photographs of them. Then one guy came over to me and said, 'We have nothing to do, so we start fighting with each other!' He was so desperate to tell someone and he had no one to tell, so he chose me. He was pleading with me, as if I had the magic key. I felt helpless, as usual."

"You're doing a lot. Just being there and taking photographs and showing you understand is immensely important. It has a huge impact. Palestinians are very in tune with who their friends are."

"What about the Migdal killing last year? Those Migdal people were on their side."

"Yes, that really was horrible. There are lunatics in every society, unfortunately."

"What will you do with this house now?"

"I'm not coming back, Dana."

"You are. Because I don't want to live here, for a million obvious reasons."

"People depend on me here, too," he said. "I can't desert them. I live here now. I don't want to go back. I don't want to see men looking at you with desire. I don't want to feel that they have a right to you and I don't."

"I never knew you were so paranoid. A nurse told me you only had second-degree burns on most of your body. Those kind of burns don't even leave scars. Is that true?"

"I do have scars on my body, but not everywhere."

"How did you know what you looked like?"

"I saw my reflection in the cutlery."

"Why did you tell them you didn't want to see anyone?"

"I didn't."

"You didn't tell the nurses you didn't want visitors?"

"No."

"How could the nurses lie to me?"

"They probably assumed you'd freak out."

"That's ridiculous. Maybe you said it while you were half-drugged."

"Maybe."

"You hurt me."

"I know you see it that way."

"What other way is there?"

"Life hurt you. Bad luck hurt you. Not me."

"I'm staying the night."

"Okay."

"I'm going to sleep in your bed."

"There's only one bed."

"Don't force me to stay here forever. I don't even speak the language. And it's not like I can just come visit you three times a week. I'm lucky I made it in this once."

"You are lucky. I was very worried."

"Once I got past the checkpoints, I felt safe."

"This isn't a safe place for anyone. There's constant shooting, people are getting killed all the time. It never stops."

"I saved up money so we could go on a vacation, just the two of us. You once said you wanted to see Ireland. We'll stay at the best hotels, we'll go sailing . . ."

"You saved money? How?"

"I write romance novels in English. It pays very well."

"Romance novels . . . I didn't know."

"I don't tell most people."

"That's really amazing, that you can do that."

"My hidden talent. Not that it takes much talent!"

"It takes a lot of talent. You have to know what other people's fantasies are. That takes a special kind of genius."

"Yes, that's me. A genius. A genius at surviving."

"I felt bad not leaving you any money, but I figured your father would help you out."

"He offered, of course. As it turned out, I didn't need him. I've put away half of what I made for our trip."

"I don't want to travel, Dana. I don't like people staring at me."

"Who cares? Who cares? So you look a little weird, so what? Haven't you noticed that everyone is a misfit? We're all weird! You never cared before what anyone thought, why would you care now?"

"I liked who I was."

"No one gives a damn. People aren't interested in anything but their own little lives."

"That hasn't been my experience, generally speaking. If people weren't interested in anything but their own little lives we wouldn't have missiles dropping from the sky every second Tuesday."

"Have you lost any students?"

"Yes. One died, and four are so disabled they can't really function anymore. One girl, the one who was killed, she was incredibly brilliant. She was a math whiz, I couldn't teach her anything. I put her in touch with a mathematician at the university—he was teaching her by email. She would have been a scientist, or a physicist, she could have done anything with her life. But she was shot down at a checkpoint, on the way to visit her brother. They shot at the car she was in—the whole family was killed. Everyone who knew her was devastated, including me. She was something special, not only brilliant but also wise and sweet. But it's always devastating."

"I brought you a photograph." I reached for my bag and took out the photo of the excited religious men and the birds in the sky.

Daniel looked at it for a long time. "Was this a funeral?" he asked.

"It was a memorial. For those thirteen Arabs the police killed. It seemed so shocking at the time, killing our own citizens. Now nothing seems shocking. We've lost the ability to be shocked."

"This is wonderful. They're getting excited about the birds."

"Yes. Do you think they thought the birds were the souls of the boys?"

"I don't know. But it's a great photograph, Dana. Thank you for bringing it. I'd like to see all your photos. You know, I probably wouldn't have ended up here if not for you. I mean in Palestine. You see how effective your lectures were . . ."

"I didn't mean for you to go this far . . ." I said, and we both laughed.

"Has anything changed in the flat? How are the plants doing?"

"They're thriving. You can't see the wall anymore. I'm thinking of trimming them a bit, what do you think?"

"Sure, sounds like a good idea . . ."

"Kitty died last year. She just went very limp suddenly, and I held her on my lap for a few hours, and she died, I guess of old age. Daniel, I've really missed you. It's been incredibly lonely."

"Yes."

"What a waste. What a waste of suffering. For nothing, for absolutely nothing."

"Most suffering is for nothing."

"It's true. This fighting . . . this fighting is for nothing," I said. "We're all dying for nothing. Come with me to bed."

"All right. But don't expect anything."

"Okay."

Daniel turned off the lights and undressed. He lay down beside me but he didn't touch me.

"Remember all the things we used to do?" I said.

"Yes. It's amazing how your body hasn't changed at all. Your face is older, but not your body."

"It's yours, my body."

"You were always a generous person, Dana."

"I've been loyal to you. I slept with a kid a year after you vanished, a one-night stand. I didn't enjoy it, it was really sad. I had no idea he was so young. Poor guy, I really hurt him. And I've slept with Beatrice. She's attracted to women, but she isn't in love with me, it was always very casual, and it's over now that we're back together."

"You don't have to tell me, Dana. I never expected or wanted you to be alone. I was hoping you'd find someone. I slept with someone while we were married, you know."

"What?"

"Remember at that first place I worked? The other woman who quit when I quit—I had sex with her a few times in the office, after hours, and also once at our place, when she did the wall painting in the kitchen."

I heard the words, they were very bumpy, like a bumpy wagon ride, but I was having trouble understanding them.

"I didn't do it to hurt you. It was the first year of our marriage, and I wasn't used to monogamy. She came on to me, and I gave in. And then I decided it wasn't worth the guilt and also it wasn't worth how you'd feel if you found out."

"How long did it go on for?"

"Just two or three weeks, I don't remember exactly. I didn't have any feelings toward her—maybe I just wanted to feel like a macho stud. Maybe I was flattered by her desire. Maybe I was afraid of how much I loved you and I wanted to cheat on you before you cheated on me. Maybe I was just a jerk."

"Does that time with the feet have anything to do with that?"

"Feet?"

"I once kissed your feet, and you got very upset and left the house."

"Oh yes . . . I'd forgotten all about that. Yes. I suddenly had an attack of unbearable guilt."

"That was the only time?"

"Yes."

"How did it end?"

"We both left the firm, and she got a job in another part of the country. But I wouldn't have continued with her anyhow."

"She was in love with you. She put your initials all over the painting."

"When did you notice that?"

"Only recently—someone came to visit, another activist, and he pointed it out."

"I was very angry with her for doing that. She ruined that room for me."

"Is that why we never ate in the kitchen?"

"Yes."

"That hurts me. Even after all this time, it hurts. Was she very beautiful?"

"No, she was very, very ugly. She had a mustache and hair on her back and warts on her chin, and she smelled of old cheese."

"Tell me."

"We're just human, Dana. That means we're fucked up and we mess up. It means we do stupid and insane things. I don't think anyone studying the human species would believe the things we do. Maybe you expect too much of people, and also of yourself."

"I don't think I expect too much. If you knew what the characters in my novels expect, that would give you perspective."

"I had to leave because I couldn't bear to lose you."

"But what did you think when you saw all those ads I put in the newspaper?"

"I told you, I thought you felt sorry for me and that you felt a sense of duty. You always had a sense of duty."

"A sense of duty! Yes, toward my country, toward my country's victims. But do you think I'd make personal decisions based on a sense of duty? How could you have so little trust in me?"

"You know trust was never my strong point."

"We're such opposites in some ways. I believed you loved me right from the word go, even though you never said it. I just felt it from the way you looked at me and ran your fingers through my hair, and made jokes about me. And you—you didn't believe it even though I let you know every way I could."

"Yes, it's true. You let me know."

"I was very loved as a child. I guess it wasn't hard for me to believe that you adored me, too. Your parents were a lot tougher with you. They're tough people, like everyone in this country. My parents were imports, they never fit in."

"I don't know what to feel."

"You made a mistake, Daniel. A very sad mistake, one which caused everyone a lot of pain. Touch me."

"Your skin was always as smooth as silk."

"Like that song."

"Yes, like the song."

"I think it's still smooth, you'll have to see for yourself."

He placed his hand on my belly. "What does my hand feel like?"

"Like it used to, only better. Remember how you always came up to me when I was washing dishes, and put your arms around my waist?"

"At first it hurt me to touch people, after the fire. It felt like physical pain, but I think it was psychological. Anyhow, it passed. I don't mind now. I look up porn on the computer sometimes, but it's so unaesthetic, it gets in the way."

"Unaesthetic! You're so funny. Even porn has to be beautiful."

"Well, why shouldn't it be?"

*"Glory be to God for dappled things,"* I quoted.

"What?"

"That's from a poem I like. Though the guy who wrote it didn't have porn in mind, to say the least."

"I've kept a diary, not that detailed, just basic things."

"I took photographs."

"If you show me yours, I'll show you mine."

"Okay."

"I'm starting to feel more relaxed."

"Me too."

"I'm starting to get excited."

"Good. I'm ready for some action."

Before, my life was orderly. I had my job, my friends, the sea. I took photographs, I wrote junk novels, I waited for my husband.

Now everything has changed. I live near the sea and I speak to Daniel on the phone every day and look for ways to see him. Maybe one day he'll move back here. Maybe one day the roads between us will be open and I'll be free to see him whenever I want.

Beatrice, Benny, and Vronsky have disappeared from my life. I told Beatrice I couldn't sleep with her anymore, and in honor of our new status as ordinary friends she invited me to her place for dinner. It was a strange, hectic evening. Dudu, who to his own amazement had made a fortune in real estate, was mildly stoned. With his hippie beard and a scrawny joint held precariously between his artistic fingers, he looked lost and dazed, as if he were still trying to understand how he'd landed on this planet, in this particular house and family. Beatrice was on the phone half the time, and the children bobbed incessantly through the evening with tenacious requests. When Beatrice and I said good-bye at the door, we both knew I would not be back.

Benny met a student, Rina, who hailed him in the middle of the night after walking out on her boyfriend, and the two of them connected immediately. Rina is skinny, high-strung, and chronically petulant, but Benny loves her, and he's happy. He moved in with her almost immediately, and I hear the two of them are now engaged. I smile in his direction when I pass him on the beach with his children and young fiancée, but we don't speak. He's still a little angry with me, or maybe just embarrassed.

Vronsky and I have lost touch.

Volvo is still here, and Jacky, and Tanya. Volvo has an American boyfriend, Tom, and he now wears long denim shorts and sleeveless tops. He and Tom fight regularly, and sometimes everyone in the building witnesses their stormy dramas, which they both appear to enjoy. Tanya's going out with the locksmith, and they seem to be getting along. Sometimes I hear the locksmith whistling in the hallway as he descends the stairs and heads out to work. Tanya says it won't last. "Still . . . live for the moment," she adds.

I talk to Rafi on the phone, but he no longer visits; I need to be loyal to Daniel. Only once, when we were helping Palestinians pick olives and two insane settlers began shooting at us, and we all lay down on the ground, terrified, Rafi crawled over to where I was and we held one another. We curled up against the wide, gnarled trunk of the tree and he placed his arm around my waist. If we were going to die, we would at least not die alone. It took the army a very long time to come—nearly an hour. A few feet away from us, Odelia was trying to help a woman from London, who had been hit in the leg.

The army arrived, finally, but they let the settlers go free, and they refused to stay with us, so we had to abandon the trees. Rafi and I drove away from the olive grove in separate cars.

I am also expecting; I'm in my eighth month. Is it Rafi's baby, or my husband's? It doesn't matter. I love them both, I can have neither.

Still, I am lucky. I am surrounded by love. Even if I can't touch it or see it, I know it is there, waiting for me.